CLAN NOVEL
CAPPADOCIAN

BY ANDREW BATES

Markus felt a rise of unease. In light of discovering Byzar, the parallel of Byzantium's destruction and Constantinople's recent sack could not be happenstance. He had seen enough of the threads of life and death to suspect any occurrence of coincidence.

"What circumstance brought you here?"

"...my childe... Alexiaaa... she... has bound us all..."

I should not be surprised, Markus thought. *But ancient though Alexia is, how could one Cainite have subdued so many others of the blood? Including her own sire?*

"This is your brood, then," he said aloud. "You are all Cappadocians?"

"...not all... emperors and lovers as well." Byzar's whispers grew more focused as their conversation progressed "...She began with my brood, many years ago. I have seen... have seen her bring more."

"Toward what purpose? Does she gather an army of Cainites?"

"She binds us into torpor. You think... that we would serve her, were we released? Alexia... would not last a moment, should we become free." The scorn that flared from the spirit became anguish. "No... not an army. She seeks to shape the future... the return of her love."

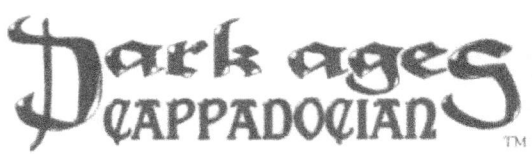

Dark ages
Cappadocian ™

Andrew Bates

AD 1204
Third of the Dark Ages Clan Novels

Fo George Alec Effinger

What Has Come Before

It is the year 1204 and the Fourth Crusade, diverted from its goal of striking Muslim Egypt and recapturing Jerusalem, has come instead to Constantinople. Over three days and nights in April, the soldiers of the so-called Army of Christ sack and pillage the greatest of Christian cities, claiming boundless treasure for themselves and making the Byzantine Empire their own. For the Greeks of the city, it is a time of defeat, outrage and despair.

Away from the eyes of men, vampires lurk on both sides of the conflict. The predators of the Byzantine night have found their city torn open and Michael, the ancient vampire who led them, destroyed. In hopes of finding the Dracon, an ancient vampire powerful enough to restore the dream of Constantinople, the vampire Malachite has traveled to Mount Erciyes in Anatolia. There he consults with Constancia, known as the Oracle of Bones, an elder of the so-called Clan of Death, the Cappadocians.

Meanwhile, back in Constantinople, rumors spread of a new crusade headed for Egypt. A powerful European vampire—Hugh of Clairvaux—supposedly hears the voice of the Virgin Mary in his visions and calls his ilk to take the Cross. For Markus Musa Giovanni, another member of Clan Cappadocian, that might prove to be a problem....

Part One: Constantinople

Chapter One

Constantinople
14 April, 1204

Markus Musa Giovanni roused his considerable bulk from slumber even as the sunset stained the western sky. He was not normally such an early riser, but this was far from a normal time. His rest during the past two days had been disrupted by the terror and pillage that swept the city above.

Standing at the center of a storm of change, he lacked a clear view of which way the winds blew. Too many possibilities existed to allow easy insight into his best course of action. Markus had spent the previous night weighing options. While he had at least narrowed his choices, none of the alternatives that remained was without risk.

Markus could return home, to Venice and to his family. Safe from the ravages Constantinople suffered this night, he could relate all that he had learned during his years in the Queen of Cities. Alas, there was precious little worth telling. He had yet to succeed at what he had once thought was a laughably simple task. And to stand before the familial patriarch, the great Augustus Giovanni, with nothing more than excuses in hand…?

Markus dismissed the thought. He could claim that the challenges he faced were greater than anyone had expected, but that was nothing more than pathetic whining. It would be tantamount to admitting he was not worthy of the dark gift given him. At the very least, he would he an embarrassment, his name a joke among the family, spurned even by the shades who whispered in the deep chambers where the Giovanni performed their necromantic studies.

Instead, Markus could remain in Constantinople. He could see what opportunities for discovery presented themselves in the wake of the massacre still raging throughout the great city's streets. The secrets he had been charged to find might more easily be gleaned under cover of violence. Yet to stay would expose Markus to mortal—and immortal—danger. His blood was more potent than that of many who bore the mark of Caine, but Markus was still young as vampires considered such things. Despite his power, he was not invulnerable. He might find that which he had sought for years, only to suffer ultimate destruction on the verge of triumph.

A third option—to flee, spending his nights far from familial responsibility and physical danger—was never more than a fleeting fancy. Markus was many things, but a coward was not one of them.

Sandwiched between the twin specters of admitting failure and chancing final death, Markus was not eager to commit to either course.

Yet lurking here accomplishes nothing. A grimace of resignation stretched across his broad features. He was a Giovanni, and a Cappadocian. In the search for the ultimate secrets of life and death, failure was unacceptable. *The time for planning is done. Now is the moment to act.*

"Look, Falsinar! A handful of Greeks approach. Ready the stone."

"You are certain they are Greeks?"

"Eyes like a hawk, my friend. You can tell by their armor; see?"

"You misremember your features, Beltramose. You have a nose like a hawk's beak, but your eyes are no sharper than a wooden spoon."

"I forgive you such a hurtful jibe, Falsinar. Your words are formed from the envy you hold for my unmatched beauty and intellect."

"Aye, unmatched indeed. I have yet to meet a man either as hideous or as ignorant as yourself."

"Poor Falsinar. Count yourself lucky that I am such a kind-hearted soul as to accept you as my friend."

"Indeed, Beltramose. God is surely punishing me for some great sin."

"Ah, look now. We have missed our chance. They have decided not to try our door."

"Do not despair. See there, just turning yonder corner?"

"What? Ah, but they look to be Venetian. Would God forgive us for striking at our own countrymen?"

"I do not see why He would bother with us now of all times. Besides, look how they come unerringly for the lone stout door that remains standing on this street. Only the suicidal would dare try to gain entry to our humble tower."

"Truly, I can find no fault with your logic, my friend. On the count of three, then?"

"I am at your command, good Beltramose."

Markus Giovanni heard pounding from the heavy, banded door two floors above his hidden lair. Even as he reached the landing, shouts of surprise erupted outside, followed by a thunderous crash. The ground shook at some impact, but lock and hinges remained firm.

Since the door remained secure, Markus spared a glance at the opposite wall of the squat tower that comprised the remainder of his home. Those who wished to gain entry from the street could not know that a significant portion of the tower's other side had tumbled in. That hole overlooked a series of ruined buildings to which the tower was once attached, part of a Venetian merchant's warehouse complex. The buildings still gave off a thick billow of smoke from the conflagration that had claimed them the previous day. Markus suppressed a shudder. Deep in his lair beneath the city, he had been safe from the deadly flames. Still, the bones of the blackened structures were grim reminder of how easily all things might fall no matter the care taken in their construction.

The cries outside of pain and panic roused Markus from contemplation. He slipped the rest of the way up the stone steps and entered the tower's top room. Peering out the jagged hole on the street-side wall, two men sniggered at one another as they levered another stone block into position.

"The city is in flames," Markus observed, "and all you fools can think to do is drop stones on looters?"

The man on the right jerked upon hearing Markus's basso rumble. The other fellow lacked the strength to hold the stone in place and barked in surprise as it fell three stories. Ignoring the renewed screams of outrage from below, the man on the left looked over at Markus.

"Ah, *Signore* awakens at last. You have a decision, then?"

"I have."

Falsinar and Beltramose huffed up the last few steps to the tower roof. Markus had sated himself with the victims of their rock-dropping stunt. It was left to the pair to remove the bodies and lessen the chances that other looters would take an interest in their abode. Markus stood at the tower's far side, backlit by the fires encroaching on the Great Bazaar. The men moved opposite their master and took a post over the tower's front entrance, leaving their lord to his privacy.

"That is something I have never grown used to," Beltramose confided. He nodded to Markus, who murmured at the air.

Falsinar looked over. "Aye, well. What is it his kind say? 'Different realms of being'?"

"It makes the things no less disquieting to be around."

"Hmm. And yet," Falsinar said, tapping a contemplative finger against his lips, "our gracious lord and master appears to have no problems trafficking with their ilk."

Beltramose frowned. "What a revelation! Truly, my friend, your insight is without limit."

"I must say that your compliment seems less than genuine."

"You know that I hold you in regard equal to that which you show me, good Falsinar."

"Indeed?" Falsinar quirked a bushy eyebrow at the taller man. "Perhaps we should each consider ourselves insulted, then."

Beltramose uttered a surprised gasp, his intended reply forgotten. He leaped to one side and shuddered, eyes darting in a mix of panic and outrage.

Falsinar cut off his chuckle in the face of Beltramose's murderous glare. "Apologies, my friend, but you looked like a distressed stork, flapping about like that. One of his pets having fun at your expense again?"

"Went right through me. Like being doused with ice water." Beltramose shuddered. "Why do they never bother you?"

"Perhaps because I am resigned to the inevitable, while you retain a sliver of hope."

"It is true that, compared to yourself, I am an incurable optimist. Yet I would never be mistaken for hopeful."

Falsinar shrugged. "Still you think that your fate will be other than that shared by our unseen friends. That our fine liege will not someday add you to his collection. You have yet to grasp that it is the price men such as ourselves must pay."

Preparations complete, Markus made a dismissive gesture. The seven shades bound to his service flitted away at speed, compelled to fulfill his commands without delay. He approached Falsinar and Beltramose with purpose, moving quietly for all his hulk. "Infantino claims that the Obertus monastery was sacked last night, not long after the crusaders breached the walls. He spied some activity within tonight, however. It is likely that some of the monks have returned to see what they may recover, now that the crusaders have moved on to the city proper."

Markus looked to the west. The Monastery of St. John Studius lay nine miles distant, within the city's outer walls built on the orders of the Emperor Theodosius II. The monastery would not have been visible from the tower, even without the thick billows of acrid smoke and clouds of ash falling like black snow around them. Although he didn't see the glance that Falsinar and Beltramose exchanged, Markus knew his men well. "You need not worry yourselves, gentlemen. Remain here and guard the tower. Infantino and the others will offer me sufficient protection."

"You are certain?" Falsinar's voice was strong, but Markus saw the bright flicker of relief in the man's aura. Reading such auras was just one more gift of the blood in Markus's unliving veins, and one more reason not to return to Venice empty-handed.

"Get some rest. I expect that there will be more than enough tasks to keep you both busy upon my return." Markus smiled. "If you get bored, perhaps more looters will oblige you with some sport."

Markus had to stoop to fit within the low underground passage. Thanks to a silent warning from Infantino, he was not surprised when two figures emerged from dark cracks in the tunnel walls. The oil lamp in his thick fist revealed two men in the simple robes of monks. One stood two yards before him, the other a similar distance behind. Monks they were, but their piety was a mockery of true faith. A sharpening of focus and Markus confirmed by the brilliance of their auras that they were mortal—ghouls, servants of the Obertus Tzimisce.

"*Isxe. Ektopizai pan sudie!*" one said.

Among Markus's many scholarly talents was an affinity for language. He translated the Greek words without effort: *Halt. Take yourself away from here with all speed.* He replied in kind, speaking like a native Byzantine. "My apologies, brother. I do not mean to trespass. I come merely to offer assistance in these times of danger."

"Danger indeed," the other sneered. "It appears you are the one in need of aid."

Markus held his tongue, considering his reply. The Obertus Tzimisce sect were scholars of a sort, not unlike Markus's own Cappadocian clan. In contrast to the Cappadocians' study of death, the Tzimisce pursued a misguided hope of finding transcendence within flesh and bone. Their so-called research being often degenerate and cruel, Markus normally had little interest in dealing with their kind. *Pentaxa pamoneros*—depraved in the extreme, as the Greeks would say. Despite this, the Obertus sect and their high abbot Gesu had gathered a most impressive collection of scholarly works—the secret Library of the Forgotten. Markus had learned of it only recently, piecing together fragments of conversation over scores of nights spent ingratiating himself to the local undead. Though eager to peruse the library's contents, he had yet to gain access to its well-protected stacks. He had hoped the chaos following the crusaders' rampage might give him the chance.

While the presence of this welcoming committee made it likely that things of interest lingered in the remains, the ghouls' antagonism suggested he would find no more success than in previous visits. Markus forced down the sudden, violent surge of frustration. Gratifying as it would be to smash his way past these mortals, giving vent to the Beast would accomplish nothing constructive. "Please, brothers, quarrels enough exist elsewhere in the city. Inform Brother Gesu of my presence—"

The monks cried out in sudden anger. Plumes of silver churned within their auras, signifying intense grief. "You are not worthy to speak that name!" the rearward ghoul spat.

Some tragedy has befallen the powerful Gesu! Curiosity gripped Markus. "I am known to him; trust that my interests—"

"Your interests are plain enough." A figure stepped into the outermost edge of the lamp's light—a lady of power and influence, clad in fine damask and with a stately demeanor that made the meager tunnel look even more dingy. Though aged, beauty had not fled her. Yet a deathly pallor revealed her as one of the undead—indeed, as one who shared the same lineage as Markus. Lady Alexia Theusa, mistress of death, elder of Clan Cappadocian.

Upon their first meeting, shortly after he had come to Constantinople, she made it clear that she did not trust the motives of his family, the Giovanni. That Alexia was the primary reason Markus had come to the city in the first place made that revelation all the more galling. Instead of being a hoped-for fount of wisdom and dark arts, she had become the main impediment to his success.

"Lady Alexia," Markus said, cursing his poor timing. *Of course she is here—she must be helping to gather whatever treasures survived the sack.*

Though Alexia had no great love for the Tzimisce's cruel practices, she held a vast thirst for knowledge that transcended matters of personal taste. In fact, as one of the vampires resident in Constantinople since its very founding, Alexia's patronage had helped establish the Library of the Forgotten.

Which made it even less likely Markus would lay eyes on a single tome. Still, he was not one to admit failure while he retained thought and purpose. Shadows flickered along the walls as the lamp moved with his bow. "I appreciate that you harbor suspicions toward my family. As I have said in the past, the Giovanni bear you no ill will. Indeed, we share—"

"We share nothing, sir." Her voice remained gentle, but held an edge that cut through his words like an executioner's blade. "As with every other offer you have made, my response is the same. Your assistance is neither requested nor desired."

Imperious crone! His lips curled in his neatly clipped beard, barely restraining a snarl. He might have persuaded Gesu or one of the other vampires protecting the Library of the Forgotten. *But she will not even allow me the chance!*

Through a growing haze of anger, Markus sensed something… an undercurrent of danger lacking in previous encounters with Alexia. She was not known to be confrontational, but she was as capable of violence as any vampire. And these nights of chaos offered the perfect chance to remove the thorn from her side that was Markus Giovanni.

His sense of the violence simmering in the elder vampire shocked Markus back to lucidity. With a voice steady only through great effort, he said, "You have made yourself very clear, Lady Alexia. I regret that we could not come to terms."

Markus backtracked after another bow, forcing the rearmost monk back into the hiding hole to give sufficient room for his massive form. Markus saw the triumphant glint in Alexia's eyes as she slipped into the shadows cast by his retreating light. Just as he could sense her surface emotions, Markus knew Alexia had read his own frustration… and his fear.

Chapter Two

Constantinople
15 April, 1204

Were he mortal, Markus would still set a brisk pace. He was a mountain of a man, legs like tree trunks eating almost two yards at every stride. Even as a youth in Venice a century before he'd been big—large but powerful and deceptively fast—earning the nickname *l'orso*, the bear. Entry into the ranks of the undead had only increased this stamina further.

Though hardier than any mortal, Markus had no interest in testing himself against the men who savaged Constantinople this night. Trained in the art of combat he might be, but Markus preferred to avoid physical conflict. He was a scholar first and foremost, and turned to violence only when logic or persuasion failed. It did help that Markus cut such an imposing figure that others were usually willing to listen to reason. Still, that was not possible this night. There was no reasoning with those who overran Constantinople, nor with those who waged a futile effort to defend their fair city.

Just as there is no reasoning with that witch Alexia, Markus thought. *Would that I could cast aside parley and take up arms against her!*

Gratifying as the fantasy was, he was not so foolish as to oppose her directly. She was far older, more powerful, and more established in the city than he. Since she operated from such a position of strength, Markus felt caution was called for. He would lair outside the city and plan in safety.

Markus spared no concern for his men as they moved north

through the dark city streets. Falsinar and Beltramose received small draughts of his potent blood from time to time. This gift made the two retainers more than mortal—ghouls, in the parlance of the undead. Stronger and sturdier than an average man, they could keep up, though they had no breath to spare for idle banter.

Silence was preferable anyway, as the sack of Constantinople had reached fever pitch. Anyone they encountered would care little that Markus and his men were allied neither with Latin crusader nor Byzantine defender. Invisible mouths whispered soundless words in his ears, guiding him around the clusters of armed men scrambling through the ash-covered streets.

Infantino and the other ghostly slaves Markus had bound into his service over the course of his unlife were assets, but they were not infallible. He and his ghouls had covered just over half the distance to the northern wall when a voice rang out. Markus bit back a reprimand; the shades would be punished later for their oversight. The hidden sentry was of immediate concern.

The cry came again, louder and more demanding.

"French," Markus murmured, eyes scanning the street with preternatural sharpness. "Crusader. There, behind the shuttered window. He demands our colors and allegiance."

"We investigated the forces when they arrived months ago, *Signore*," Falsinar said. "Choose a name and we are on our way."

"Unless I happen to choose the very ones we have just run into. No; we have no time for delays. Beltramose, shut this fool up." Markus stepped forward, calling out in French a few delaying platitudes that covered the sound of leather swinging in the darkness.

The sentry forgot some of his caution upon hearing the familiar tongue of his homeland. He opened the shutter a crack for a better view of the strangers below. An iron pellet sped through the crack and smashed into the crusader's temple, cutting off his final words in mid-sentence. Beltramose stuffed the sling back into his belt and hoisted his pack even as the watchman fell to the attic floor in a clatter of armor.

Their destination, the Port of Neorion, was but a short distance past the city's northern wall. Markus hoped to slip through, take a small boat, and traverse the Golden Horn to a hiding spot less likely to be engulfed in flame or overrun by frenzied Latins. A score of enraged crusaders thundering after them had other ideas.

Markus ordered the ghosts ahead as he led Falsinar and Beltramose on a mad dash. Their chances were poor if the shades did not find what he needed. Luckily, Rina, the ghost of a young Pisan girl Markus had very carefully murdered and bound some forty years ago, came back with a promising option. Markus did not hesitate. He dashed after the spirit, smashing through a partially collapsed shed, down a side street, and into a burned-out building. Once part of the Byzantine military barracks, the building was long ago refitted as a warehouse for Latin trade goods. Most recently, it had served as a poor hiding place for some of the neighborhood's Latin residents hoping to avoid the rampage engulfing the rest of the city. Someone had put the place to the torch. The dozen or so unfortunates had barred themselves within too securely to escape the hungry flames.

Sharing lineage with the invaders offered these poor souls no protection, Markus noted. *No matter. Their bodies will serve my needs as well as any Greek.*

"Apologies," Beltramose gasped as he crouched, hands on knees. "Did not... realize—"

"Save your breath." Needing to breathe only to converse and pass for the living, Markus spoke as easily as if he were lounging in the family estate. "The fault lies with the spirits for missing that cursed sentry."

"Not to mention... the fellow's... companions... on the... floor below," Falsinar added between gulps of air.

A glare from Markus made it clear this was not the time for levity. It was bad enough that the watchman, felled by the pellet from Beltramose's sling, had tumbled from the attic atop his compatriots and roused them to action. Even worse, Markus and his men had stumbled across two additional groups of Frankish crusaders as they fled. It would make for an amusing story some other night, but now the possibility of disaster remained too immediate. "The damage is done. Now we deal with the consequences."

"How... long?" Falsinar managed. He slumped against one soot-covered wall, like Beltramose trying to recover from their mad sprint.

Markus pulled a thin blade. "A few minutes. Infantino and the others should delay our vengeance-minded friends sufficiently. Still, you must protect me if we are interrupted before I finish."

The two mortals nodded. Despite their having run so far with laden packs, Markus's blood gift was fast returning the ghouls' breath and strength.

Falsinar and Beltramose left their packs by the wall and moved to the building's scorched doorway. The fires scattered through the Latin Quarter cast sufficient light on the area. Falsinar took a pull from a wineskin as he loosed his falchion in its scabbard. Handing the skin to Beltramose, he unhooked his crossbow from its strap and readied a quarrel. Beltramose drank as well before checking the edge on his long sword. He leaned the blade against the wall for easy access, then withdrew the leather sling from his belt and loosened the drawstring on his pouch of iron pellets.

Behind them, Markus gave the sprawled, blackened bodies one more look, then drew the long knife across his opposite palm. The cut was a cold white mouth until he willed forth the blood. Reaching out, he sprinkled vitae upon the corpses. A string of Latin words tumbled from his lips as the red pearls fell upon the dead, and the corpses jerked as if each phrase and each droplet were a hammer blow.

Compelled by Markus's will, vampiric blood suffused the bodies and forced scorched muscles and ligaments to re-knit. Channeled by Cappadocian magic, dark energy was drawn from the netherworld to quicken carbonized flesh...

...and the first of the corpse knights stirred to action.

Falsinar and Beltramose chuckled to one another, enjoying the cries of confusion as frustrated crusaders chased phantom sounds.

"Still harbor unwelcoming thoughts toward the master's unseen slaves?" Falsinar inquired.

"Hrmph. They have their uses. But I shall never grow used to trafficking with things I cannot see or touch."

"And yet you never tire of the company of women."

"Do not strain yourself so much attempting humor, my friend."

"My apologies. True, you have no trouble *seeing* the fairer sex. And their disdain *does* differ from being bereft of physical contact."

"Curious." A wicked smile bloomed upon Beltramose's face. "I never faced any such disdain from your sister."

Falsinar choked out a noise between hilarity and outrage. He covered his mouth when a trio of armored forms turned the corner. "Ah, my fraternal indignation must bide for the moment," he muttered as the crusaders began systematically checking the ruins. "Our Frankish friends appear to have tired of chasing phantoms."

"Indeed. They will be on us within moments. See if—" Beltramose stopped. Falsinar had also heard the noises from further within the darkened room. Sounds of scraping and uneven footsteps, of hollow grunts and groans, that multiplied and drew closer.

"You may find ghosts disquieting," Falsinar whispered, his face pale and devoid of the humor of a moment before, "but perhaps it is better *not* to see our allies."

Sir Eustace of Vendôme was frustrated. His lord, Count Louis of Blois, had entrusted him with guard duty. Protect the Gate and Port of Neorion. Watch for any heathens trying to flee with treasures that rightfully belonged to the Church. Dispatch any reinforcements coming to aid in Constantinople's defense.

Truly, "entrusted" was much too generous a term. Eustace knew the duty for what it was: punishment. The handful of refugees he and his men had encountered in the Latin Quarter this night had little more than the clothes on their backs. As for reinforcements, there was no chance of that. The crusaders had broken Constantinople. Individuals remained, but nothing approaching a force to be feared.

No, this pedestrian detail was meant to remind Eustace of his place. Count Louis liked to play his men against one another, subtly encouraging them to jockey for position and favor, like some living chess game.

Eustace had little problem with that. He was born with more than his share of ambition and he played the game well. But ever since the crusaders put Isaac and Alexius on the throne as co-emperors of the Byzantine Empire the previous summer, Eustace could seem to do no right in the eyes of his liege. This scut work was simply the latest in a string of menial tasks he'd suffered through. He had come to the conclusion that Louis was testing his mettle, just as God tried Job. It only made sense, considering Eustace's proven talents. Still, it didn't make enduring the dull tasks any easier.

Especially tonight. Louis and the others were advancing through the city, gathering untold riches—for the glory of God and the Church, naturally. Eustace and the unfortunate men lumped into this assignment with him would be lucky to collect the odd goblet when their brethren were through.

He was at last coming to terms with his duties when three men of martial skill and laden with large sacks slew a sentry while Eustace and his men took a rest from their patrols. The shouts during the chase had brought more men to his aid, but the three cowardly Greeks had gone into hiding at the base of the walls that separated the quarter from the port. They were slipping from one burned-out structure to another, making just enough noise to send Eustace's increasingly angry warriors dashing hither and yon in pursuit. Toying with them, like Count Louis himself.

Suffering Louis's caprices was one thing; being the sport of a handful of stinking heathens was another altogether. Eustace corralled his men and began a more systematic search. Those Greeks had to be carrying something of value, and Eustace was determined to possess it.

Eustace and his lieutenant heard the clash of blades from the next street over. He called out to the rest of the men and charged. A worm of disquiet squirmed in his belly when he heard screams—screams in French and German. Had the Greeks launched some kind of ambush?

Rounding the corner, Eustace choked back a cry of his own.

Blackened horrors out of nightmare attacked the crusaders. Things with skin split and cracked like a boar left too long on the spit, tendons creaking and bone grating with every movement. They swung with blade and clawed hands at Eustace's panicking men, advancing without pause despite the Franks' flailing efforts to beat them back.

Eustace heard a torrent of prayer and realized the words came from his own lips. Faced with the unholy, the young crusader worshipped in earnest for the first time in long memory. The prayer bolstered his quavering soul. He raised his blade high and bellowed praises to God. Eustace's lieutenant stood fast as well and joined in the cry. A handful of the fleeing crusaders stumbled in their retreat as they heard the words of faith and purity.

The dead things came forward—at least a dozen, their notched swords and hooked fingers dripping with crusader blood. Yet the knight from Vendôme held his ground. His voice grew stronger and his surviving soldiers came to the call. They formed a ragged line against the monstrous enemy, voices rising in a unified call to the Lord.

Distant fires in the burning city cast faint illumination on the nameless Byzantine street as warriors of Christ clashed with the soulless dead.

Markus watched his corpse knights tear into the crusaders. One of the Franks made a valiant attempt to rally his men, but the gesture proved futile. The animated bodies fought with a ferocity that defied description.

Less than ten minutes after it had begun, the battle was done. Freshly slain remains littered the street along with the blackened corpses of the temporarily resurrected. Markus Musa Giovanni stepped from the burned-out warehouse and summoned the remaining five corpse knights to his side. Murder incarnate, the walking dead hungered to be free from the one who, through dark ritual and power of his cursed blood, had woken them and now bound them. He maintained iron control to hold them in line. He would dissipate the death energies after the corpse knights cleared a path through the Port of Neorion.

Falsinar and Beltramose shouldered their packs and, with not a little trepidation, ventured onto the street. Stepping gingerly to avoid the many splashes of gore, the men followed their lord from the city of Constantinople.

Chapter Three

West of Constantinople
23 April, 1204

Eight nights in the wilderness not far from ravaged Constantinople left Markus and his men in poor spirits. Venetians were renowned as traders, willing to travel anywhere in search of new markets. These three were no different, although Markus journeyed in search of scholarly knowledge rather than conventional trade goods.

Travel aboard ship and in caravans involved a certain lack of luxury, to be certain. But hunkering in the chill and damp of spring with no creature comforts and on constant guard for marauding crusaders and fleeing Byzantines? It was a new experience, and by no means a pleasant one. Markus weathered the ordeal better than his mortal retainers did by dint of his preternatural constitution. Falsinar and Beltramose bore up as well as two city dwellers could, but days of guarding the rude hole that served as Markus's lair and nights of shivering, fitful sleep in the same small cave took their toll.

Markus spared little sympathy for their discomfort. The men had endured more challenging circumstances in the past, and would surely do so in the future. A more pressing matter commanded his attention than listening to Falsinar and Beltramose complain.

During his years in Constantinople, Markus had learned of many items that his extended family would be eager to possess. In the nights following the flight from the city, his bound spirits—Infantino, Vesta, Hartmut, Viator, Domnola, and

Rina—were his eyes and ears in the chaotic Queen of Cities. The ghosts gathered information on the condition of various estates, churches, libraries and their contents. Their observations confirmed that almost everything of note had been looted, destroyed, or spirited from the city. Unfortunate, to be sure, but Markus was confident that a certain cache remained hidden within the bowels of Constantinople.

Problem was, he'd been stymied in every attempt to date to track that particular cache to its source. The reason was simple enough: Markus sought the lair of his fellow Cappadocian, Alexia Theusa. He had hunted Alexia's haven for years, ever since her adversarial position became clear. Markus continued trying to win her over, of course, but he was not adverse to raiding Alexia's lair if that's what it took to uncover her secrets.

It was proving quite a challenge. Vampires were paranoid about keeping their havens secret. They had no greater fear than being exposed during the day, while they were at their most vulnerable. Still, with the secret resource of phantoms at his command, Markus had reasoned it was only a matter of time before he found Alexia's private nest. After losing two shades in the course of his investigations, he had been forced to reevaluate the matter.

Now, at last, it appeared that the perfect opportunity to make his move had come.

"You are certain she is gone, then?" Beltramose asked around a mouthful of rabbit fresh off the spit. Markus had forbidden any fire from the first night of their bivouac, lest smoke during the day or light during the night reveal their position. Arising this evening, he found that Falsinar and Beltramose had staged a minor revolt. The fire was small, barely sufficient to roast a rabbit felled by a bolt from Falsinar's crossbow. The ghouls were quick to point out that they only considered building it due to the overcast sky. Markus gave them their little victory. This was their last night at the hideout anyway.

"I am reasonably confident, yes. Infantino and the others have spied her from time to time over the past few nights, in the rare moments she does not conceal herself from their sight."

Falsinar washed down his own rabbit with a gulp of bitter wine. "Given the trouble they have tracking her, how can you be sure she has left Constantinople?"

"Lady Theusa is powerful, but she is not omnipotent. Considering the pains I have long had in keeping her under surveillance, a better use of resources was in order. Rather than trying to follow her, I directed Infantino and the others to watch those she might have reason to contact."

"And one of them said that she was leaving?"

"Better. She left with one of them." Falsinar and Beltramose passed the wineskin between them, sharing a toast to their lord's cleverness. "From what Infantino and Hartmut reported, the Nosferatu Malachite has undertaken a journey, with Alexia lending some assistance as guide."

"Nosferatu," Beltramose said, lips curling. "Compared to them, lepers are as appealing as fresh-faced virgins."

"'Judge not,' my friend. Unpleasant to look upon the Nosferatu may be, but they hold great influence here. Or they did, prior to the city's fall."

"But they are not even Latin," Falsinar offered in Beltramose's defense.

"Latin. Greek. Petty labels in the larger scheme. Few recall we were once all part of a single great empire. The Greeks may worship differently than we do, but our God is the same. As is our Devil." Markus began pacing, the long, slow burn of frustration flaring into anger. He continued, more to himself than to his retainers. "Yes, it is all simple perception. Perception that bears no impact upon truth. Greek or Latin, mortal or Cainite… *knowledge* is what truly matters. Knowledge begets power. And with sufficient power, all things are possible.

"Ah, but wisdom. The odd man out. Without wisdom to temper power, failure is assured. It matters not the task, from the simplest chore to the greatest venture one can imagine." The vampire spun to face his men. "Yes, Falsinar. The Nosferatu in fallen Constantinople are not Latin. Nor is their scion, Malachite. But this makes them no less worthy of respect. Only a fool assumes he is superior without first taking close measure of his opponent. Why do you think I was always the polite visitor in this land? Why is it that I never pressed the reputation of Clan Cappadocian or the power of my family upon those with whom I dealt? Because whatever my power, a score of others there could render me to dust with but a flick of the wrist!"

Falsinar and Beltramose exchanged a look. Markus was known for lapsing into lecture, a byproduct of his mortal years as a scholar. Yet the ghouls had seldom seen Markus vent to this extent. Unsure of their role, they remained mute while Markus prowled like the bear that was his nickname. Silence, punctuated by the occasional crack and pop from the fire, stretched for a minute or more.

Regaining some measure of equilibrium at last, Markus returned to his seat by the fire. "Apologies, gentlemen. It has been a difficult time for us all. But please; Malachite should be accorded respect. I have had few dealings with him, but he was always considerate. More than can be said for my clanmate, Alexia."

Falsinar nodded. "So do we follow her, then?"

"I had considered it, but no. Alexia is skilled enough at keeping things from the phantoms that even Infantino could not glean where she and Malachite are headed. Besides, I do not think she would be any more forthcoming with me elsewhere in the world than she has been here." Markus scratched at his dark beard, considering the constant frustration he had faced in dealing with the ancient vampire. "No, I will learn more by finding her lair. She has dwelled in Constantinople for as long as anyone can remember. She must have amassed a most impressive store of knowledge in that time, some of which is certain to have direct bearing on my mission."

"And anything else will at least be educational, yes?"

"Indeed."

Beltramose looked east in the night. Layers of hills and trees obscured sacked Constantinople, which lay like the carcass of some mammoth beast of legend. "A fine plan, *Signore*. And what is our role to be?"

"To remain in safety—or as much as is possible, given current circumstances. Viator discovered an abandoned cottage not far from the road to Adrianople. I have made a map. Wait for me there." He removed a fine iron chain from around his neck. Attached to it was the wedding band of a foolish Venetian merchant murdered by Moorish pirates when he made one too many disparaging comments about Mohammedan women while at port on Majorca.That sailor's young wife had thrown herself into the Grand Canal upon hearing the news and even in death could not quite bring herself to wander far from the symbol of their doomed union. Of such foolish attachments were ghostly slaves born. Markus handed the chain to Falsinar. "Domnola will go with you. If there is trouble, call her name with a message and she will find me. Otherwise, I shall meet you once I have completed my task."

Slipping back inside the city walls was an ordeal, since only the sewers offered undetected entry. Markus was far too large to fit through most of those passages, which were much trafficked by the Nosferatu. And were he not, he had no desire to become fouled with the noxious effluvium that churned through the underground tunnels. While he discounted subterranean egress for the moment, getting back into Constantinople was not an insurmountable challenge for one who could command the spirits of the dead. An hour's patience and a sentry provided an opening, stepping away to add to the output of the sewers. Markus followed Infantino's whispered guidance up and over the walls of Theodosius.

Once inside, Markus used the system of cisterns and aqueducts that ran through much of the city's interior. Like the sewers—though larger and far cleaner—these routes allowed him to travel unnoticed by Constantinople's conquerors. Within an hour, he slipped from the cistern hole connected to the Aqueduct of Valens, not far from the Church of the Holy Apostles. That grand basilica was the first stop in his investigation to locate Alexia's haven. It might not be her actual resting place, but this particular church held great importance for her, and he himself had noted that she visited it regularly. Not surprising, given that the emperors of Constantinople were laid to rest here. Lady Alexia Theusa was fascinated with death like any Cappadocian—"graverobbers," other Cainites called their kind in less polite moments. Markus figured that she studied the corpses of the dead emperors to discover distinctions between the existence of divine royalty and common folk. Did the imperial mantle leave marks on the flesh and bones and the echoes of life within them? It was a question of more than idle curiosity for Markus also, but he had not yet had the opportunity to pursue the matter.

He approached the Church of the Holy Apostles with trepidation. The multi-domed cruciform temple radiated the residue of generations of worshipers' faith. The holy aura was a tangible pressure even from where he stood at the courtyard's outer edge. Not unlike the heat from a blazing furnace—a comparison that was not mere hyperbole. Markus could well be burned by this holy place if he did not first reaffirm his acceptance of God's limitless power and infinite mercy.

The irony of his circumstance—one of the damned, daring to enter a temple to God—was not lost upon him. He had chosen his course willingly, with full belief in the Lord and in the peril to his soul as a result. Still, it was not intended as a challenge to the heavens. Standing at the far edge of the courtyard, Markus bowed his head and prayed. It helped to settle the tremble in his long-dead heart. He squared his broad shoulders and walked a measured pace across the courtyard.

The bound spirits assured him that no one guarded the basilica. Coming upon the large main entrance, it was clear why. The doorway was a ragged opening, the glorious marble blackened with soot and the wooden door hacked almost to kindling. His preternatural senses cut through the darkness to perceive the destruction inside. He knew the place had not been spared the sack, but seeing it firsthand was startling nonetheless. A church, even a Byzantine one, represented faith and learning, a desire to commune with a higher power and to achieve greater comprehension of the self and of the world. Seeing the place desecrated awakened a cold anger within him. He contemplated using his power to glean the identities of those who had committed this act. It would be difficult, but with effort he might discover some residue of an aura that could be tracked.

No. It is not my place. I leave it to God to exact vengeance. A *more pressing matter lies at hand.*

Bracing himself against the aura of the divine, Markus entered the Church of the Holy Apostles. Struggling to retain focus against the church's spiritual pressure, he plodded with a scowl of concentration toward the western wing. He did his best to ignore the gooseflesh rising on his neck and arms, and the deterioration of his usually strong sense of balance. Fever was not something a vampire was accustomed to, but he could manage.

During a previous investigation of the church in his ongoing effort to find the lair of Alexia Theusa, Markus had learned of a secret panel that led to the true resting place of the Byzantine emperors, from the last to the very first, Constantine himself. The door was disguised as a carved likeness of Constantinople's great Cainite lord, Michael, in the guise of an angel. Though Markus was more than a little curious about the wealth of secrets the catacombs must contain, he was unable to investigate. Some force lurked within the crypts, something of a power formidable enough to give him pause. A creature of Alexia's, placed to guard against intruders—perhaps even put there to challenge him specifically. Markus learned that much from a ghostly slave in the final moments before it disintegrated into spectral effluvium.

He never discovered just what caused the wraith's destruction, and the remaining ghosts were not eager to find out. Ironic in a way, since being in the church appeared to invigorate them—indeed, Markus had less trouble than normal perceiving their thick, smoky auras. Nonetheless, they were loath to venture into the crypts. Infantino, strongest of the shades, would go no further than the bottom of the twisting stairs that opened to the catacombs. Lacking sufficient information on what awaited in the darkness, Markus had let the matter lie… until now.

Let us hope the guardian went with Lady Alexia and the Nosferatu Malachite. Markus allowed himself a cold smile. Even if it remained below, he felt more comfortable taking on whatever-it-was without worry that the elder Cappadocian would appear at an inopportune moment.

Coming upon the atrium that housed the secret panel, he found a pair of bodies—a monk and a crusader, each advanced a week in rot and decay. The corpses gave Markus little pause. He had seen enough death in his time. Such a tableau was even unremarkable within a church, given the slaughter throughout Constantinople. Instead, his attention was on the secret crypt entrance. The wall panel was open. He couldn't tell whether it had been left ajar at the same time the men were killed, or if someone had passed this way moments ago.

Did the guardian from below slay these men? Markus wondered. Given that the crusader was decapitated in particularly grisly fashion, some supernatural agency was likely involved. He looked around the atrium but found nothing to provide further context. He commanded the shades to investigate the catacombs, but was no more successful than before. He could subjugate them entirely to his will, but the effort would leave him weakened—not an appealing condition if danger lurked below. Markus would have to see for himself what, if anything, awaited beneath the church.

Muttering imprecations at the timidity of spirits, Markus squeezed into the narrow passage. The church's supernal aura faded as he descended, reduced to a lingering afterthought at the base of the staircase. He commenced a cursory search in the darkness. The oil lamp remained unlit in one hand so that he did not announce his presence prematurely.

Only a few paces in, he was pleased to discover scattered patches of sickly green fungus and pale light filtering from narrow air ducts. Moonlight and fungus gave off the most feeble of illumination, but it was sufficient to one of his unnaturally keen senses.

After some minutes of careful shuffling, Markus realized he'd been hearing a voice for a while now. He paused and cocked an ear. It offered a hypnotic murmured cadence, its rhythm as seductive as waves lapping the shore....

Markus slumped, cracking his head against a wall. Startled back to clarity, he marshaled his wits. *The voice.* It had lured him into a kind of stupor. It was seductive and repulsive at once, lacking rising intensity but nonetheless containing great urgency. Concentrating on interpreting the sound rather than being seduced by it, he soon determined that he was not its focus. Still, even with over a dozen languages at his command, Markus could not place the muttering that echoed through the crypts. He stole forward, the voice growing somewhat louder but hardly more distinct.

A *mélange of languages,* Markus realized. *Greek, Latin, Arabic, Chaldean, Aramaic... at least two others. Many tongues, but spoken with one voice.*

Caution and curiosity battled within him. He moved his bulk as silently as the narrow tunnels allowed, determined to find the source of this mystery. A glimmer became visible further down one corridor. Torchlight, from the reflected flickering. Aided by the illumination, he moved with greater confidence. Another turn and he saw a large chamber—the tomb of the Emperor Constantine.

A single guttering torch revealed a sarcophagus in the center of the room. The heavy lid was pushed off, lying forgotten on the floor to one side. A long sword in an unadorned sheath leaned against the other side. An armored figure—unmistakably someone other than the long-dead Constantine—sat in the open casket. He was large, not as thickset as Markus but formidable nonetheless. His chain mail gleamed dully in the torchlight, under a white mantle embossed with the red eight-pointed cross of the Knights Templar. His apparel was so clean in comparison to the musty chamber that it veritably glowed. Fair hair fell from a wide brow that suggested intelligence and compassion. Yet the figure's mouth hung slack like a simpleton's, a string of pinkish drool marring his otherwise impeccable attire. His eyelids fluttered over pupils rolled up to reveal nothing but white. His large, mailed arms hung at the elbow over the casket's edge, hands twitching in irregular counterpoint to the ongoing murmur.

Markus might have pondered the incongruity of a warrior of Christ desecrating the burial place of Constantine, had not even greater puzzles presented themselves. Firstly, the knight's pale aura revealed him to be of the blood, a fellow Cainite. Secondly, he was in the grip of a fit, likely related to the chanting. Thirdly, whatever the source of that voice, it did not come from the Templar's lips.

This undead knight cannot be Alexia's guardian. The voice... He is ensnared by whatever lurks down here.

Markus was on the periphery of the effect, but its potency was clear. But what was the thing itself, and how could he avoid becoming its victim as well?

The Templar stirred. Eyes still showing white and mouth slack as before, the vampire knight hoisted himself from the open tomb. He moved with a speed that was easily a match for Markus at his fastest. Standing tall in the chamber, his sheathed blade grasped in one fist, the Templar extended his free hand toward the sarcophagus. A pale arm the color of the surrounding stone emerged from within the casket, then another. The Templar drew out the grasping form—an inhumanly emaciated woman clad in a simple shift. She moved with the lithe sensuality of an asp, clutching at the Templar, twisting her lean body to wrap her legs about his waist. Her limbs clung to the stoic knight with disquieting intimacy. Her face hovered close to his, her lips a hair's breadth from the knight's cold cheek as she sustained the whisper of strange words.

What is this creature, that she can hypnotize an undead knight? Markus was too enthralled by the bizarre union to retreat as he surely should. Her aura was as pale as the Templar's or Markus's own, yet shot through with pulsing veins of red-gold that fascinated the eye. Markus tore his gaze away with an effort and slipped back down the passage. A *Cainite, but of a kind I have not encountered before.*

Then, at last, Markus heard a word in the chant that provided the answer... while calling forth entirely new questions.

Chapter Four

North of Constantinople
24 April, 1204

He was called Sir Hugh of Glairvaux of the Knights Templar. He was also of the Ventrue, a clan of vampire nobles who considered themselves best-suited to rule of all the undead. Markus learned the vampire knight's identity later, after following him from the crypts beneath the Church of the Holy Apostles. The Templar left Constantine's tomb moments after Markus stepped away, cramming himself into an alcove in a hasty attempt to hide. Sir Hugh wandered by, still in oblivious thrall to the guardian of the catacombs.

After a brief internal debate, Markus went in pursuit. With the aid of his spectral slaves, Markus tracked the knight to a military camp outside the walls of Constantinople. Strangely, the ghosts were as unwilling to approach the knight as they were to descend into the crypts. They did, at least, glean the Templar's name when the knight was greeted by an underling.

It was clear that Sir Hugh of Clairvaux was a creature of some power and influence. Though secretly one of the undead, he led an entire troop of Templars. Markus had sensed the knights' piety; true warriors of Christ were they. The same could be said of Hugh, despite his undead condition.

The night had grown short by then, so Markus tracked down Falsinar and Beltramose. The ghouls had encamped in the tumbledown ruin of a cottage, and were hard at work preparing a suitable resting place for their lord. Markus just had time to slip into his new lair before the lethargy of dawn overtook him.

"The guardian under the church is a... what, *Signore*?"

"She is one of the Lamia."

Falsinar frowned. "I am unfamiliar with the term."

"Understandable. It is an uncommon one. I myself have never met one of the Lamia bloodline." Markus shrugged with his hands. "A lesser breed of Cappadocian are they—in numbers, influence and ability. A select group, women mostly, who began as a mortal cult worshipping Lilith."

"As in..."

"Adam's first wife, yes." Markus allowed a smile. "One wonders why the witches did not name their group in her honor. Rather, the name comes from folklore, an honorific bestowed upon their high priestess, who was Embraced by one of my clan."

"So they are of the blood, then?" Beltramose wondered.

"A divergent path, but yes."

"Ah!" Understanding lit Falsinar's features. "Not unlike the Giovanni, then."

Markus turned a cold glare on his retainer. "My family enjoys full and unreserved status within the clan. The witches are little more than attendants and bodyguards. There is no similarity between Giovanni and Lamia beyond sharing the blood of Cappadocius."

Falsinar bowed his head. "Of course not, *Signore*. It was foolish of me to assume so."

"Yes, it was." Markus rubbed at his temples, an old habit from mortal times. He continued in a calmer tone: "Most Cappadocians are scholars, like myself. In contrast, the Lamia make their claim as fierce warriors. My sire, Guisseppi, told me that is why they were inducted: to provide the clan with a measure of martial support. A Lamia often pledges her skills to protect a Cappadocian—usually an elder of some stature.

"I should have known," he muttered with some chagrin. "They are rare, seldom seen outside Mount Erciyes. Still, I should have known that Lady Alexia would have a Lamia in her charge. One could not ask for a better watchdog."

"But if this is some warrior woman, what of this business of whispering in diverse languages?" Beltramose asked.

"I do not know, yet. Her kind have their own style of dark arts that is said to enthrall with a mere touch or even with seductive whispers. I do not know what she intends in using it against the Templar. I shall puzzle that out in time, but already it has been of benefit. Had I not heard her speak of Lilith, the Dark Mother, I would still be at a loss as to her nature." Markus paused, recalling the encounter in the catacombs. "I am disturbed even to recall the intimacy she displayed toward the Templar. And there was an aura about her…. My sire said nothing of the witches acting so strangely."

Markus shook off the memory. "It comes down to this: I am certain, now, that the Lamia guards the entrance to Lady Alexia's haven. Alas, even with you men to support me, only Christ and Caine may say who would be the victor were I to face her directly."

"Then what do you propose, *Signore*?"

"Good Beltramose, I see no need to engage in conflict when another can be found to do so in my stead." The ghouls shared a timid glance. Markus gave a hearty laugh. "Not you, gentlemen! There is another. Better suited than any of us."

"The Templar?" Falsinar offered after a moment's thought.

Markus's teeth flashed sharp and white in his dark beard. "The Templar."

Markus established a routine to monitor Sir Hugh of Clairvaux. As one night passed to another in the ensuing weeks, it became clear that the Ventrue knight planned a new crusade in the ashes of the one so recently aborted. Sir Hugh relocated for a time to the growing refugee camp outside Adrianople. There, he set about gathering forces under his banner. Once he reached sufficient numbers, the army would sail for Egypt. Richard the Lion-Hearted himself had observed after the Third Crusade that Egypt, the center of Muslim wealth and power, must be broken before Jerusalem could be reclaimed. The Fourth Crusade had been formed for this very purpose, only to spend itself upon Constantinople instead. But Sir Hugh and his Templars—a collection of fellow undead and ghouls loyal to the cause through the twin influences of vampiric blood and righteous faith—had not forgotten their purpose.

And they soon drew the attention of others. Rumor had formed in the wake of Constantinople's fall that the Nosferatu Malachite would be the city's savior; but he was gone for weeks now. Sir Hugh championed a different cause, but his charisma was undeniable and his presence was obvious. In the absence of one to uphold the dream of a golden Constantinople ruled by refined and potent vampires, Cainites and mortals alike gravitated toward the Templar's quest. Markus watched from the shadows as the Egyptian Crusade gained ever more champions.

The Lamia's growing influence upon Sir Hugh had more than a little to do with this venture. The creature's whispers reached the Ventrue knight no matter how far he ranged from the catacombs, and even spewed from Hugh's own lips during so-called "holy visions." Markus knew these were far from divine events, but he decided to keep his own counsel until he better understood the Lamia's motives.

Having generated support among the disaffected and desperate, Sir Hugh left the sprawling camps outside Adrianople for an estate near the docks of Galata, a few miles from Constantinople's imposing walls. It was home to one Gabriella of Genoa, a Cainite of the Lasombra lineage who offered Sir Hugh her patronage. Masters of shadow and manipulation, the Lasombra held great influence in Latin territories, including Markus's home of Venice. Markus had heard of Gabriella, but the woman was not of a status to exert much influence within Constantinople. Thus, Markus had never seen the need to establish contact with her. Given the speed with which Gabriella joined forces with Hugh, it was apparent that the Templar was not alone in taking advantage of the flux that Constantinople's fall had created. Gabriella surely hoped that the Egyptian Crusade would result in a greater power base for herself.

With Sir Hugh's relocation, Markus returned to his ruined tower in Constantinople's Latin Quarter—though, since the sack, the whole of the city could be considered Latin. The conquering forces had not hesitated to install themselves. It was a boon for Markus and his men, who hadn't mixed with their fellow Latins since their retreat in April. The homesick Falsinar and Beltramose considered the camaraderie of other Venetians, of Lombards and Pisans, a greater benefit even than sleeping in real beds and enjoying regular hot meals again.

Even so, Constantinople was much changed from the bustling city of mixed cultures it had been but two months before. Despite the efforts of the new emperor, Baldwin of Flanders, the city and the surrounding lands remained in tumult. Latins ruled Constantinople, but Byzantines lurked in the outlying regions. Factions gathered forces in hopes of retaking the city. Tension hung in the air like a haze in summer, and violence flared often throughout the city and beyond.

Mortals were not alone in their interest, either. Vampires from a variety of clans returned to or arrived for the first time in Constantinople, each with his own agenda. The Queen of Cities served as a particularly desirable arena in which Cainites could indulge themselves. Sir Hugh and his Egyptian Crusade were but one example of the never-ending machinations of the undead.

After brief encounters with others of the blood, Markus found the irony rich indeed. Constantinople had long been ruled from the shadows by the vampire Michael. The city had come to symbolize a dream the ancient had of a vampiric utopia, an unparalleled example of Cainite prestige and achievement. His dream found expression in the grand city itself, thanks in no small part to the influence through the centuries of Michael and his two erstwhile companions, Antonius and the Dracon. Though from different clans, Antonius and the Dracon shared Michael's dream without reservation. So profound was the Toreador Michael's vision that it gained proper status—mention of "The Dream" brought forth knowing nods from vampires throughout Europe and Byzantium.

Only now, the Queen of Cities was fallen, ancient Michael and Antonius were destroyed, and the Dracon was vanished like the promise of the Dream itself. In its place, Cainites representing clans high and low crept in, hoping to carve out a supreme position. Many claimed to resurrect the Dream, but Markus found in their words and actions a sad attempt at make-believe.

He'd given Michael's Dream little thought, busy as he was pursuing matters for the Giovanni elders. But now that the city was fallen—now that he saw the rude parody that replaced a profound and enlightened realm—Markus felt the sorrow of loss.

It was for this reason, as well as to keep his actions veiled from possible rivals, that Markus directed his men to keep a low profile. Falsinar and Beltramose were to be on their guard even when they caroused with fellow Venetians. Markus had a dream of his own—not as grand a one as Michael's, perhaps, but Markus was intent on avoiding his own destruction in the course of seeing it realized.

This was not always an easy thing, determined as he was to observe Sir Hugh and the strange Lamia. The Ventrue knight and the Lamia guardian were quite powerful. It would not go well for Markus, were he discovered spying on either one. As it was, he inadvertently exposed himself to Sir Hugh's underlings once or twice and made a panicked scramble from the catacombs another time when the Lamia caught a whiff of his aura. And now that Sir Hugh was again close to Constantinople, the Templar resumed his clandestine visits to the crypts beneath the Church of the Apostles. Markus was frantic to know what secrets the two shared during these meetings, but he dared not follow.

The Lamia's influence upon Sir Hugh left Markus in a quandary. On the one hand, the longer he delayed in breaking her control, the more difficult it would be to accomplish. There would be no problem turning the pious Ventrue on the pagan Lamia after that, for Sir Hugh surely was not its willing thrall. Markus was confident that the Templar would be quick to destroy the guardian in a fit of righteous vengeance—or, at the very least, weaken her enough that Markus could finish the job with a minimum amount of danger to himself and to his men.

On the other hand, Markus was ever more curious as to just what the Lamia was up to. He saw no connection between the Egyptian Crusade and Lady Alexia's interests. The Lamia manipulated Sir Hugh to strike at Egypt, but why? What interest did the Lady Alexia have in that ancient land? Or did the Lamia act of her own interests? Regardless of which woman was behind it, holy wars were of little moment to Cappadocians. There had to be some other goal worthwhile to the Clan of Death. Markus had come across several mentions of the fascination the ancient citizens of the Nile Valley had for death rites, so he could guess in general terms what would draw a Cappadocian's interest to Egypt, but he was a man of details and fact, not generalities and supposition. Observation would reveal more than action at this juncture.

"There is no question that your knowledge and wisdom are great, *Signore.* Yet is this continued waiting the best course?"

Markus quirked a thick brow. "It is as if you have plucked the very thought from my mind."

Half expecting anger at voicing such presumption, Beltramose was thrown off his stride. "Ah. I assure you that I lack such an ability, *Signore.*"

"That may change, should you prove yourself worthy to receive my Embrace." Markus waved that topic away for another time. "Worry not, gentlemen. I have considered this matter with some intensity these past weeks. Curious as I am to know what Lady Alexia wants with an Egyptian Crusade, we lack the luxury of waiting indefinitely for understanding."

"So you think the Lady Alexia is behind the Lamia's influence?" Falsinar asked.

"Like as not. The creature has been content to do nothing more than guard Alexia Theusa's lair for… well, for how long, only God may say. It is possible that the witch seized the opportunity of the recent chaos to enact some plan—but it may be that Lady Alexia did the same." Still ignorant of the source of motivation, Markus was nonetheless gripped with increasing unease as he witnessed its effects. The Lamia had become more than a simple impediment to his interests. She was a corrupting force out of proportion with the power he sensed. Memories of heaped corpses and degenerate ceremonies in the darkness under the Church of the Apostles flashed through his mind. Markus shook off the visions with an effort of will. "Whatever the case, we have reached a point where simply watching from the shadows gains us nothing.

"The time has come to act, gentlemen."

Chapter Five

Constantinople
15 July, 1204

It was now almost three months since Alexia Theusa had left Constantinople. She might return at any moment, and Markus would have wasted his chance.

He had spent a week preparing a blood ritual he hoped could snap Sir Hugh of Clairvaux from the Lamia's control. Cappadocians knew many secrets of the dead, from accelerating decay to inducing the rigidity of death. He was confident he could immobilize Sir Hugh long enough to bind the Ventrue with more conventional restraints. Then he would attempt a rite known to transform some of the properties of the vampiric form, hopefully changing Hugh's humors enough to snap the Lamia's hold. He had never tried the rite before and was unsure if it would work, but it was the best plan he had. Alas, Sir Hugh was never alone long enough for Markus to make his move.

This night was his last attempt. If Sir Hugh could not be turned, Markus was resigned to making a direct assault against the Lamia. He could find help from a few of the disaffected Cainites that slouched around Constantinople. The pretense of hidden treasures would be enough of a lure, and they would make better fodder against the Lamia than kine mercenaries would. It was far from a preferred plan, but it would have to do.

In the end, the choice was made for him.

During a stroll near the docks at Galata with his confidante, a strange Arab girl named Amala, Sir Hugh encountered a fellow Templar. Markus's preternatural hearing was more than sufficient to hear their introductions from a dozen yards away. He assumed this Sir Ingolt of Wolfram was another Templar inducted into the secrets of Cainites—until Hugh actually swooned when the man stepped forward to embrace him in greeting. Markus sharpened his gaze and saw Sir Ingolt's aura blazing in a blinding nimbus of gold.

By Christ and Caine! His soul quaked as when he stood before the Church of the Holy Apostles. *He is imbued with such piety—his mere presence wracks Sir Hugh with agony!*

Markus watched as the shock and pain of Sir Ingolt's holy aura threw the Ventrue knight into a frenzy. Losing any semblance of humanity, Sir Hugh lunged forward. Ingolt showed remarkable bravery, facing down a slavering fiend with pure heart and steady hand. Hugh triumphed but barely, skewering the true Templar with a savage thrust of his blade just before collapsing himself.

Markus slipped away as the girl Amala rushed to Sir Hugh's side. The Ventrue was unharmed physically, but it would be some nights before he recovered from the spiritual wounds Sir Ingolt had inflicted. Hugh was useless now, committing Markus to another course.

Moving down darkened streets, he headed to a sewer grate. Though he had sought to avoid using them before, the sewers were the only feasible means of keeping an eye on Sir Hugh. The Nosferatu had long ago developed an extensive network of tunnels that wound through Constantinople's sewers and extended past the city's walls to the docks of Galata and beyond. Thanks to Infantino and the other bound spirits, Markus had discovered a few of these passages. They suited his needs well, once he learned to ignore the waste.

His other concern—running into the sewers' original Cainite residents—had proved negligible. It turned out that most of the Nosferatu had relocated to the Adrianople camps after Malachite left with Lady Alexia and a handful of his ranking clanmates. The sewer system was mostly empty but for the ubiquitous excretions that flowed throughout its countless tunnels.

His heavy brow was knotted in contemplation as he

squeezed through the sewer opening. Although necessity had set his course of action, Markus still felt keen disappointment. Sir Hugh of Clairvaux had offered such a tidy solution to the problem of the Lamia. Markus did not look forward to facing the creature himself, even with fellow undead, blood-enhanced ghouls, and bound spirits to aid him.

Others like Sir Ingolt would offer an interesting alternative, he thought. Depressing a concealed lever exposed the tunnel behind a false wall. A *squad of such knights armed with righteous faith would surely crush the Lamia!*

Markus allowed himself the flicker of a smile as he stepped through and lit a torch. Of course, approaching such pious warriors would be to flirt with his own destruction. And that assumed he knew where to find—

The world did a cartwheel. Markus slammed against the ground, the torch tumbling from his grasp. He was flipped on his back like a landed fish just as suddenly, then shoved against the muck-covered sewer wall. Kneeling with a blade at his throat, he saw his attacker at last. A wizened figure of advanced age, his skin was a rich mahogany covered with myriad wrinkles. A beard of pure white framed a long face from which shone two excited, predatory eyes. A pale violet aura shot with streamers of emerald flickered around him. Given the attacker's stealth and the ease with which he had tossed Markus, this spindly Arab was assuredly a fellow Cainite—one of the feared undead killers known as Assamites, Markus felt certain. Calling themselves the Children of Haqim and disavowing ties to Caine, these vampires were said to be the ultimate masters of murder. Killing was an art form to them, a religion—as death was to the Cappadocians.

Fear gripped his dead heart, but Markus offered a disarming smile to the Assamite standing over him—well, before him, anyway. Even kneeling, Markus was so large compared to the slight Arab that they were almost at eye level. He said in Greek, "I think you're making quite a mistake here, good fellow."

"No, no, no," the Assamite replied in the same tongue, showing his own teeth. "I know from your speed at our last encounter that you are Cainite, and now you know I am as well."

The "last encounter" was probably one of the times Markus had been seen near Sir Hugh's camp. *Too confident; he overplays his hand and reveals too much.* Despite the compromising situation, the Assamite's words and demeanor showed that he was far more interested in learning from Markus than in harming him. "Then the little dagger is still pointed at the base of my throat because—?"

"To keep you in check while we talk, of course."

"I'm disappointed you would think such a thing could stop me," Markus said. He shifted as if to stand. The Saracen held him fast with strength out of proportion to his frail limbs. *Not so eager that he forgets himself, however.*

In a confiding tone, the Assamite explained that he used a maneuver common to his clan's training—the thin blade, coated with Assamite blood poison, promised a most effective means of rendering Markus a drooling idiot even if it did not prove sufficient to destroy him. "It is my turn for questions, and I have so many," the Saracen concluded. "Who are you?"

Markus offered his name, and was surprised to see recognition spark in the Assamite's eyes. It was not exactly common knowledge in the undead community that some fledgling Venetian necromancers had joined the secretive Cappadocians. *This gnarled creature is exceedingly well informed indeed.* He wondered what treasures were stored in the Saracen's mind. His thoughts speeding like a galloping horse as he considered ways to reverse their roles of interrogator and captive, Markus missed much of the Assamite's subsequent rambling about Clan Cappadocian.

"But tell me quickly," the old man said at last, "why you are here in this fair city."

"Curiosity about this place, about the Church of the Apostles, and what special treasures it might hold." In hopes of forming a bond of shared interest, he added, "I have a penchant for wanting to sate my curiosity, I'm afraid."

"That, I can certainly understand," the Assamite replied, his aura suggesting that gathering knowledge bordered on obsession. "And, perhaps most pointedly, what is your interest in dogging the steps of Sir Hugh of Clairvaux?"

A question I would ask of you as well, my friend. "Yes, that, well... he has a connection to this place."

"These tunnels?"

"Not the tunnels exactly."

"By Ar-Rahman, you should not play so with an old man's curiosity. It is difficult to tell when such games might get out of hand."

"I meant no disrespect," Markus said, smiling despite the Assamite's threat. The wizened vampire's hunger for knowledge was unmistakable. Now to gamble if this could be steered to benefit Markus's agenda. "It simply occurred to me that you and I might not be at cross-purposes. Assuming, that is, that you're here to stop his mad crusade, and that you haven't done so yet out of concern that something might be behind him."

"Perhaps."

Seeing the Assamite's thinly veiled eagerness, the final elements of a new plan fell into place. "Yes, well, then 'perhaps' there is something of interest I can show you in these tunnels. It's not too far off."

The aged figure hesitated but a single mortal heartbeat. He withdrew the knife and gave Markus room to rise. "Show me," he said.

"Those beloved shades of yours were of no use at all! You could have been destroyed!"

"I appreciate your concern, Beltramose. But as you can see, I am unharmed." Despite his dismissive manner, Markus was chagrined and not a little unnerved. Having discarded Sir Hugh from his plans, he had likewise forgotten caution as he left the Ventrue knight to his Arab concubine. It was no surprise the old man had caught him so easily in the sewers. Even a vampire lacking an Assamite's mastery of stealth would have had little trouble sneaking up on him. Anger bubbled up then, drowning the thrill of fear Markus felt in recalling the compromising situation. He had been distracted, it was true, but his spirits *should* have noticed the Cainite assassin approach. *Unless they saw a chance to slip free of my yoke.*

Bound to service by necromantic rites, the ghosts were far

from willing servants. They sometimes took advantage of circumstances in hopes of escaping their spiritual shackles. Yet aside from balking at investigating the Lamia's catacombs or spying upon Sir Hugh, they had seemed resigned to their fate ever since Constantinople fell. Markus had grown lax in keeping them in check without even realizing it. He recognized his error during those first moments in the sewer, when his unique senses showed the ghosts' agitated anticipation as they watched their master kneel before the Assamite.

Markus glanced at the smoky forms cowering to one side of the tower room, quite a change from their recent eagerness. The Turk Viator was apparently feeling especially weak and miserable this night, the spectral echoes of his blisters seeping ectoplasmic ichor on the floor. He had died of the beatings and brandings crusaders gathered on Cyprus had seen fit to deliver him, and then found himself enslaved by Markus for another twenty years, revisiting the agony of his death again and again. *It is a shame*, the necromancer thought, *but such were the wages of sin.*

Markus decided he would let the spirits stew for the time being. They would be punished for their insolence once he dealt with more immediate concerns. "Had the Saracen wanted me dead, I would have been a pile of ash in the sewers without ever knowing I had suffered final death. The creature, Fajr, wanted answers. Answers I was quite happy to supply."

"Thanks be to Christ and Caine, *Signore*. But you imperil yourself, spying upon the Templar without our aid."

"Gentlemen, already you guard my slumber and pursue errands on my behalf in the day. You must rest sometime." Markus patted the man's shoulder. "Besides, despite your martial skills, even you could not observe a Cainite undetected for long. And, since my 'beloved shades' balked at approaching Sir Hugh, who was left to perform the task?"

Unable to argue this logic, Beltramose looked to Falsinar for assistance. The stocky man shrugged. Beltramose chose another tack. "Matters have grown more complex than is safe for us, *Signore*. The city is still in turmoil as Baldwin of Flanders secures the throne. This Lamia guarding Alexia's haven remains a mystery. And the means by which you had hoped to deal with her, this Sir Hugh of Clairvaux, you now declare is in the grip of madness and is useless to us. Then you are accosted by a Saracen killer! What good does it do us to traffic with him? He will surely turn on us at the first opportunity!"

"The Assamites are not merely bloodthirsty killers. Though unchristian, I grant you, they follow a code of conduct as rigorous as any Templar." Markus had seen more than one Templar fall from his vows to satisfy base desires, but that would send the discussion on a needless tangent. "And they are possibly the most skilled in the art of killing of any creature that exists. Who better to send against the Lamia?"

"As you say, *Signore*," Falsinar put in. "But I must agree with my emotional companion. How can you be certain this Assamite is here to stop the Egyptian Crusade? How can you trust that he and the others he claims are with him will put an end to the Lamia?"

"In the tunnels, I described to Fajr the Lamia's influence upon Sir Hugh. The Assamite is a learned man; he knows what the witches are capable of. Most importantly, he is now aware of how great a threat this one poses." To ensure that the Saracen vampire would not underestimate the danger that the Lamia promised, Markus had revealed the residue of her corruption. Remains were scattered in the sewers around the Church of the Holy Apostles. There were dozens of corpses, offerings Sir Hugh had led to his mistress as their couplings grew ever more depraved. Worse than simply sucked dry of blood, the bodies exploded with disease that inflicted a most painful death on the vermin that came to feed upon them. Markus had not needed to explain to Fajr that the Lamia carried an infection of great virulence as corrupting to mortal flesh as her dark arts were to Sir Hugh's mind. The quick-witted Assamite understood the implications at once. With Sir Hugh's forces to lead the way, the Lamia might spread the infection of flesh and will throughout Muslim lands.

"And you are certain that, like the Templar, the Assamites are not also in league with the Lamia?"

"The facts say otherwise. Consider that Assamites pray to

Allah, as any good Muslim would. Egypt is a Muslim land..."
Markus arched his heavy brows, encouraging his men to make
the connection. At their blank looks, he spelled it out: "Sir Hugh
mounts a crusade to strike at Egypt. He has been put up to this
by Lady Alexia's guardian, though I know not why as yet. This
Fajr as much as revealed that he and a few others are here to
stop it. But if they destroy Sir Hugh, might not the Lamia simply
find another proxy?"

"Ah... But if the Lamia is destroyed, the Assamites need fear
no subsequent campaigns once the present one is dealt with."

"Exactly, Falsinar." Markus noted that this logic did little to
reassure his men. "I do not discount your concerns, gentlemen.
But the Lamia must be destroyed, and I must find Lady Alexia's
haven before she returns. The Templar is useless to me, as are
his men. Fajr and his associates, however, are of the blood. They
possess the necessary skills."

"But Saracens, *Signore*? Especially Cainite Saracens! You put
us in peril, dealing with ones such as they."

"I grant that it is a risk, making an arrangement with these
creatures," Markus replied with some heat. "But I must take
such chances if I hope to fulfill my obligations to the family.
Do not forget, gentlemen, that we are charged with gathering
any knowledge that will help secure the Giovanni as equals
within Clan Cappadocian. Lady Alexia has proven unwilling
to form an alliance, but that in no way lessens her usefulness
to our cause. I will have no better chance of entering her lair,
and learning what secrets she keeps there, than now. And the
Assamites offer the best chance for me to accomplish this."

The ghouls were silent in the face of their master's rebuke.
After a frown of contemplation, Beltramose said, "I cannot dis-
pute your logic, *Signore*. But I confess to unease at making a pact
with Assamites. Who is to say they may not decide you are a
threat to their plans once they destroy the Lamia?"

"I am confident Fajr's primary desire is to remove the Lamia
from this world. There is no doubt that she is the instigator of the
Egyptian Crusade, an affair of far greater interest to Assamites
than a single graverobber." Markus paused, his agile mind considering a number of variables. He was confident enough that

his plans remained on course, but the Assamites' involvement must not be underestimated. Their focus was on stopping the new crusade, but that did not mean Markus should consider himself forgotten. As Beltramose suggested, the masters of assassination might want to tie up other loose ends after dispatching the Lamia. Simply taking extra care would not be sufficient protection against the Assamites, given their prowess. Granted, now that he was certain they were in the area, Markus could guard against the Children of Haqim to some degree. The same preternatural clarity of senses that enabled Markus to register the presence of ghosts likewise gave him a chance to detect a vampire otherwise concealed from normal perception. There were no guarantees when dealing with the many and varied disciplines of the undead, however. And although Markus might sense a lurking Assamite—or Nosferatu, for that matter, as those hideous creatures shared the rare talent of obfuscation—his mortal retainers could not say the same. "Your concern is warranted, Beltramose. It is best we stay out of sight until the matter is dealt with. Collect your things; we will find another resting place."

As the Assamites might not be alone in having an interest in where he rested, Markus explained that they would wait until just after dawn to move from the ruined tower. Falsinar was sent to appropriate a cart on which he and Beltramose would load their master, packed securely in a sealed casket, and hurry to a new lair. Markus had searched the area a few nights previously and found a suitable bolt hole—a cellar beneath a burned-out building on the edge of the Latin Quarter. Few stirred in the dawn, which should make the move easy enough.

Markus fell into contemplation as Falsinar and Beltramose gathered what little remained of their belongings. One reason the pair had been in his employ for so long was that Markus appreciated their frank attitudes. They forgot themselves at times, but on the whole the men gave Markus worthwhile advice and spoke up when his scholarly eagerness took him too far afield of prudence.

Beltramose was right about the Assamites. It was folly to take Fajr's claims that they were only interested in stopping the

Egyptian Crusade. Fajr watched Sir Hugh from the shadows. Who knew how many other Saracens did the same, or had even infiltrated the crusader's camp? The Arab woman Amala, perhaps? And what other plans might they be exploring? After all, if they simply wanted to stop the crusade, why had they not already slain Sir Hugh and the rest of the core leadership?

Frustrated at his lack of firm answers, Markus shook off the thoughts. In the end, it was of no matter. The important thing was that Markus had set the Assamites on the trail of Alexia's guardian. Soon enough, the Lamia would be dispatched, clearing the way at last for Markus to discover what secrets Alexia kept in her haven.

"How can he be certain the Lamia is destroyed?"

"By Saint Sebastian's eyeteeth, Falsinar! You have pained my last nerve this day. He is not certain. That is why we blaspheme by entering a house of God with drawn blades."

"Well, at least I do not blaspheme by uttering *vulgarities* in a house of God."

"The Lord will forgive me, for He knows what a trial you are to me."

"And I had thought it was the other way around."

"You may ask for clarification when you stand in judgment—which I may hasten along if you continue with your tedious questions."

"An idle threat, considering your blade is too dull even to offer a decent shave."

"That explains your face then, my friend."

"Give me strength, Lord. Good Beltramose, let me clarify my previous query."

"Let me be the last to stop you. Speak, and I shall lend a willing ear. Gift me with the pearls of your wisdom, that I may grow rich with understanding—"

"Grow silent, that I may speak!"

"I await your words with unparalleled eagerness."

"Listen: Our lord says the guardian was attacked last night."

"So he was told by a pair of his damnable shades, my perceptive Falsinar."

"But the spirits do not dare the catacombs, correct? How can they know in certainty what transpired?"

"Ah, well. Did they not see the attackers emerge afterward?"

"They left one less in number, but otherwise you speak truly, Beltramose. Still, a curious thing, that. Three attackers seems a paltry number if we are to believe in bands of Saracens readying to strike."

"Perhaps they hold forces in reserve, or perhaps three is all the task required. Alas, it shall remain a mystery, as I have the impression that the ghosts provide little in the way of details. This is your question, then?"

"Indeed no, 'twas merely a preface."

"Shall I take my rest upon this broken statuary while your epic unfolds?"

"With the breath you have spent dragging the conversation hither and yon, Beltramose, I could have told you my question twice over."

"And yet I still have not heard it."

"Then prepare your senses, for here it is: Is it not possible that the two figures did not emerge victorious, but were in retreat? Could it not be that the Lamia did survive, wounded but still very active? Or that she routed her attackers entirely, with nary a scratch upon her? And so may she not still lurk beneath this church, on guard for any further trespassers?"

"Hmm..."

"Indeed."

"To my chagrin, I must admit your query has merit. But I put forth that our lord reasoned similarly, else why would he charge us with investigating the catacombs now, in the daylight hours?"

"I grant you that, Beltramose. But though sunlight is anathema to their kind, are not the catacombs underground?"

"You speak truly, good Falsinar. But what do you suggest? That we stop here, in sight of the panel that leads to the lair of the guardian? That we return to our lord without confirming the creature's status?"

"We would find ourselves joining the ranks of Infantino and his ilk. No, I merely wished for you to feel the same quaking of the bowels that I have experienced since this thought occurred to me."

"You are a fine friend indeed, Falsinar, that you would share such things. In turn, then, let me offer you first entry through yon secret passage."

"Your kindness knows no bounds, Beltramose. I could not possibly take such an honor from you."

"I insist. And dawdle not, my friend. The sun passes the zenith as we speak."

Markus Musa Giovanni looked over the chamber with interest. Four sarcophagi were set low in the floor, only their lids above floor level. Each stone lid was carved in the likeness of one of the four emperors who had taken the throne after Constantine. Four statues were set in alcoves in the far wall: women, from the delicate limbs and style of dress. It was not apparent who the statues were meant to depict, as the head of each had been crushed to fragments. Noting similarities in elements of clothing and jewelry that matched the emperors' depictions, Markus figured that the statues represented wives of the respective emperors. The empresses were buried elsewhere, but their images stood vigil over their fallen husbands. Touching, but not what Markus had come for.

Of far more interest were the two vampiric corpses. Crumpled against a wall like some forgotten toy, the desiccated bundle of bones was nonetheless easily recognizable as the Assamite Fajr. He must have been a vampire for a comparatively short time—a century at most—since his remains hadn't crumbled to dust upon his final death. In contrast, the other vampire had been quite ancient indeed, given the pile of delicate ash in the middle of the room.

Though educated on the process of undead decay, Markus had never seen the actual remains of a vampire before. The ashes were especially fascinating—an innocuous pile of thick gray powder mixed with fragments of bone. A *small amount of substance left for a creature of such power.* "Immortal we may be, yet still we remain subject to God's will."

"*Signore?*"

"Nothing, Falsinar." Markus faced his retainers. "The Lamia would have made her stand where she was strongest. I will begin my search for Lady Alexia's lair here."

"Shall we assist you, then?" Beltramose offered, raising high the lamp as if mere illumination might reveal a hidden passage.

"Your skills are better suited to war than to investigation. And there may be traps harmful to mortals. Take Falsinar and make another circuit of these catacombs. Make certain there are no other active residents. Do not forget to mark your way with the chalk."

Falsinar dug a piece of soft chalk from a pouch and handed it to Beltramose. Then each hefted his lamp and, after a look at the Lamia's remains, moved into the corridor. It was silent for a moment but for the scrape of their boots, then came the murmured echoes as they took up their perennial chattering.

Markus took his own lamp and approached the wall to the left of the chamber's entryway. It was nondescript, but that meant little. Lady Alexia was cunning in the extreme. A panel or lever could be hidden as anything, even a simple stone block in the wall. A measured, scientific investigation was the best approach to be sure he missed nothing.

Still, though the guardian was destroyed and Lady Alexia was gone three months now, Markus did not assume he could investigate at his leisure. His instincts said that she would be gone for some time—yet reason suggested that since he did not know where Alexia had journeyed to, whether she had reached her destination, or if she was already returning to Constantinople, it was safest to assume she might come back any night. Given that, he would much prefer to have already gone through Lady Alexia's haven by the time the elder Cappadocian returned.

Setting aside the distracting thoughts, Markus extracted a thin iron probe from his belt and began testing each block in the chamber's wall.

Two nights later, Markus was in a state. An exhaustive search of the catacombs under the Church of the Holy Apostles had revealed a number of clever, hidden levers. Manipulating them triggered a surprising and extensive reconfiguration of the underground complex and revealed a handful of secret chambers, including the destroyed Lamia's resting place.

Yet not a single one opened upon the lair of Lady Alexia Theusa.

Markus raged through the crypts for hours when he could no longer contain his frustration. The blood of Caine pounded in his veins, fueling him with preternatural energy. In the grip of the Beast, his huge form thundered down the ancient corridors and through the scores of crypts. He smashed statuary and shoved at sarcophagus lids. He tossed aside decayed corpses and flung about buried riches. Black velvet doublet torn and streaked with grime, dark hair wild and thick beard bristling, eyes glaring red and mouth spitting blood-tinged froth, Markus lunged into the chamber housing the Lamia's ashes.

"Where?!" Markus roared. "Where have you hidden it?! I will not be denied, witch!" He grabbed one of the headless statues and strained to topple it. The marble form levered forward after a series of brutal tugs. Markus fell back, his left shoulder wrenched from its socket, as the statue crashed to the ground. The impact expelled a gust of fetid air that scattered the Lamia's ashes.

The pain of his dislocated shoulder helped Markus regain some measure of control at last. His strength faded fast as the Beast retreated to the dark depths of his soul. Through a combination of physical effort and focusing the healing power of his immortal blood, Markus reset his shoulder. He gasped at the flare of pain and collapsed, exhausted, atop the felled statue. Hunger gnawed at his belly. The thirst for blood grew ever stronger as he wound down from his exertion, but he was too spent to rouse himself to feed.

Where is your haven, Alexia? he wondered. *Ancient you may be, but do not dismiss me. My blood is potent, my wits sharp. Better that you had been willing to accept my alliance, crone. For you have roused the anger of a Giovanni. I will uncover your secrets, every last one.*

Markus sensed something then. A presence. Had the Assamites returned to finish him as they had dispatched the Lamia? Panic sent a new surge of blood through his veins, the effort spiking his hunger dramatically. His eyes narrowed,

searching through the dimness of filtered moonlight and phos-
phorescent moss for an aura that would reveal the presence of
another. He was not sure what good it would do, since he lacked
the strength to put up much of a fight, but it was all he could
think to try. Minutes passed. *Surely if Fajr's cohorts were here, they
would have attacked by now.*

Yet something tugged at his awareness. Something was...
there. In the Lamia's scattered ashes, a fragment of stone from
the statue, a wedge barely larger than a finger. It offered just a
moment's will-o-the-wisp flicker to his sight. Markus levered
himself to all fours and looked at the shard with frank curiosity.

On closer inspection, he saw it was not broken from the
statue. Indeed, it was not marble at all, but a stone of some yel-
lowish cast. Sandstone, perhaps? Clay? It matched nothing else
Markus had seen in the catacombs. A character was carved on
it, but even with his acute senses Markus lacked sufficient light
to read it. *Some charm of the Lamia's, perhaps, or an amulet given her
by Lady Alexia?*

Desperate for any lead, Markus snatched up the shard.

Cold engulfed his hand, a chill that sank all the way down
to his long-dead bones. It swept up to his elbow with terrifying
speed, leaving his forearm numb before he even realized what
had happened. Markus flexed his fingers in a panic as the cold
overwhelmed him, but his hand would not release the shard.
Whispers and images carried on the wave of cold assaulted his
mind. Splinters of the past hammered him in a blizzard of sensation. The fragment shrieked of knowledge beyond his greatest imaginings. He had but to surrender to the lure of the abyss
and omniscience would be his.

Even as his will crumbled, a defiant spark flickered inside
Markus—a burning hatred of Alexia Theusa. *So close, but again
I am denied! No! I will not succumb; she will not beat me this time!*

He called forth the last dregs of strength. It was agony to
move, but he reached with his other hand for a piece of the broken statue. With a roar that was equal parts pain and triumph,
Markus smashed his hand with the chunk of marble. The shard
fell from his crushed fingers, and the chill vanished as quickly
as it had come over him.

Though cracked and shedding small chunks from the blow, the fragment was remarkably intact. It lay overturned amid the Lamia's remains, the mysterious character on its face hidden as if to tempt Markus into reaching for it again.

He was as still as the surrounding statues while his mind struggled to process what had transpired. Markus cradled his shattered hand and trembled at echoes of memory that were not his own.

Chapter Six

Feeding and a day's rest left Markus in a better frame of mind to address the matter of the mysterious shard. It contained tremendous power, but what was its nature? Its promise of omniscience was no mere taunt. The simple fragment somehow retained impressions of events surrounding it; perhaps even more than that.

Whatever the case, Markus was sure it was an object of some value to Alexia. The Lamia must have been a valued servant indeed to be trusted with the shard. Or perhaps Alexia had used it to help hold the Lamia to her will. Given that Markus suffered a kaleidoscope of impressions after only brief contact with the thing, it was evident that tremendous power was required to keep from being overwhelmed by the shard's influence. Markus had to admit he lacked such potency; it was quite possible the Lamia had as well. That would explain why she had acted bizarrely even for one of her kind. Despite this danger, a part of him yearned to take up the shard again. *To harness the power of such a thing; to learn its secrets... With sufficient control, it can be done.*

He was certain of it, for he had captured a single complete memory in the instant when his rage overwhelmed the fragment's chill. The image shone through the tumult of remembrance even now.

—Lady Alexia Theusa stands in a large chamber, examining a

corpse with great interest. The shadowed alcoves surrounding her hide a multitude of secrets, and nearby tables hold all manner of devices and curiosities—

His will was strong enough in that instant to command the fragment—albeit inadvertently—to show a specific thing: Alexia in her lair. Though offering no point of reference, it inspired him. It could also be made to lead him to her haven!

Markus wasn't foolish enough to take up the shard again himself, though.

He emerged from his chamber to find Falsinar napping in the next room. "Where is your compatriot?" Markus asked, nudging him with his foot.

"*Signore!*" Falsinar struggled to wakefulness. "It is his turn for watch."

"Very well. Gather your weapons. Beltramose will join us on our way."

"Where are we going?" Falsinar asked as he grabbed for his sword belt.

"To test a theory."

Markus hung his lamp from the praying hands of one of the headless statues. Falsinar and Beltramose held lamps of their own, thereby illuminating the crypt from three directions. The men fidgeted, unsure of their purpose. Beltramose looked especially uneasy, having felt the chill of an agitated spirit. Markus had applied his full necromantic abilities to force one of his wraiths, Vesta, to accompany them into the catacombs. The ghost was quite disturbed, though Markus remained unable to determine the source of her anxiety. It could be any number of things in a place as old as this, but it caused her spectral neck to stretch out in emulation of the hanging that had claimed her life for a crime she did not commit. Her head now hung over her left shoulder and her tongue lolled out of her mouth, mostly bitten though in her dying moments. Had she the will to appear to the living, she'd be terrifying indeed. As it was, only Markus could see her, and he had enough mysteries on his plate. Ignoring the ghost's distress, he focused on the shard that still lay amid the Lamia's scattered ashes. Markus had been too exhausted and shaken the previous night to risk taking it with him.

It rested amid the ash, as unremarkable to the eye as before. In better lighting and with a clearer head, Markus saw that the shard was, in fact, a portion of clay tablet. Having touched it once, Markus could sense its influence, a whispered siren's song to his mind. He flexed his fingers, the hand restored to wholeness after he had fed upon a hapless looter who searched for riches in a city long ago picked clean. With a nod to himself, Markus kneeled to perform his first test.

"Falsinar, set aside your lamp and ready your knife. If I cannot release the shard, you must pry it from my grasp." Markus then took out a piece of heavy velvet—cut from the garment he'd ruined in his rampage the night before—and used it to pick up the fragment. Its whispers grew somewhat louder in his thoughts, but otherwise Markus felt nothing unusual, not even the slightest chill. He nodded reassurance to Falsinar and carried the shard to the nearest sarcophagus. Kneeling by the lid, Markus set the fragment down on the relief covering the first crypt, nudging it over with the cloth to look at last upon the symbol carved on its surface.

It was a single word, written in Chaldean, translating to *Lilith*. From the worn condition, it could well have been carved when the ancient Chaldean race still dwelled in southern Babylonia, seven centuries before the birth of Christ. It could have been done more recently, given that Chaldean was often used among current Babylonian cultures for the working of spells and enchantments. Still, it hinted at great age, a time at least before the foundation for the first church to Christ was laid.

Lilith, the Dark Mother. Worshipped by the Lamia and long tied to the greater realm of the undead. Some Cainite legends claimed that not only was she Adam's first wife, but that she became Caine's consort after he suffered the curse of vampirism for slaying his brother.

It did not surprise Markus that the Lamia would have such a keepsake.

"Return opposite Beltramose," Markus told Falsinar. "Remain still hereafter, each of you, unless I say otherwise."

He took the hanging lamp and placed it near the Lilith shard, then exposed the flame. Reaching under his doublet, he untied one of the leather cords from around his throat. Hanging from the cord was a bone—a segment of vertebra, taken from the broken-necked corpse of a Greek woman named Vesta during the ceremony Markus had performed to bind her soul to his service. Holding forth the necklace, he commanded Vesta forward. The bone ensured the spirit's loyalty, or at least her obedience. It had other uses as well.

Next, he took a sachet of waxed parchment from his belt. The small envelope contained a portion of Vesta's heart, dried and ground to powder. With necklace in one hand and packet in the other, Markus began a murmured chant. The words were Latin, but spoke to something far older. He sensed Vesta's increasing unrest as the ritual progressed, but that was to be expected. The wraiths were furious about their service to Markus to begin with, and he was crushing what little independence remained to her. He spared it no reflection. It was all part of the study of death and the soul, the very reason Markus had accepted the gift of unlife almost a century before.

Reaching the end of the chant, he held the edge of the sachet over the lamp until the waxy parchment started melting. The corner split open and the sachet curled black fingers toward his hand. He tipped the packet forward and the dust fell into the flame. A blast of cold blue fire erupted with blinding intensity. Markus was prepared, his hypersensitive eyes turned away at the last instant, but the curious Falsinar and Beltramose were not so lucky. Ignoring their surprised cries, he dropped the smoldering sachet.

"*Monstra mihi portum*," Markus commanded as he lowered the necklace. *Show to me the haven.* The Latin words gave Vesta direction and formed the final step of the ritual.

The bone dangled just above the Lilith shard. Then the vertebra shot down to the stone like a lodestone seeking iron. Vibrations coursed up the leather cord as Vesta's spirit was drawn far enough into the physical realm to touch the clay fragment.

The room was still but for the thrum of the necklace. Then

the bone shattered with such force that fragments ripped myriad lines across Markus's flesh. The pain was a momentary distraction, and he healed the tears with an instinctive application of will and blood. Of greater moment was the frigid air that blasted into the chamber's ceiling, leaving a film of frost on the stone.

"That was unexpected," Markus admitted, as he contemplated the residue of Vesta's exit from the catacombs.

Vesta's spirit lacked the strength to sustain itself after encountering the Lilith shard. She was torn to nothingness, but not before fulfilling the last command Markus had given. Lurking aboveground in the Church of the Apostles, the other wraiths followed the psychic scream and ectoplasmic residue of Vesta's passage out of the crypt and across the length of Constantinople. Had they not been bound by necklaces similar to the one that had shattered in the crypt, the five remaining ghosts would never have returned to relate what they had seen.

The wraiths milled about in distress as they reported to Markus. Their aura of unease bled through to the physical world, making Falsinar and Beltramose tense as well. The men couldn't perceive their ghostly counterparts, so Markus related the details. "Vesta fled eastward. Infantino said she went underground near the Acropolis. He found her before she was lost to the shard's effect."

"What does all this mean, *Signore*?"

"Triumph, Beltramose," Markus replied, eyes bright with excitement. "Triumph! I have found it. I have discovered Lady Alexia's lair!"

The First Hill held Constantinople's heart, some said, for the city had found its start here, at the peninsula's tip. Through the centuries, many venerable structures, including the Church of Hagia Sophia and the Senate Basilica, remained of significance in the affairs of the city's mortal inhabitants. Yet other portions, notably the area surrounding the Acropolis, languished in obscurity. The Acropolis had fallen to ruin long before the sack. The great pagan temple dedicated to vanished Greek gods was reduced to broken columns, fragments of walls, cracked floor-ing, and shattered altars. The ruins held little interest for the Orthodox Greeks of past nights, nor for the Catholic Latins who now commanded the city.

Treading up the thoroughfare of Tzycanisterion Street, Markus considered the distinctive profile of ragged columns. The grand Acropolis was one of the earliest structures erected here. It held a commanding view of the city and of the surround-ing seas. Constantinople itself stretched to the west, wrapped in a watery embrace. The Marmora lay to the southwest, the Bosporus to the northeast. The Golden Horn was a gentle arc extending from the expanse of the Bosporus. Amazing as the vista was, few people came to enjoy it. Markus sensed that the Lady Alexia encouraged this neglect through her subtle influence.

He felt the disquiet while still some distance from the Acropolis itself. He might not have noticed it, merely decided it wasn't worth the effort, if he hadn't been prepared. His will and his eagerness to unlock at last Lady Alexia's secrets were more than enough to overcome any hindrance.

Falsinar and Beltramose shook off the sensation with less ease, as did the spirits. Markus snapped his fingers, an explosion in the silence that blanketed the area. "Be alert. Lady Alexia has taken great care to hide her lair. Should you relax your atten-tion, I suspect you would fast consider this a fool's errand and wander elsewhere." The hypothesis seemed borne out, from the startled looks the two ghouls exchanged.

"We are with you, *Signore,*" Beltramose replied, determina-tion clear in the set of his jaw. A similar expression found a home on Falsinar's face. Markus heard the lackluster whisper of Infantino's assent as well.

They moved through the rubble of the temple, alert for any-thing. Aside from the nagging aura of distraction, the place was devoid of threat. Markus followed Infantino through the moon-lit shadows to an altar.

Vesta's spirit had plunged into the earth during its com-pelled flight the previous evening, bypassing conventional access to Alexia's haven. Infantino had followed, despite the stress it caused the spirit to move through physical objects. The ghost had then backtracked through the first entrance he found and returned to Markus. That entrance was hidden beneath this altar. Aside from the cracks and wear from the passage of centuries, the altar, dedicated to Athena, looked no less solid than the surrounding temple. Markus was certain he could not budge it.

Alexia was older than he by many centuries, but even so Markus doubted the entrance was gained through brute force. Cappadocians were not especially strong as vampires went. Recalling the catacombs beneath the Church of the Holy Apostles, he commanded Infantino, Domnola, and Viator to search for levers and catches aboveground, while Rina and Hartmut passed through the stone to see how the altar was situated. Falsinar and Beltramose kept watch.

An hour later, Markus increased yet again his opinion of Lady Alexia. Hoped-for ally turned cryptic nemesis she was, but Markus gave her his unreserved respect, this time due to the complex arrangement of levers required to move the altar. It was an ingenious design: five triggers, separate from one another within the area around the altar, pushed in sequence. If any one was attempted out of order, the remaining levers would not even budge. A single lever inside the passage set the sequence in motion as well, but Rina and Hartmut lacked physical substance to move it. After noting the design in the pages of his journal, Markus opened the passage and led the way down a series of steep, sloping tunnels that extended far beneath the Acropolis.

The narrow passage opened on a large, vaulted chamber. Alexia was not present, nor was there a body in the center of the room; but otherwise it was just as Markus had seen in his vision. Crystal spheres in the ceiling reflected their lamplight, casting roving spotlights as they moved and revealing the blocky shapes of shelves and furniture. After some tentative stumbling due to the disorienting reflected light, Markus found a series of sconces. Recalling a detail from his borrowed memory, he lit them. Illumination flooded the room as the newly cast light reflected along a series of cunningly placed mirrors to the spheres and chased away the shadows.

Five passageways led off from the chamber, including the

one they'd just used. Markus ignored these for the moment, enthralled as he was with the central chamber. The place was originally a crypt, although one expanded from its initial dimensions and decorated as some semblance of a residence. The floor was strewn with an assortment of rugs and reed mats. Parchment screens in wooden frames were arranged here and there, dividing the space into discrete sections. Shelves and tables filled much of the space and held books, small chests and ornate boxes, figurines of deities from diverse cultures and religions, jars of things suspended in thick fluid, stacks of bones tied with dried gut, rolls of parchment with arcane markings, stones and clay tablets scored with a dozen different languages, and other things not as easily identified.

The walls were filled with cavities in which lay bodies—bodies that, in Markus's rarified sight, flickered with the telltale aura of the spirit. "By Christ and Caine," he whispered.

"*Signore*?" Falsinar grasped the hilt of his falchion, ready to come to his master's aid.

Markus was too fascinated with his discovery to respond. As he didn't appear worried, Falsinar and Beltramose stood to one side and waited for their lord to give them direction.

Markus moved to the nearest body and was surprised to find he recognized it. The body was dried out, leathery skin stretched taut over bone, but that mattered little. A person's features were formed of skin, muscle, fat, and cartilage built upon a foundation of bone. Like any Cappadocian, Markus could see through the subtleties of this fleshly map to the true visage underneath, no matter the extent of decay.

After some brief thought, he matched the face to one of the corpses in the catacombs beneath the Church of the Apostles. He had spent long hours looking through every portion of the catacombs. Markus had not given the bodies much attention in comparison, but his eager mind had catalogued much about them nonetheless. With that connection made, he recalled in which crypt the body had lain—the one dedicated to Basil II, who ruled Constantinople in the first quarter of the eleventh century.

Puzzled, he looked at the corpse lying in the cavity to the

left. He recognized another of Constantinople's emperors, recalled the name on the sarcophagus under the Church of the Apostles—Phocas, a tyrant from the early seventh century. Markus moved from one body to the next, peering at each with increasing excitement. As with the bodies that resembled Basil and Phocas, the others were drawn and mummified forms resembling closely the emperors interred beneath the Church of the Holy Apostles.

Markus saw more berths when he passed by the tunnel openings. He snatched up his lamp and hurried down the corridor. It opened on a circular chamber with still more corpses. Returning to the main crypt, he continued his investigation along the far wall. The bodies here carried a greater sense of age than the others. Also, Markus did not recognize their features. They had no look-alikes in the catacombs beneath the Church of the Holy Apostles. He might not recognize this part of the collection, but Markus knew they were like the rest.

They were not mere corpses at all, but undead. The lair of Lady Alexia Theusa was filled with scores of vampires.

"Each one of them, *Signore*?"

"That I have seen thus far, Beltramose." Markus cast a critical eye around the lair's central chamber. "I can sense the spirits that remain linked to the flesh. Their auras are consistent with that of Cainites. They can be nothing other."

The ghoul looked around, his unease apparent. "Are they the Lady Alexia's, then?"

"Of that, I am not certain. The manner in which they are kept suggests that they have been bound. Against their will, I would presume. Note the cloth wrapped about this one in these separate places. I thought at first that it was homage to the Egyptian practice of mummification. It may be, in fact, but only as a secondary intent. If you look closely, you can see faint markings upon the cloth. A Cappadocian ritual, this. It forces the subject into torpor, held deep in the dreamless sleep of the undead."

Falsinar returned from poking through the contents of the shelves and tables. "So we need not fear their sudden waking?"

"I do not think so. The bindings have been in place for some time. And were they meant as guardians, I hazard that they would have roused themselves to action long before now."

"What do you make of them, *Signore*? Who are they? Why do they look like the emperors?"

"Why indeed?" Markus hooked a thumb through his belt and pursed his lips as he considered the mystery. "Their presence here, and their condition, speaks to a great deal of effort on the part of Lady Alexia. I expect that she would not be forthcoming as to why, were she here. My best chance to gain understanding must be from the bodies themselves. This may take some time. Go and rest now."

"Leave you unprotected, *Signore*, here in her lair?!" Beltramose looked mortified. "We could not!"

"You have been awake day and night of late. Even partaking of my blood, you have grown weary. I can see the fatigue in you both. Worry not; I have the wraiths to warn me of any threats."

Beltramose bit back a plea. He and Falsinar looked unhappy, but they accepted the command without further protest. Taking up their lamps, the ghouls went back up the tunnel.

Markus approached the oldest grouping of bodies. He spent an hour, then another, applying the full extent of his intellectual and mystical talents to their study. Beginning a third hour of investigation, Markus at last felt he had found the best candidate. The corpse was unremarkable enough to look at, average in build and as dry and wasted as the others. But Markus felt a potent spirit was contained within.

His blood quickened as he began the complex and demanding ritual. Necromancy was a new and exacting art. It showed tremendous promise, but much remained unknown, even to the Giovanni, about the art of communing with and commanding spirits. Markus's family had but a few centuries of study behind them when Cappadocius inducted the Venetians into his clan. Markus took great pride in his skill with it.

He felt the resistance as the ritual progressed. Whatever Lady Alexia had done to these Cainites, she had taken great pains to ensure they did not regain consciousness without her leave. Markus allowed himself a tight smile. She had used variations on ancient Cappadocian flesh rituals, fashioning the body as an anchor to the soul. Necromancy was a fledgling discipline in comparison, but it offered him an advantage. His ritual ignored the powerful protective auras that surrounded the flesh, and sought the spirit itself.

The stronger the soul, the easier it was to contact. Unfortunately, that also made it all the more difficult to control. This was especially true of a vampire, Markus now sensed. His subject's spirit was warped and magnified by the curse of Caine. Though long held in torpor, Markus's efforts roused it to a great agitation. The Beast, the darkest part of the vampire soul, clamored for release. In the shadow of its roiling fury, Markus sensed the higher consciousness was just as desperate to be free.

Markus had no intention of indulging it. He had no interest in binding this shade to his service, powerful though it was. He continued the ritual, drawing the soul ever farther from its shackled flesh. Awareness increased within the spirit as it emerged, the Beast gradually receding to a storm on the horizon of consciousness.

The roused spirit remained tied to its undead flesh, but enjoyed enough mobility that it could turn a hint of features toward Markus. "...*wwhhhoo...*" it asked, a whisper at the edge of Markus's mind.

A dialogue between souls, the speech of ghosts transcended any particular tongue. Still, Markus could sense something of the physical character behind the shade's soundless voice— Greek. He responded in that tongue, speaking aloud. "You may call me Markus. And whom do I have the privilege of addressing?"

"...*naaame... Byzzaarrr...*"

Markus frowned. The name was familiar—too familiar. "Byzar of Clan Cappadocian?"

"...*yes...*"

Markus was as surprised as he was confused. Prior to his mission, he had studied as much as he could of the Cappadocians and of Constantinople. He was aided in this by one Nepotian of Galata, a Cappadocian who had arrived in Venice fifty years earlier to exchange knowledge of death with the new members of his clan. Nepotian had spoken of a Cappadocian, Byzar, who had first settled the region that would one day become Constantinople. Indeed, Nepotian claimed that the colony of those times was named Byzantium in his honor. But Nepotian said Byzar and his brood had vanished at the twilight of the second century, when Byzantium was razed in civil war. Some thought Byzar met with final death in those nights; others that he and his followers slipped away to a less turbulent locale.

How could Byzar have come to be here, bound in torpor beneath the city that had borne his name so many centuries ago?

Markus felt a rise of unease. In light of discovering Byzar, the parallel of Byzantium's destruction and Constantinople's recent sack could not be happenstance. He had seen enough of the threads of life and death to suspect any occurrence of coincidence.

"What circumstance brought you here?"

"*...my childe... Alexiaaa... she... has bound us all...*"

I should not be surprised, Markus thought. *But ancient though Alexia is, how could one Cainite have subdued so many others of the blood? Including her own sire?*

"This is your brood, then," he said aloud. "You are all Cappadocians?"

"*...not all... emperors and lovers as well.*" Byzar's whispers grew more focused as their conversation progressed "*...She began with my brood, many years ago. I have seen... have seen her bring more.*"

"Toward what purpose? Does she gather an army of Cainites?"

"*She binds us into torpor. You think... that we would serve her, were we released? Alexia... would not last a moment, should we become free.*" The scorn that flared from the spirit became anguish. "*No... not an army. She seeks to shape the future... the return of her love.*"

"I do not understand."

"*Alexia exists to be reunited with her lost love... Andreas... long dead from her mortal life. I had thought her turned from the path after her Embrace. Instead, she trapped us here… so we would not hinder her."*

Markus still did not see how interring these many Cainites would help bring back Alexia's lover. "What of these, who resemble the emperors interred beneath the Church of the Apostles?"

"Not simply resemble. They are Constantinople's emperors. A vision… she had a vision of Andreas returning to life… to rule a golden city. So she gives each emperor the gift of Embrace as death approaches, binding his soul to undead flesh so that it will not be recycled into a new royal birth." Byzar's aura pulsed the faint vermilion of amusement, anticipating Markus's next question. *"The corpses buried in place of the emperors are commoners, bodies she has molded to pass for the true rulers of this city…. In this way, she has maintained her secret through the centuries."*

Astounding. Alexia's subtle influence upon the Byzantine court, her secretive nature, amassing powers beyond those that most Cappadocians would ever develop—it was all for a love long dead. It made a sort of sense, Markus supposed. Constantinople's many names had included the Golden City, an apt label until recently. The city still stood, but it was a shell of its former glory. The fires of enlightenment and culture were extinguished in the aftermath of the crusaders' assault. It was a gilded capital no more. Alexia must be in a panic, wondering if Constantinople had ever been the city of her vision. Perhaps that was why she'd left with the Nosferatu Malachite, to search out some other place to match her dream.

Marveling at Lady Alexia's madness, Markus also noted that Byzar must have a potent soul if he could observe Alexia's actions so clearly through the veil of torpor. "She truly believes her efforts will return this Andreas to her some night?"

"It is of no matter what Alexia believes. She has committed treachery against her clan. Release me and my brood, that she may be dealt with."

All spirits asked for release soon enough. "I cannot. This ritual allows only for communication, and I know too little of how Alexia bound you to attempt a reversal. You must tell me all that you know, so that I can better address your circumstance."

Reddish-brown whorls of frustration blossomed in Byzar's aura. *"Who are you to command me? I am Byzar, childe of Cappadocius, keeper of the secrets of death, master of the art of decay—"*

"I have heard of you, venerable Byzar." Markus would not release the ancient without first consulting his own sire. It was possible, though unlikely, that Guisseppi and his fellow Giovanni would decide to leave Byzar to his current circumstances. Assuming that, Markus could dispense with tact and force the shade to respond. It would benefit him in the short term, but would give rise to trouble in future nights. Byzar wielded great power, despite having been trapped in slumber for centuries. Markus doubted the ancient could utilize these abilities in his present condition—otherwise he would have long before now—but he was sure to be released at some point. Markus did not want to be the subject of Byzar's revenge when that time came. The alternative was to destroy Byzar after Markus extracted the needed information. But then he would have to inflict final death on each of the Cainites here, in case any was also aware of what transpired and would pursue revenge upon gaining release in the future. No, most likely the Giovanni would want to free Byzar and his brood. As the direct offspring of Cappadocius, Byzar would make a powerful ally. He could help the Giovanni attain the respect within the clan for which they strove. But until Markus knew for certain, extreme caution was the safest course. The challenge came in making Byzar see the wisdom of this as well.

"Understand that you have my respect. But understand also that I am likewise progeny of Cappadocius, and scion of the Giovanni. We are become of the blood only recently—in times after your imprisonment—but do not presume us to be the lesser for it."

"You spell your doom should you not release me and mine. Mark what I say!"

Markus had heard such bluster before. "I would rouse you fully from torpor if I was confident I could do so safely. As it stands, I must learn all that I can before I take action."

Silence for a time, then: *"Giovanni. You are Markus Giovanni.*

I recall…. Upstarts, manipulators and destroyers of souls. So said Alexia."

"She is mistaken. My family has long studied the spirit, but to understand the course of death. Just as the Cappadocians study the flesh—"

"It is not the same. Improper, an affront to God."

Markus noticed Infantino and the other ghosts fidgeting. They dwelled in the same ethereal realm as Byzar's spirit, and had no trouble hearing his words. Markus wanted to send them away so that they would overhear no further inflammatory comments, but he had to keep his focus on sustaining the connection to Byzar. "Did the Lady Alexia say this also?"

"Yes… but I concur. The secrets of death are found in the flesh. The immortal soul is inviolate. You risk your own destruction by presuming to command that which is God's province alone."

This sentiment was not uncommon among Cappadocians, much to the Giovanni family's frustration. Markus saw irony, at least concerning Alexia. She spurned contact with those who might best help her recover the spirit of her lost love, all for some limited interpretation of Cappadocian doctrine. A doctrine that was flawed anyway, given the Giovanni family's presence within the clan. "Yet your sire brought us into the clan for our expertise, to better understand the ways of death. Do you question his decision?"

"Cappadocius is wise and powerful, but even he is fallible. Indeed, it is the greatest flaw of our kind, more so than the visage of death that comes upon us after the Embrace."

"What do you speak of now? What flaw is this?"

"The visions that arise in certain of our kind. Even beings like us have a role in the larger scheme, else God would not suffer us to exist. We seek answers in death… the rare oracles among our kind look for insight in visions. But in doing so, they lose sight of the greater boundaries. They overstep these boundaries at our peril. Even Cappadocius has gone too far… striven for knowledge that was not his to possess."

Byzar was falling into riddles and opaque references. The ancient's spirit was tiring, and Markus likewise grew weary from sustaining the ritual. He was running out of time. He ached to learn all he could from Byzar's trove of knowledge before the elder Cainite's soul fell back into torpor. A torrent of questions flooded his thoughts, but Byzar's latest statement was too tantalizing to disregard. "Cappadocius is said to experience unparalleled revelations. How could he be subject to boundaries of any sort?"

"In a time before Christ, when the clans themselves were aborning, Cappadocius encountered a powerful seer. This man, a mortal named Sargon, heard the voice of God with unparalleled clarity. In the grip of these visions, the man transcribed His words... creating a codex of matchless insight into the divine.

"Cappadocius and Sargon debated matters of theology and spirituality. Each... was fascinated by the other's interpretations and insight. These talks were not sufficient to quench the thirst for ultimate understanding that gripped Cappadocius. My sire learned of Sargon's divine codex. Overcome with the promise of omniscience, Cappadocius was determined to possess it.... The two had a falling out. It may be that, in his fevered state, Cappadocius slew the mortal. Or perhaps Sargon s potent magic drove him off. This I do not know...." Byzar's voice trailed away, and his aura was reduced to the faintest gossamer wisps. A frantic Markus poured out the last of his own waning strength to sustain the connection. The spirit responded with a flicker of movement. *"...friendship... Their friendship was destroyed, and Cappadocius never even glimpsed the codex. A great folly, for had Cappadocius commanded his visions instead of being commanded by them...in time Sargon may have given him the codex without reservation."*

"I understand, now, the flaw of which you speak. But surely Cappadocius has amassed great wisdom in the time since. I cannot see that inducting the Giovanni was a similar mistake."

"Of course, you would not. Yes... Cappadocius learned from his folly... began a... more reasoned course of study, his discussions with Sargon the basis of a curriculum that became the foundation of our clan. But... his pursuits through the centuries... never strayed far from a desire to discover the insights that Sargon had inscribed in his clay tablet—and an ultimate hope to someday recover the codex itself...."

Byzar's tale smacked of a cautionary fable, but still... a tablet rumored to contain the knowledge of apotheosis, power sufficient to make one equal to God Himself. What a wonder to behold it would be, if it truly existed. *Did Byzar mean to say—*"You suggest that the Sargon Codex may be found? That Cappadocius strives for it even now?"

There was the distant echo of a chuckle as Byzar started again to fade. *"...most surely... You carry a piece of it now... a key... removed for caution."*

"I carry what?" Markus felt for the irregular shape in the pouch at his belt. "The Lilith shard? It was the amulet of a maddened Lamia."

"What do you think... drove her to... madness?" Byzar's words were but the memory of a whisper. *"Lamia ssstole... from her own mistressss... recover... Lazzzaareenes..."*

"What? What of the Lazarenes? Not even a crazed Lamia would traffic with those heretics! Tell me what you mean!"

"...braaave the... desert... asssk them... yourssself..."

Then there was nothing but the silence of the grave.

Chapter Seven

Constantinople
30 July, 1204

"Egypt, *Signore*?"

"And immediately, Falsinar."

"Lady Alexia's haven did not hold the information you sought, then?"

"Alas, I have left her haven untouched. I lack the time to catalogue her secrets, and I would that she not know I have found it. I shall send Guisseppi a report relating all I have discovered, including the Lady Alexia's penchant for ensnaring Cainites. Of greater moment is the Sargon Codex."

"...Of course."

"There is no need to feign understanding. I have never spoken of the Sargon Codex before now. Suffice to say that it is a treasure for which any Cainite would kill to possess."

"And it is in Egypt?"

"Correct, Beltramose. I was puzzled before that the Ventrue knight would move so aggressively to mount a new campaign to Egypt, so soon after the debacle of this latest crusade."

"You suspected the Lamia's hand in it, did you not?"

"Yes, but her *motive* was a mystery. I understand now: the Lilith shard. Having spoken with Byzar, I have devoted my full critical and mystical faculties these past few nights to studying this bit of fired clay. I am confident that this fragment is a piece of the Sargon Codex. If Byzar is to be believed, it was removed intentionally."

"Toward what purpose, *Signore*?"

"To act as a key, I think. If even half the rumors are true, the Sargon Codex holds secrets that could change the world forever. Yet without this key element, I suspect it is impossible to form an accurate interpretation of the greater work."

"So the Lamia influenced Sir Hugh to mount an Egyptian Crusade, that she could place the key with this codex? But she is now destroyed; there should be no need for haste on our part."

"Would that it were that simple. What did you learn when I sent you to the camps near Galata these last two days?"

"That forces have gathered in great numbers for a campaign to depart by ship from the Golden Horn, as soon as the end of August... ah."

"Indeed. Even with the Lamia gone, and regardless of whether Sir Hugh knows of the Sargon Codex, an Egyptian Crusade will throw the entire region into turmoil. There is no telling where the Codex will end up if we do not track it down first."

"'Track it down'? Then you do not know where it is kept, *Signore*?"

"Not yet. I believe I could use this shard to find it. Given how it affected the Lamia, I am reticent to attempt any direct contact with the thing. I will try to glean what I can from it through other means. The fragment aside, we are not without more conventional avenues of investigation. We gain nothing by remaining here, however. I can perform further tests as we sail, and any answers that remain will be found upon our arrival in Alexandria."

"Apologies, *Signore*, but do you not think this action hasty? I am not eager to travel to a land filled with nothing but Saracens and sand."

"I am little more eager than you, Falsinar. Things of far greater threat than Saracens lurk in that ancient land. Still, many Latins dwell unmolested in the trading cities of Alexandria and Cairo. We shall be safe enough, posing as a Venetian merchant and his loyal retainers.

"With any luck, we will recover the Sargon Codex and be on our way to Venice before the Egyptian Crusade is halfway across the Mediterranean."

Markus Musa Giovanni steadied himself with one hand on the rail as the ship crested a wave. The walls of Constantinople were a slab of darkness, blotting out the stars across the northern horizon. It was not even four months after the city's fall. From this distance, Constantinople looked just as it had before those fateful nights in April.

Contemplating the receding city, Markus said a prayer for the dead. The words were long overdue, a eulogy for a place of wonders and limitless promise, now deceased. It had died months ago, the body left to rot in the sun as maggots of humanity burrowed into its flesh and picked its bones.

I am one of chose parasites, he thought. *I pride myself on being a refined thinker, yet I have dug through the corpse of Constantinople with the same hunger as the rest of the Latins.*

Fellow Cainites said that Constantinople personified a utopian ideal. Markus was too much a pragmatist to succumb to the idea of the Dream. But now he wondered if it might not have some merit. Venice would always be his home. Still, as his ship sailed south across the Marmora, he realized how much he would miss Constantinople.

Markus had come here hoping to secure his family's position among the luminaries of the Clan of Death and larger Cainite society. It was not to be, but he did not leave the Queen of Cities in failure. Rather, the promise of success greater than he could have imagined rested in a pouch on his belt. Once he returned to Venice with the Sargon Codex, the Giovanni would finally attain a place of honor within Clan Cappadocian.

Then, at last, would the ultimate secrets of death be theirs to master.

Part Two: Mount Erciyes

Chapter Eight

Mount Erciyes
26 June, 1204

The woman was on the threshold of the darkened temple when the vision came upon her. She halted in mid-stride, taking in the sensations without protest. The visions often occurred without warning, coming unbidden and vanishing just as quickly. It was the price for centuries devoted to becoming attuned to the ceaseless flow of prophecy.

A vision's meaning was not always clear, even to one as skilled as she. They could appear as if actual events unfolding before her eyes, or as abstract impulses. They might be phantom voices or mysterious portents. She was known to spend weeks puzzling out especially obscure insights. This one was easy enough to interpret: a pair of travelers coming out of the west, a light dimming on the horizon behind them. One carried within him a portion of the light, a fitful spark buffeted by winds of doom. The other wore a mask of bone.

It burned upon her mind for but an instant and was gone.

"They will arrive within a week," the woman said. "Remember, none may enter but the Nosferatu and his charge."

Long familiar with the random nature of her mistress's visions, the bodyguard Qalhara stood patiently two paces back. "It shall be done, mistress. And Alexia Theusa...?"

The woman's smile was as cold as her long-dead flesh. "All loyal Cappadocians are welcome in these halls, Qalhara." Gathering her dark robes about her, Constancia—childe of Japheth, grandchilde of Cappadocius, High Priestess of the Temple at Erciyes, Oracle of the Bones—stepped into the darkness.

The Cappadocian monastery was well prepared when the Nosferatu Malachite and his coterie reached the base of Mount Erciyes six days after Constancia's flash of precognition, some nine weeks after having left Constantinople. Cainite and mortal guards observed them from narrow watch windows ranged about the face of the mountain that housed the monastery in its very belly, and passed word to Qalhara. The dark-skinned Lamia warrior assembled a selection of initiates at the main gate, the blunt silhouette of Mount Erciyes filling the night sky behind them.

Qalhara spared the massive edifice a glance as she awaited the visitors' arrival. The Cappadocian monastery wasn't simply built in the squat mountain, it *was* the mountain. The exterior was carved from the living rock, great columns and sweeping arches framing hieroglyphs and iconography that celebrated divinity and mortality both. The interior descended from entrances near the jagged peak deep into the bowels of the earth. Stairs snaked up to the mountaintop and down into the darkness belowground. Winding passages, a compromise of practical concerns and arcane needs, ranged for miles in a complexity that defied any attempts at mapping.

Qalhara felt a surge of pride. This stark place was far different from the land of her mortal life, the lush wilderness that gave birth to the mighty Nile. Yet it was her home in a way that Nubia had never been, a monument to a most unique lineage. Qalhara played a most vital role in sustaining that lineage. She was guardian of the oracle, protector of the high priestess Constancia. The coveted post fulfilled her as nothing had in the short years of her mortal life.

She stepped forward as the travelers reached the main gate, ready to discharge her duties. With the barest handful of words, she greeted them and indicated the wishes of the Cappadocian high priestess. Malachite's Nosferatu companions were somewhat distressed to learn they would not be admitted to the temple. Her dark features as impassive as the stone rising behind her,

Qalhara pointed out a number of openings in the surrounding rock that would suffice as resting places during daylight hours. She then promised herself to Malachite's safety during his stay.

From first greeting to the final ascent inside the monastery sans her unlikely Nosferatu entourage, the Lady Alexia Theusa was as silent as the surrounding stone. Though the Byzantine vampire was an elder Cappadocian, Constancia did not trust her or her apparent remove from the intrigues of Constantinople—and neither, by extension, did Qalhara. The Lamia spared Alexia hardly a glance, but she was nonetheless aware of every movement the woman made as they entered Mount Erciyes.

"You have played the role of attendant these past three nights, Qalhara. What have you learned of this Malachite?"

The Lamia warrior inclined her bald head, the deep ebon skin gleaming almost purple in the lamplight. "Mistress, he is withdrawn and distracted."

"Not due to discomfort with his accommodations, I hope." The Cappadocian monastery was not intended as a place of opulence or comfort. Acolytes and adepts ranged through the endless halls throughout the night, minds filled with the vast mystery of *thanatos*, the condition of death. Their chants formed a constant susurration that reached even the most distant corners within the mount. Yet so subtle and soft were the whispers that they seldom actually pierced the veil of monastic silence. The chants were like a tickle in the mind, a teasing echo of thought. Visitors—of which there were very few—often had trouble concentrating due to such fleeting sounds. Neither did the stark corridors and chambers encourage calm with its decor dedicated to death—altars of bone, tapestries depicting stages of decay, statuary replicating various manifestations of death. It would be no surprise to Constancia if Malachite found the environment unsettling. Still, she suspected Qalhara spoke of something more.

"He is no more bothered by his surroundings than any other supplicant," Qalhara confirmed. "His unrest lies within."

"A tortured soul indeed. And you saw no sign that he bears loyalty to Alexia?"

Qalhara curled her full lip. Her head moved just enough to the left and right to indicate the negative.

"Good. I am confident that he is not her latest pawn, but one cannot be too careful in these times." In truth, the unrest of current nights had little to do with sparking her suspicions. She had seen a breathtaking array of danger and deceit down the march of centuries. Trust from Constancia was a treasure hard won and easily lost.

Some minutes passed, during which time both women could have been mistaken for finely crafted statuary—one alabaster, one ebony. Constancia's perceptions drifted inward. She was not much surprised by reports about the disastrous Fourth Crusade, though the specifics were disturbing to hear. She had known that great turbulence was in the offing, but the portents were too widespread to glean a comprehensive picture. She also enjoyed correspondence with many fellow Cainites throughout the known world, but few had passed along anything new in the short time since Constantinople's fall. With Malachite's arrival at Mount Erciyes, she would have the opportunity to cull revelations from a mind not her own. *What secrets have you brought, little leper?* she wondered. *Was Constantinople the end, or is it only the beginning?*

Constancia roused herself from contemplation. "Malachite has traveled far in body and spirit. I will honor his request. Prepare him for the oracle."

A slight bow of the head and Qalhara stalked from the meditation chamber as silently as she had entered.

Constancia stood, still as death, as Qalhara led the supplicant into the Hall of the Dead. Malachite had the subdued, lost look common to one emerging from the long nights of the purification ceremony. His gnarled and pockmarked skin was drawn taut around the oversized bones of his skull. His eyes seemed sunk so far into his head as to be two orbless black pits. Even for one of the disfigured Nosferatu, vampires turned hideous by the curse of their low blood, Malachite seemed uncomfortable. The cavernous chamber did nothing to put supplicants at ease, its every surface—walls, floor, ceiling—layered in twining rows of bone. The dead were not forgotten or ignored here. They were celebrated, their remains forming a hallowed hall in which the Cappadocians performed one of their most sacred rites. A hundred torches, each a femur with a skull at the end, lined the walls. Within each skull, a saucer of human fat held a lively flame. The light flickered and danced, making shadows jump and lending a semblance of life to the millions of bones surrounding it all.

Qalhara murmured some last instructions and retreated into the shadows by the chamber exit. With a first few faltering steps, Malachite approached Constancia. Along the way, the random and overlapping whispers ubiquitous within Mount Erciyes became, here, a rhythmic chant. Fifty initiates, a mixture of ghouls and vampires inducted into the study of death, sustained a mantra from their positions along the chamber walls. Their words bolstered the trance that lingered at the edge of Constancia's mind. She would draw upon this synergy to tap into a deeper reality and call forth the secrets of fate.

Malachite stopped a pace from where Constancia stood next to a large hole. The Well of Bones. Constancia sensed his distraction turn to unease as he looked upon the abyss.

Would he remain so close if he knew just what the pit holds? she wondered with cold humor. Familiar with the myriad manifestations of life and death that dwelt in all things, Constancia heard the Well of Bones call to her. The circular opening was a lover's mouth, promising to reveal all, to bestow ultimate knowledge, if she would but give herself to its embrace. Her will stronger than that siren song, Constancia stood resolute.

Turning from the well, she saw that the Nosferatu had recovered some measure of equilibrium. He stood straight, his hideous visage in startling contrast to her own cold beauty. *He is ready; now it begins.*

Constancia removed her ceremonial robe. Her taut alabaster skin was marked with ceremonial designs of henna, ink and blood, the secret markings of death. She drifted further into trance, unhindered by the physical world but for the petty concern of her own undead flesh. The spirit world pressed against her with increasing force, and the whisper from the pit became an eager howl.

Awakened fully to her undead nature, she straddled the barrier that split living from dead and commanded both realms to attend her. Neither truly alive nor fully dead, Constancia walked a spiritual path she called the Road of Bones. Metaphysical and empathic connections formed a quicksilver web that overlaid her sight. Threads of fate extended all around. A blinding array of possibility flowed from Malachite. Constancia hungered to explore each strand, but the supplicant was to be accorded respect. She filed the configuration in her mind for later study.

"You bring a token," she observed. Malachite opened his hands, displaying a small ceramic icon. *A trifle, but what import it contains. It bears one of the faces of the Dracon!*

She knew of her old companion's connection to fallen Constantinople, but the link to Malachite was a curiosity. Distraction led her from the trance, so she relaxed back into the chant. Her questions must wait, for she was Malachite's conduit to the visions.

Constancia faced the Well of Bones, her bare feet resting on a femur just at the edge. Another step—nay, a mere flex of toes—and she would succumb to the abyss forever. Regaining the equilibrium of the trance, she stood firm upon the fragile bone as if it were the widest slab of marble. As the chant adjusted its rhythm, she called forth the grave cups. The pair of gold chalices, stained black with dried blood, rested in hidden alcoves and seemed to appear in her hands, the power of the temple made manifest. Immersed in the totality of the vision state, high priestess and initiates spoke as one:

"All that is dead carries the echoes of life."

Constancia tipped her left hand, the chalice she held pouring forth the ashes of the dead placed there after the cremation of ritual victims. The cloud of ash swirled into the pit, buoyed by the whispers that coursed through the temple, calling the spirits that awaited rebirth.

"All that lives hears the call of its death." The second grave cup tipped, rich blood pouring in a stream to sunder the swirling ashes.

"We, who stand on the threshold of the grave, frozen in the moment between life and death, seek these echoes and callings for guidance. We call to the remains of the dead and the cries of the dying to answer us."

Constancia felt the final parting of the veil. The gateway to the underworld was open. A multitude of whispers spilled forth from the Well of Bones.

Though standing firm at its edge, Constancia swam through the sea of ethereal voices that clamored for a return to life. She spared them no pity. Death was part of the cycle to which they were bound. In time, they would find their way back to the realm of flesh. Until then, they held command of insights that would serve her well. With the supplicant's request as her beacon, Constancia would search through the myriad of whispers for those whose words held truth.

But the spirit world demanded one last offering before divulging the mysteries that were its provenance. Robed initiates brought forth a mortal woman. Malachite looked upon her, his servant, and said her name. The chant took it up, paving the road to oblivion. Constancia lowered her arms. The grave cups fell from her fingers, dispersing as they cascaded into the Well of Bones.

And then the mortal was sent into oblivion after them.

Chapter Nine

Mount Erciyes
9 July, 1204

Constancia reclined in her private chambers, pale dead skin washed clean of many of the tattoos she had worn during the previous night's oracle, ceremonial robe exchanged for a simple white belted shift. She sat still as stone, though her thoughts ran in turmoil.

Malachite had made his query in the Hall of the Dead: He sought the Dracon, hoping that elusive ancient could give answers as to the future of the Dream. The vision of utopia that Constantinople once embodied had long served as an anchor of sanity for scores of vampires desperate for meaning in the eternal nights of unlife. Constancia sifted through the clamoring voices, culling the rare truths from the legion of falsehoods, those chosen calling out their revelations in the vast chamber of bone.

But a voice called out that Constancia had not chosen, a voice that spoke not to the Dream of a Cainite utopia but to destruction of a kind Constancia had never contemplated. It spoke barely two sentences before she silenced it. The Nosferatu was upset at the denial, though he found no sympathy in Constancia. *The words were not part of the payment due from his offering. They were for my ears alone.*

She made the voice silent to the others in the Hall of the Dead while its whispers coursed through her soul:

"I see bones crumbing to dust, the well collapsing in upon itself.

"I see the doom of the Clan of Death, swallowed by its own desire.
"I see the end of the father, destroyed at the hand of his son.
"I see a new legacy, built upon the ashes of the old."

But that was all. In silencing the whispers, she had driven off the voice before the message was told in full.

While she lacked the full message, Constancia had little trouble interpreting what she had. The art of divination was rare, but Constancia was its accomplished mistress. Her insights were second only to those of Cappadocius himself. Indeed, some initiates whispered that the high priestess had surpassed her grandsire and plumbed the vastness of revelation with unmatched expertise.

The desire of Clan Cappadocian was clear enough, for it was the journey upon which the clan's founder had trod since the earliest nights after his Embrace. Venerable Cappadocius sought the ultimate knowledge of *thanatos*. Often deep in self-imposed torpor, the ancient vampire floated from vision to vision. He was seldom completely free of these portents, even in the rare times he returned to consciousness. He walked through the physical world as if it were a dream.

The followers of Cappadocius pursued this interest also, though few with any appreciable skill in divination. Instead, they investigated death in their own way, through mystical inquiry, scholarly research, and scientific experimentation. They all felt assured that some night, though it might be centuries from now, one of their number would find a means to unlock the ultimate secrets of death.

But is the portent accurate? Will this study someday result in the destruction of our clan? The possibility tickled something in her memory, only to slip away when she tried to focus on it.

The third line suggested the heart of the matter. Cappadocius was sire—father—to the clan. His blood flowed through the veins of every Cappadocian. His was a power unrivaled by any but his fellow Antediluvians, the ancient vampires who had each sired one of the clans that lurked in the shadows of the new century. *And surpassed by Caine, of course,* Constancia allowed, *the father to us all.*

But Cappadocius's eldest childer were nonetheless mighty. Under certain circumstances, one might well prove able to slay his maker. But did any possess the resolve to make an attempt?

The answer came to her in an instant: *Lazarus*.

"Mistress, it has been but a single night. You must feed before attempting another oracle."

"The matter will not bide, Qalhara."

"And the Nosferatu makes ready to leave. He—"

"Then see him off in safety. Watch for Alexia Theusa. She manipulated him to the mount. She will not allow him to leave before she gets her due."

"Yes, mistress. I shall return as soon as I am able."

"Yes, yes. You! Assemble a score of initiates in the hall at once!"

Twenty ghouls ringed the Hall of the Dead, voices raised in meditative chant. The skull sconces flickered weakly, lit anew for the ceremony.

Constancia stared into the well's hypnotic emptiness. Hunger and doubt coiled in her belly like a pair of snakes. Portents were not absolute, she knew. Circumstances might change, the future altered by acts in the present. But doing so often brought great risk, and the alternative course was not always the better one. So she stood again before the Well of Bones, to glean all that she could of this mystery.

She wasn't channeling anyone else's queries, so the ritual required fewer initiates. A price must still be paid, however. After calling forth the grave cups, Constancia called one of the ghouls to her side. She made the proper obeisance with the stained chalices, then turned to the initiate. Piotr, a youth from the northern steppes. Though mortal, his skin was almost as pale and drawn as her own, a legacy of long months spent deep within the mountain. With one slender hand, she grasped the crown of his close-cropped black hair. Constancia tilted his head back and sank her teeth into his exposed throat. Her fangs tore at Piotr's jugular and she suckled at the rich blood that pumped from the wound. She felt his throat vibrate as he sustained the chant while she fed.

Constancia took enough blood to erase the fatigue from the earlier ceremony. She straightened and tugged Piotr to his feet. He swayed, lightheaded, and his chant was a mumble as blood coursed from his neck in regular spurts. Constancia felt the warmth spatter her naked flesh, obscuring both permanent tattoos and markings applied anew for the ceremony. Taking up the mantra again, she pushed Piotr into the well. The ghoul struggled to continue the chant as he fell into the swirling darkness. As ever, there was no impact of a body on cold ground, for there was no ground, no bottom at all, in the well. Just the abyss.

Constancia focused on the rising spirits, searching for the one who spoke out of turn. She recalled the timbre, the weight of the tone. *Feminine, young, strong… Near. It is near.*

"Speak in full measure of our fate, we who spring from Cappadocian roots," she commanded the soul.

In the thrall of the high priestess, the spirit was eager to please. The words contained no hint of falsehood. With her full power committed to calling forth the oracle, Constancia heard the echo of others confirming, supporting the vision. They spoke again of dust and doom, of the Clan of Death suffering from its own folly, of the destruction of the father at the hands of his own progeny, of the rise of something new in place of his brood.

"Why will this come to pass?"

"The Dream…" Echoes resounded from the ivory walls as a multitude took up the words.

So this is *linked to Malachite's query*, Constancia reflected, trying to suppress the surprise that could ruin the trance. *He seeks the Dream's last remaining architect and somehow this quest will spell our destruction.*

This was a serious matter, Constancia conceded, but it was not necessarily a problem. She was well acquainted with the cycle of destruction and renewal. The Road of Bones, the morbid vampiric faith she preached among her clanmates, espoused a belief in a never-ending sequence of life and death. Those who walked this Road cultivated a scholarly dispassion regarding the living and the dead. As two sides to the same coin, neither state held inherently greater interest. Every thing that lived would some day die, and all that was dead would some day be reborn.

As high priestess of the Road, Constancia enjoyed intimate familiarity with the many shades of life and death, and even understood secrets of the vampiric condition. She had also come to recognize that the cycle occurred on many levels. Not only did individuals live and die, but also cities, kingdoms, empires—even cultures and ideas. There was a link between the cycle of individual existence and the greater realm of being.

So it may be here. Constancia had assumed that the clan would endure for many nights to come, experts as its members were on death. Yet knowledge was not tantamount to an exception from universal rules. Vampires were unique, it was true— like flies in amber, they were caught in the moment between life and death—but ultimately they were subject to the cycle, like all other creatures. Death would claim and recycle even the ancients one night.

Still, Constancia was not eager to see her clan end up on the dust pile of history. *Why does the Dream require the destruction of Clan Cappadocian? Our discoveries could be of unimaginable benefit to living and dead alike. Is there not another way?* She put these questions to the murmuring souls.

The weave of cause and effect was difficult to parse even from the spirits' unique perspective. But an answer came at last. Upon hearing it, Constancia understood that Clan Cappadocian was not the only thing that must die.

Chapter Ten

Mount Erciyes
1I July, 1204

"Attend me, Qalhara."
    The Lamia warrior moved to the foot of the couch of bone. Her face, marked with a mixture of tribal tattoos from her mortal days and clan markings from her undead nights, was impassive as ever. Yet, behind this dark mask, Constancia felt her guardian's loyalty and expectation as clearly as if Qalhara shouted the words aloud. The two vampires liked to speak as much as they desired the caress of the sun. Alas, speech was unavoidable at times. "Tell me of Malachite's departure."

"There was an altercation at the outer gates, mistress. Alexia Theusa accosted the Nosferatu."

"She demanded word of Andreas?" At Qalhara's nod, Constancia remained as still and pale as the divan, though anger stirred within her. *Given the second epiphany's revelations, it is paramount that Malachite survive. He, and two others. Yet Alexia would threaten the very stability of the cycle—all for a single soul!* "And?"

"One of the Nosferatu's coterie suffered injury. The wound was not grievous. I interceded and sent Malachite away. Alexia Theusa spent these past two days and nights in an empty initiate's cell. She awaits you now."

"Bring her. I will speak of her beloved Andreas."

Alexia Theusa entered, casting a curious eye about the sparsely decorated meditation chamber. She remained clothed in the style of the Greeks, a robe of exquisite embroidery over a gown of rich brocade. Bands of silver adorned her wrists and a necklace glittered with tiny gems. Although Embraced in her later years, Alexia retained a beauty that shone through even the extreme deathly pallor common to Cappadocians.

In contrast, Constancia was barefoot in a simple, dark-belted robe. Her only adornment was the collection of tattoos that peeked from her sleeves. Though young at the time of her rebirth into the Cappadocian ranks, Constancia had long lost any definition of physical age. She looked made of porcelain, slight and fragile compared to Alexia's statuesque form.

Despite their physical differences, the two women shared a number of personality traits. Poised and supremely confident, each was a skilled practitioner of the disciplines of death. Constancia far surpassed Alexia in oracular ability, however—a detail which was lost on neither woman. It was one detail among many that formed an antagonism between the two. Due in large part to this mutual distrust, this meeting was the first time they had spoken to one another in three hundred years.

"I understand that you suffered an outburst last night," Constancia jibed. Emotional displays were a distraction to adherents of the Road of Bones. The mind required discipline, strict focus, when plumbing the mysteries of death.

Alexia responded with a beatific smile. "A momentary lapse."

"And to spend nights in penance as a lowly acolyte. I am most impressed by your adherence to the Road." Constancia quelled her pleasure at noticing the turbulence flicker through Alexia's aura, well aware that the other woman could sense her emotional state in turn. She went on in the same calm tone: "It is good that your actions caused no lingering harm, my sister. But that makes them no less unwise. The same may be said for manipulating a supplicant."

"Do not lecture me on wisdom, my *sister*," Alexia spat, her smile curling in scorn. "Your mastery of the Well of Bones is most impressive, but it does not make you omniscient."

"At least I do not focus upon a pinprick, forsaking all that remains of possibility."

Alexia was swallowed by a nimbus of red. Constancia had sensed this anger, lurking beneath a surface calm, when Alexia arrived with Malachite the previous week. Alexia's aged beauty turned harsh and cruel as she pointed an accusatory finger. "Do not taunt me. I know that Malachite learned the truth of my Andreas. Yet you remain petty and secretive. You force him to silence and deny me the knowledge that is my right!"

"You are mistaken, sister. It was the Nosferatu's choice, and his alone, what he would reveal. Is it my fault that your manipulations deny you the truth you seek?"

"How dare you! I would not be forced to such measures had you not usurped command of this monastery. I stand as close to Cappadocius as you—"

"I usurped nothing," Constancia shot back, heedless of restraining her emotions now. Her body trembled, still weak from the two recent vision ceremonies, as she struggled to stand. She contented herself with leaning forward aggressively, and declared, "I have attended Cappadocius and this clan with ceaseless dedication. While you? You have hidden, pining for a love gone in another lifetime. All things succumb to the cycle, Alexia. Your precious Andreas passed from flesh to spirit long ago. That is the way of it, or have you forgotten?"

Blood tears welled in Alexia's eyes, a mixture of loss and outrage. "I know better than most how the cycle turns! Life passes to death, only to be reborn again. But why does my Andreas not return? Even have I cleared the way, even have I called for his return to life, yet still he—"

"You have called for *what?*" Fear of the greatest heresy possible within the clan brought Constancia to her feet, despite her lingering exhaustion. "What do you mean, Alexia? Do not tell me you speak of resurrection!"

Constancia's cry froze Alexia on the brink. She trembled like a rope about to snap, pink flecks of saliva staining her chin and madness dancing behind her eyes as realization flickered across her face. A hand, curled to a gouging talon a moment before, cupped her mouth in shock. "No..." she whispered.

Constancia did not wait for an answer. Calling for Qalhara, she leapt at Alexia with the last of her strength. Instead of the wrist she aimed for, Constancia caught a handful of heavy fabric. Alexia cried out and tried to pull her sleeve away just as Qalhara burst through the chamber door.

Constancia gave the robe a furious tug. Alexia stumbled, her garment spreading like the wings of a great dark bird as she fell. Qalhara was upon her a moment later.

"Restrain her!" Constancia commanded, falling to her knees in a wave of vertigo. Then Qalhara gave a yell of her own, rising with surprise to hold an empty robe in her dark hands. Startled for only a moment, she swept the robe about, hoping to catch the vanished Alexia. But the delay was long enough; the room was empty, Alexia gone.

Qalhara rushed out, shouting commands to her sister warriors. The clamor spread quickly as the residents of Mount Erciyes mobilized in search of one of their own.

"She fled over the wall, mistress," Qalhara announced. She held out a small piece of cloth. "This caught on the battlements. We have begun a hunt, but it goes slowly."

"That is of no surprise. Alexia Theusa is more than a simple scholar. She has learned other arts in her time away from Mount Erciyes. Cloaking herself from even our perceptions is far from the most remarkable of these tricks, I suspect." Constancia took the cloth with a bitter smile. "I admit to some sorrow in this, Qalhara. There was no love lost between us through the centuries, but I had hoped Alexia remained true to the ways of our clan. But now..."

Qalhara said nothing. She simply waited for her mistress to say the words that would condemn one of the eldest of the clan to destruction as a heretic.

Constancia spoke again after a long, pregnant moment. "Now, it seems that my suspicions are confirmed. In the madness of her loss, Alexia Theusa has begun traffic with the Lazarenes."

Chapter Eleven

Mount Erciyes
15 July, 1204

"The strands of fate have become tangled knots," Constancia said. "Would that you might gift me with your wisdom, venerable Cappadocius."

Silence hung heavy in the small room; the creature remained still upon the simple stone bier before her. Cappadocius, patriarch of Clan Cappadocian, had not heard a word she uttered. Constancia was not surprised at his silence. He was deep in self-induced torpor. His consciousness was far from the shackles of his undead flesh, searching for the ultimate truths of existence.

This chamber, deep in the bowels of Mount Erciyes, was known only to a few—trusted clan elders like herself. Even they ventured here but seldom. It was a trial to stand in the presence of the ancient. With his small stature, the Antediluvian hardly looked like one of the most powerful beings on earth. Yet even in deepest torpor, the ancient vampire radiated strength that made her shudder. His body projected a sense of being so much more *real* that the surrounding bedrock seemed as flimsy as parchment.

Wondrous and terrifying as her grandsire's presence was, it stripped away all extraneous thought much like a crucible burned impurities from precious metal. Constancia was left with only the most vital matters on her mind.

The recent oracles presented two possible futures. Dramatic repercussions would affect Clan Cappadocian either way. One future promised the clan's destruction at the hands of one of its own. Another future would see the clan survive, though in a world transformed by a power rivaling that of God Himself. But which future might be realized? As was often the case in such matters of destiny, the answer rested upon the actions of a lone Cainite.

"An upstart Venetian," Constancia murmured. "A figure of no note within our society. I doubt he even knows the role he shall play."

Burdened with the knowledge of the oracles, Constancia could not stand idle as events unfolded. She must take action, but her own course was not an easy one to choose. Much as it pained her to consider the end of her clan, the alternative was even more unbearable. *I wish that another of the elders could aid me. But Taddeusz, Kiril—even great Japheth himself…*

"They lack sufficient mastery of the *Via Ossium* to grasp the full import of what we face," she said to the dormant ancient, as if explaining herself to an irate teacher. "They would strive to save our clan no matter the cost."

She fell silent for a time, once more pondering that course herself. But the message of the oracles would not be denied. "No. Such would be folly. In ignoring the truth of revelation, an even greater tragedy would occur. I have dedicated my unlife to studying the Road of Bones. I have become its high priestess by your grace, founder. I cannot blind myself to its lessons as they would. It is our fate, is it not? Surely you would not remain in torpor if you knew of another course?"

She made a tentative gesture toward Cappadocius. Though his soul was adrift far in the ether, he looked as solid and immobile as ever. Constancia might not have expected a conversation, but a part of her had hoped for something; some sign from the Antediluvian that she went forth with his blessing.

Instead, she was left with solitude and the cold comfort of her convictions.

Qalhara scanned the bizarre, rocky terrain with uncanny intensity. They were five nights' travel from Mount Erciyes and had yet to encounter the slightest sign of life, but the Lamia warrior never relaxed her vigil. She stood down only when she and her mistress sought shelter from the rising sun. Aside from the sear-ing destruction it promised Cainites foolish enough to tempt its rays, the sun also triggered overwhelming lethargy in the undead. It mattered little how valiantly a vampire struggled to retain consciousness within crypt or tomb. As the sun climbed the heavens, slumber exerted its inevitable pull. Still, Qalhara's slumber was uneasy. Four ghouled initiates watched over them during daylight hours, but she was loath to rely on others, for she alone could offer the high priestess adequate protection.

It didn't help matters that Qalhara was unsure just why they sped westward at such a pace. Constancia was never one for conversation, but she had become even more brooding and withdrawn than usual after her two visits to the Hall of the Dead. The encounter with Alexia had spurred her to action, but the brusque commands she gave Qalhara hinted at little of her plans. Their present course would eventually lead them to the Strait of Bosporus—to Constantinople. Were they trying to catch the Nosferatu and his band? Did Alexia flee along this route? Was there some other reason they were headed for the fallen city? Qalhara's subtle queries had been rebuffed consistently so far. And, being ignorant of Constancia's plans, she was worried that she wouldn't be adequately prepared for any encounters.

She'd been told only that she was to assemble a small reti-nue that would travel with some haste. Qalhara and her mis-tress were the only Cainites. The four mortals—Akil, Hamarta, Dhanep and Palladius—were chosen primarily for their martial skill. Their horses were ghouls just like the initiates, fed Cainite blood to enhance their strength and to make them more easily controlled. Invigorated by the blood, the mounts could traverse Cappadocia's blasted landscape at an alarming pace. Each night Qalhara hoped that Constancia would disclose her plans. And more than once, on the rare occasions when they stopped to rest the horses, she sensed that her mistress was about to speak. But, in the end, the high priestess said nothing.

Qalhara spied a rocky outcrop that would serve well as camp for the coming day. She steered her mount toward the overhang, the others following her lead. The initiates well knew their duties and started digging out a pair of shallow graves over which they would erect a tent. Qalhara watched Constancia dismount and walk a few yards away. The Lamia followed suit.

"If I read the maps correctly," Qalhara offered her mistress, "a caravan crossroads lies roughly along our present course. We should reach it some time tomorrow night. Should we plan to turn south, or do we continue west?"

Constancia was silent as a breeze toyed with the simple pilgrim's robes she wore.

"Forgive me, mistress, but if you have in mind a destination other than Constantinople, it would be best I know now."

"We do, indeed, travel for Constantinople," Constancia admitted.

Emboldened by getting a response at last, Qalhara asked, "And what is your intent once we arrive there?"

Constancia gave her champion a look which, among ancients who had not needed to breathe since Diocletian was emperor, was tantamount to a sigh. "Very well. I will tell you this much. As you know, Malachite requested an oracle in his search for the Dream. In the second vision, I saw one who has a bearing upon his quest. We must steer him to the Nosferatu."

"Malachite was still near when you performed the second ceremony. We could have sent him a message, let him find this person himself."

Constancia gave her head a decisive shake. "This is not a task left to underlings. The stakes are too high."

"I do not understand, mistress. What have we to do with the Dream?"

"That is not a question I choose to answer, Qalhara."

"Mistress? I am your guardian. How can I protect you if I do not know your plans?'

Constancia turned away, her white-blond hair stirring in another gust of wind. "I was a Cainite for over one thousand years before you met your sire in Nubia. I am quite able to look after myself."

The Lamia was stunned. There was no question that Qalhara was subordinate, but never had she been treated like this. Unsure whether to apologize or continue her pleas,

Qalhara watched in mute surprise as Constancia walked away without a backward glance.

The week that followed was an unwavering routine. They stopped to rest the horses only when necessary, and words were spoken only for matters requiring immediate attention. Qalhara had never felt more distant from her mistress than she did during this time. It was frustrating and unnerving, to be thought unworthy to help Constancia bear the burden of the knowledge she carried. But what could she do? She was the servant, subject to the wishes of her mistress.

She had just crested a low ridge when the initiates cried out. Qalhara turned in time to see Constancia slumped over and tumbling from the saddle. The men maneuvered their horses to defend against attack while she rushed to the high priestess's side in the blink of an eye.

It would take a powerful blow to strike her down. How could I have missed it?! Qalhara thought, then almost laughed with relief. The high priestess had not been attacked. Rather, she'd been caught in the grip of a vision, one intense enough that it overwhelmed her sense of the here and now. Even as Qalhara reached her, Constancia was coming back around. But she was far from happy, given the dark expression that fast replaced the disoriented look she wore.

"I am already too late!" Constancia cried, bounding to her feet so fast that Qalhara had to scramble out of the way. Possessed with frantic energy, Constancia lunged for her mount. "He will be on the Mediterranean before I reach the Bosporus! Hurry; I must hurry!"

"Mistress!" The relief Qalhara had felt a moment ago was gone. The sour copper tang of blood-sweat filled the air as her mistress leaped into the saddle. Constancia had been wound tight with tension for weeks; whatever she had just experienced had put her over the edge. *She will succumb to frenzy if she does not calm down at once!*

Constancia was too far in the throes of panic to hear Qalhara call out. Having no other alternative, the Lamia whispered a prayer to her ancestors and to Lilith, the dark queen of her line. Her mouth filled with a bloody, phlegmy spittle, which she promptly spat onto the high priestess's exposed calf. Unlike most other Cainites, the Lamia were mistresses of all four of their humors, not just their blood, and among other dark doings, they could use them to affect others, even ancients like the High Priestess of Bones. A lethargic calm swept over Constancia the instant after the phlegm hit and was absorbed into her skin. She relaxed visibly, leaning against the powerful neck of her horse. She was not completely docile, however, as was clear when she leveled an accusatory glare upon her bodyguard.

Expelling the calm had aroused a contrary anger in Qalhara—her own humors were now out of balance. She stared back in defiance, at last giving vent to the frustration she'd kept in check for so long. "I will not apologize for using my arts against you, mistress; I did so only to protect you."

"And that gives you leave to attack me?" Constancia asked, her words all the more menacing for their quiet tone.

"When you might come to harm if I do not, yes. It is my duty—one that you have been keeping me from fulfilling these past weeks. Please, mistress, it is past time I knew what you intend. Whom do we hunt, and why?"

No longer in thrall to her fevered emotion, Constancia pondered her guardian's demand with her normal placid composure. After a long minute, during which Qalhara had plenty of time to think through just what she had done, the high priestess finally nodded. "Very well. Malachite came to me seeking guidance on how the Dream might be sustained in the aftermath of Constantinople's fall. More than simply pining for the Dream, he hunted for it. Indeed, he hunted for the last person who had helped give the Dream form so many nights ago."

"The last? You speak of the Dracon. I have heard you mention him."

Constancia nodded. "He is truly ancient, a childe of the founder of Clan Tzimisce, and at least as much my elder as I am yours. But he went into seclusion long ago; not long after you first came to Mount Erciyes, I believe. It is telling that, of the three who shaped the Dream from vague wish to clear possibility, only he survives. Unlike most of the fleshcrafting Tzimisce that comprise his clan, he never had much interest in manipulating his own form. Rather, he saw himself as a catalyst, bringing change to the world around him. Some have said that, when he left Constantinople, he took with him the chance that the Queen of Cities could complete its transformation from Dream to Reality."

"And you. What do you think?"

"It is not a matter of convenient opinion for me."

Qalhara nodded. She was not well versed in such esoteric matters, but she had learned enough in Constancia's service. The high priestess was more than a mere observer of the Dream and its architects. She and the Dracon had maintained a correspondence for ages, even before the mysterious Tzimisce had joined Michael in Constantinople. Qalhara did recall something of the Dracon's visit to Mount Erciyes. She was new to the clan then, and had known only that he was a guest of great influence. Hindsight gave her greater context now. "Did he request an oracle?"

"No. He had just left his companions, Michael and Antonius. He simply conveyed his plans to roam the world for an indeterminate time." Constancia paused, a thought forming from the spark of memory. "I wonder if I might have seen the threads of these converging events if I *had* beseeched the Hall of the Dead then. Alas, pondering might-have-beens will solve nothing, and I am distracted from what I meant to tell you.

"Malachite seeks to sustain the Dream, and he hopes that the Dracon will make it possible. I have discovered that he is mistaken. If the Dream survives, it will warp into a nightmare from which none of us will awaken. And the architect of this nightmare shall be none other than Lazarus!"

Qalhara felt her blood chill at mention of the heretic's name. Like everyone else in Clan Cappadocian, she had heard of Lazarus's schism with his sire, Cappadocius. She knew that Lazarus and a handful of followers had fled to the desert waste of Egypt. He and the so-called Lazarenes had been gone for so many centuries that they were little more than legends and ghost stories. "There is no question, mistress. He must be stopped! Why would you think I should not know of this?"

Constancia straightened in the saddle and stared to the west. "It is not that which I kept from you, but the future that will unfold if Lazarus is denied. For if the Dream dies, so too does Clan Cappadocian."

"How can that be? The clan was never concerned with the Dream."

"It comes back to Lazarus. I believe that if he is denied the chance to usurp the Dream, he will take his revenge upon the rest of his kind."

"What if Lazarus is destroyed instead? Surely, then, a different future may unfold."

"If only fate could be steered so easily." Constancia smiled bitterly. "I asked that question and many others. Only these courses now lie before us, and the danger of Lazarus's success is by far the greater of the two. Before starting this journey, I set some of our best adepts to divine how Lazarus may be destroyed— or even returned to the fold—but he has long avoided even my attempts at scrying. As there is no guarantee that they will learn anything of import, I decided that action was necessary."

"And rushing to Constantinople... Has Lazarus left Egypt? Do you seek to confront him yourself?"

"I would not presume to match my powers to his. Lazarus is a childe of Cappadocius. He is of an older generation than I, and he has correspondingly greater power. Even my own sire Japheth may not be his equal. No, I had a much simpler solution in mind. A figure of far less power and influence than Lazarus is the lynchpin to these future courses—an adopted cousin, one of the Giovanni."

Qalhara frowned. Like her mistress, she did not trust the upstart necromancers. It did not surprise her to learn that one might have ties to Lazarus.

"I have not learned why as yet, but one Markus Giovanni is the key to Lazarus's plan. If the Giovanni can be turned from that encounter to meet the Dracon instead, the Dream will pass to distant memory. Then we may yet find a way to keep Lazarus from destroying the Cappadocians in the future." Constancia pointed a delicate finger westward. "Alas, I have just seen that the Giovanni will be long gone by the time we reach Constantinople."

"But do you know where he is headed?"

"To Egypt, of course. Lazarus is secure in his power there."

"Then is there not time still? We are many weeks' ride from Constantinople, but we could make for the Mediterranean to the south instead. With a fast ship, we could reach Alexandria before this Markus Giovanni."

"You are right, of course. I forgot myself in the haze of the vision." A rueful smile tugged at the corners of Constancia's mouth. "And there is one with whom I have long shared correspondence who may be found in Outremer. We should get what we need with his aid."

Qalhara mounted her horse and wheeled him around. Constancia had not moved; she sat tall in the saddle, her pale blue eyes locked onto Qalhara's own. The Lamia felt the stirrings of unease. Whatever else had been accomplished here, she had attacked the Oracle of the Bones. Surely a punishment was due.

Constancia urged her steed close to Qalhara and spoke in a low tone that barely carried to the Lamia's ears. "I offer you an apology, Qalhara. I did not want you under the same burden of knowledge that I suffer. I had felt that no one could be trusted to react objectively to these dire portents. I was wrong. You are my guardian. As you may share my fate, you deserve to know where destiny shall lead us."

Qalhara did not trust herself to speak. Instead, she gave her mistress a single sharp nod, then dug her heels into the horse's side.

The four initiates watched the entire strange scene in shock. Servant challenging mistress, calm discussion of the clan's destruction—or worse! It was a lot to grasp, even for initiates blessed with a much larger view of the world than that of the common man.

The men shared a baffled look when Qalhara rode off, Constancia riding just behind. Palladius shrugged after a heartbeat and nudged his horse forward. A moment later, the other three followed suit.

"

Andreas!"

It was a croak more than a whisper, the only word spoken for many nights. Rather than lose all meaning with the constant repetition, the name proved the only anchor in a turbulent sea of madness.

The creature that slipped into the Cilician city of Tarsus two hours before dawn bore little resemblance to the elegant woman who had entered Constancia's private chambers five weeks earlier. Frantic travel by night over unforgiving ground and slumbering during the day in holes scratched into the earth had taken its toll on Alexia Theusa. Weeks of wild flight with no blood—other than occasional vermin—for sustenance had reduced her to little more than a skeleton within a skein of gray flesh and wrapped in tatters. This assemblage of bone and rags was mobile through sheer force of will. But it was the turmoil within Alexia's mind, unleashed after building up for more than a millennium, that was the source of greatest strain. She had come to Mount Erciyes desperate for answers, but had fled in panic and ignorance.

The fall of Constantinople had triggered her mental unraveling, but the pattern was woven long before. Born to affluence in ancient Athens, Alexia had found true love in a lowly slave—handsome Andreas, gentle Andreas. They stole time together when they could, but in the end the secret grew too great to bear. One a slave, the other of the elite—they could never truly be together in this world. Andreas and Alexia agreed on a pact of suicide, that they might be joined in the afterlife. But they were denied that as well. Alexia's father discovered them; he restrained her even as Andreas succumbed to the poison he had taken. Subsequently shamed and exiled, Alexia chose suicide a second time.

Then came a vision: Andreas promising his return in new flesh—not as slave, but as emperor of a city of blinding gold.

"Andreas!"

Alexia Theusa searched the known world for such a place, at the same time learning all she could of the ways of death, that she might hasten her love's return. After years, she encountered the Cappadocian Byzar, who grew fascinated with her. Noting Alexia's advancing years, he offered her unlife, that she might endure for eternity until Andreas returned. She accepted. Reborn as a Cainite, Alexia saw the vision of her love again. Then she saw the city, a golden phantom that arose from the ruins of Byzantium, the colony in which she dwelled with Byzar. The vision that had sustained her after Andreas's death renewed her hope. The city for which she had searched did not yet exist, but in becoming a vampire Alexia had acquired the means to bring it about.

She spent the years that followed encouraging the destruction of Byzantium and the subsequent cultivation of Constantinople. She had little interest in the Dream that enraptured so many Cainites, including its current champion, the pensive Malachite. Her dream of utopia began and ended with her lover. Yet the centuries passed and he did not return. Doubt and madness crept around the edges of her consciousness. Had something gone wrong? Had she misinterpreted her vision? But the answers would not come, no matter what she tried. A master of the Cappadocian mystic discipline of death—and highly skilled in certain other vampiric arts—Alexia Theusa had never mastered the rare art of divination. Despite extensive attempts, she saw but a single vision—Andreas and his promise of return to rule a shining city of gold.

Worse still, she could not seek aid from those who could grant her the answers she needed. Cappadocians were known for their knowledge of death more than their skill with divination. Some few were powerful enough that they could glean the future from the great beyond—none more so than Constancia, High Priestess and Oracle of the Bones. But Alexia could not approach them. They would fast discover what she had done to Byzar and the others. She would be destroyed for her heresy, and would never be reunited with her love.

Alexia was not alone in diverging from the traditions that Cappadocius had handed down. Others had broken from the clan; others had been declared heretics and worse. The greatest of them all was Cappadocius's childe, Lazarus. He studied death as his sire did, but with a vision that discounted nothing.

Deep in the deserts of Egypt, Lazarus and his followers pursued the arcane secrets of resurrection. It was considered an abomination by the rest of the Clan of Death, but Alexia came to see it might be the only means to restore her Andreas to life.

She had kept her dealings with Lazarus as secret as her usurpation of Byzar and his brood, but Alexia feared that Constancia's oracular sight would reveal her efforts. Every time she communicated with the high priestess, Constancia seemed more and more weary of her. Alexia retreated ever further from her dealings with others in her clan, her focus steadfast upon that shining vision of Andreas. He was her sole enduring hope, the golden city an enduring promise of happiness. Then came the Fourth Crusade. When the crusaders breached the walls of Constantinople, when the keepers of the Dream—Michael, Antonius, the Dracon—were destroyed or vanished, Alexia felt her hope disperse like dust in a breeze... and with it, her very mind.

"Andreas..."

Alexia's vision had not visited her since Constantinople fell. Despair was a dark pit that yawned wider beneath her with each passing night. Her vision was lost with the city. She had to recover it, had to find a new oracle if she could. One that would at last lead her to Andreas. Even if she could bring herself to request one of Constancia—impossible as making the sun reverse its course in the sky—Alexia was certain the high priestess would deny her. But the Nosferatu Malachite; he yearned for the insights of a seer as well. She had thought him a promising proxy for her question as to Andreas's fate, but he must have discarded any effort at subtlety in his desperation to seek out what remained of his precious Dream.

So what of *her* dream? What of Andreas?

Alexia's thoughts worried at the question each moment of her flight from Mount Erciyes, a ravening mongrel with a well-chewed bone. She paid little attention to her course, headed ostensibly for Constantinople but with no recollection of the way. She had come upon a road some nights—weeks?—ago, and held close to it since it offered easier passage than going directly over unforgiving terrain. That road led to a river and down it toward a small but fortified river port: Tarsus. Caught up in the turmoil of her mind, she paid no heed to the streets she now stumbled through. Somewhere in the back of her mind, she knew the Apostle Paul had been born in this very town, but theological esoterica did not have the weight to snap her out of her dementia.

A shape appeared before her—a thin brown man with sharp features. Other figures stood on the periphery. The blood rose within Alexia. Her lips curled, fangs unmistakable in the moonlight. "Andreas!" She snarled, a promise of destruction of any who would keep her from her love.

"You see, lord?" someone said. "She calls your name."

"So she does," the figure before her replied. His voice was the gentle caress of a breeze in summer. "From your manner, lady, one might think you mean me harm. Pray tell me how I have wronged you, that I might make amends forthwith."

Bafflement roiled within Alexia. What was this? She struggled for clarity against her Beast. This man was a stranger. His garments, though of rich fabric, were of a simple cut. His features spoke of an Egyptian lineage, though his words were in flawless Greek. Yet while she did not recognize his physical form, she sensed something in his spirit. A light surrounded him, a quality to which she felt an immediate connection. Could it be, her love was returned after all? "Andreas...?"

Alexia succumbed to exhaustion as confusion leeched the last of her strength. Strong hands gripped her as she fell. Eyes the color of gold stared into her own. "I beg pardon for handling you thusly, lady, but the ground would not be as forgiving. Rest now. We will ponder the mystery of our meeting soon enough."

And thus the soothing voice carried Alexia Theusa into unconsciousness.

Chapter Twelve

Principality of Antioch
23 August, 1204

The Silk Road had seen its share of troubles in recent years. On more than one occasion, the Christians had poured through the isthmus of Anatolia in ostensibly pious desire to capture the Holy Land. The border region of Antioch-Tripoli, located along the route from Byzantium to Palestine and one of the western terminus points of the Silk Road, was especially sensitive to these incursions.

Being in this no-man's-land, Antioch—a region of fertile plains twenty miles from the Mediterranean Sea—had cultivated the habit of shifting allegiances. It would enjoy an arrangement with the Frankish barons to keep invading Saracens at bay one year, only to seek support from the Turks in a bid for political autonomy from the west in the next. This did nothing to encourage long-term stability, which is why Antioch's present circumstances were rather precarious. The crusaders' arrival in Constantinople the previous fall had stirred things up across Outremer. Unwilling to be caught in the middle of a clash when the crusade eventually crossed the Bosporus, Bohemond—current ruler of the County of Tripoli and the Principality of Antioch—distanced himself from the Seljuk Turks he'd been courting just a few months earlier. Then the crusade spent itself on the sack of Constantinople, leaving Bohemond in a desperate scramble to reaffirm his friendship with the Seljuks. Few slept easily, least of all Bohemond himself, as Antioch struggled in the purgatory between alliances.

Despite this unrest, merchants continued to ply their trade and Antioch remained a key stopping point. Men were willing to chance mortal danger when there was money to be made. Traders worked not just the Silk Road but also sea routes that used the nearby Mediterranean port of Saint Symeon.

Of course, where riches might be found, there were those who sought to take them. Raiders lurked all along the Silk Road, happy to descend upon caravans that traversed its routes. Given its current state of flux, Antioch proved an appealing home for a number of brigands. They gave the courtesy of leaving the resident merchants' caravans unmolested for the most part—in fact, it was not unheard of for some men to be hired as guards, or to be sent against competing traders.

Bedri and his men—Kutuz, Tabib, Hami and Memir—were of a type such as this. The Seljuk warriors had no strong ties but to one another and moved as the will of Allah required. This had brought them to Antioch a few months before, and the work that followed had been steady for the most part. Having just finished an uneventful escort from Kashgar, Bedri and his fellows sought the soothing calm of a narghile. They were not alone in seeking relaxation at day's end. Many merchants and shopkeepers were gathering in open-air cafes around the Antioch bazaar, eating, drinking, and exchanging lies. Having selected a prime spot to sit with the water pipe and watch the bustle of the town, Bedri and his men could hardly miss the pilgrims' arrival.

That the pilgrims were mounted was cause enough for the five Seljuks to take notice. That the steeds were clearly from Cappadocia, a region renowned for its fine horses, was remarkable indeed. And that the pilgrims were led by two women, one of whom was as black as the night that had fallen just an hour before... well. The mystery held sufficient appeal that Bedri, tired of listening to Tabib's long-winded fables, felt compelled to investigate.

"I have never seen a mounted hajj before," Bedri called out as he neared the travelers. Tradition called for those making the journey to Mecca to travel by foot in all humility. But, drawing close, he saw that the four men and two women did not look to be Muslim. He supposed they were Christians. Bedri chuckled as inspiration struck. They might prove an hour's sport; for a few coins, he could pass off some open sewer of a back alley as the site of St. Paul's first sermon.

"You are Christians, then, eh?" Bedri continued. "And your fine steeds; have they found Christ as well?" Kutuz and the others sauntered after Bedri, chortling amongst themselves. Their leader was known for his clever wit, and they didn't want to miss a moment.

The pilgrims heard his words, but none bothered to reply. The four men were servants, it seemed, for one deferred without question when the pale woman handed off her horse's reins. Bedri was drawn to the females, even though they merely stood silent in the simple robes of mendicants. He was put out. Where was the entertainment if they did not rise to his bait? It was just a bit of fun, after all. "You have taken vows of silence, is that it?"

The pale woman—her unhealthy pallor was as startling up close as was the other's ebon skin—gave Bedri a cursory look. The glance lasted the barest instant, then she turned to the dark-skinned one. Bedri had never felt so completely dismissed. He was a warrior, a man. He towered over this slight little woman! So why did he feel as insignificant as a flea in her presence?

Bedri turned to his companions, unsure of what had just transpired. Tabib and Memir were doing a poor job of concealing their stares at the dark woman's tattooed skin, but Hami and Kutuz had witnessed the snub. Rather than sharing Bedri's outrage, they found it amusing. Was everything a joke to them? Intolerable! Incredulity turned to anger. Bedri was not about to let this go unchallenged. How dare she turn from him?

Bedri advanced—no more than a step!—and the black-skinned woman was suddenly in his way. This one was as small as the other, but she blocked his path as effectively as a wall. He would not dream of laying hands on a woman, even one that looked so strange he scarcely believed she could be human. "Step aside, woman," Bedri commanded, struggling to retain his tattered dignity before his men—whom he could now hear sniggering amongst themselves!

"We have no business with you. Begone," the dark woman responded in a preemptory tone.

A surprised burst of laughter erupted behind Bedri, followed by unpleasant mutters. It was humorous enough before, but the other Seljuks were now agreed—where did this strange woman get the authority to speak to a man that way? Emboldened by the support from his men, tardy though it was, Bedri drew himself tall. "You bring shame to your family and to Allah, acting in this manner. Step aside or bide the consequences of your insolence!"

"Deal with this, Qalhara," the pale one said. "We are delayed from more pressing matters."

Bedri opened his mouth to retort, and the dark woman mimicked his action. Her full lips opened wide, revealing small, sharp white teeth. She cleared her throat with a thick, wet sound… and spat! A wad of yellow, bilious gunk hit the slab of his cheek. Bedri discarded any pretense of posturing as he wiped at the bile with frantic hands. What kind of savage was she, to do such a thing—? Bedri felt his hands grow clumsy and uncoordinated, and a livid rash spread quickly over his skin. His head felt swathed in cotton, with more shoved down his throat until he could not breathe. Gasping, Bedri turned to his men for aid—only to see that they were overcome by the same disease. They stumbled about, their skin raw, clawing at their throats for air. Then the cotton began covering his eyes, and he felt himself falling into the dark haze….

"A brittle mind to that one," Constancia observed as the heavyset Seljuk fell to the dirt and twitched in the grip of morbid hallucinations. Qalhara offered the ghost of a shrug, her attention on the remaining four men. Their shocked expressions were fast turning to angry determination.

"I know not what you did, witch," said the leftmost man, so like the one who'd fallen that they could have been twins. "But you will not leave this place alive." Constancia found the turn of phrase amusing, but the continued delay was beginning to irritate her. She nodded to Qalhara, then advised the initiates to keep a firm grip on the horses' reins.

"Tabib, Memir," the man continued, "make sure those do not flee. Hami and I will deal with this thing."

"We hear you, Kutuz. Beware her tricks."

Qalhara moved forward with a dozen rapid paces. The man right of center—Hami—was first to free his blade. With a yell, he swung down at the Lamia with a heavy, two-handed blow. Qalhara moved into it, her hands darting up to catch the blade flat just above the hilt. She crouched and wrenched the sword over and down to one side. Hami still gripped the weapon tightly and was flipped from his feet. He slammed to the ground, losing both his breath and his grip on the sword.

Tossing the heavy Turkish blade in the air, Qalhara caught it by the hilt just as Kutuz lunged with his own weapon. Qalhara parried the blow with ease, sending the thickset Kutuz stumbling past to trip over his downed friend. The other two Seljuks forgot their directions and charged in to protect their friends.

Qalhara spun, adjusting to a crouch that took her under Memir's guard. Her stolen blade ripped across the mortal's abdomen with such power that he was almost cut in half. Seeing such a vicious strike startled the other man for a heartbeat—his last, as Qalhara reversed her blade to skewer up into his chest.

The other two men had regained their feet and came at Qalhara from either side, Hami with a knife and Kutuz with his sword extended to get the most from his longer reach. With a feint toward Kutuz, Qalhara kicked aside Hami's knife hand and swept her weapon to chop deep into his opposite shoulder. Leaving the blade stuck in the bone, the Lamia tucked and rolled just in time to avoid Kutuz's attack. She flipped into a crouch, her arm moving in a blur. Kutuz was as surprised as anyone to see the bone handle of Hami's knife protruding from his clavicle. He gulped like a fish, translucent red bubbles popping from between his lips. Then his knees buckled and Kutuz dropped to the ground, dead.

The bazaar was silent but for gasps from Hami. Having wrenched the sword from the wound, the Seljuk warrior struggled to stanch the bleeding.

Qalhara strode toward him, hungry eyes glittering in her stoic face.

"Qalhara."

The Lamia stopped, looking where Constancia inclined her head. A man moved with fluid grace through the crowd of surprised onlookers. He was of middle years but fit, with skin the color of caramel and possessing a learned look. He paused a few feet away and surveyed the carnage, then turned his attention on the small group of Cappadocians. With courtesy undercut with anger, he said, "I am Zakariah, vizier of—"

"I know where your allegiance lies, Zakariah," Constancia interrupted, "and it is he with whom I would speak."

Dubious of her claim, Zakariah indulged in outrage. "You allow your pet to commit violence here, only to demand of me such a thing?"

"I do so because your place is as servant to your betters. I do not seek audience with you, Assamite, but with the master of shadows. Tell him the Lady of the Bones awaits."

Constancia faced Zarathustra across the dim chamber. Even her keen senses barely detected him. The vampires of Clan Lasombra were known for one of the more arcane Cainite gifts. Control of shadow required great skill, but with proper focus an adept could overwhelm the brightest torch with darkness, animate tentacles of concentrated night, or even make a shadow attack the very person who cast it. Zarathustra, the hidden ruler of Antioch-Tripoli, was truly a master of this art. He was also secretive and paranoid to a degree notable even among Cainites. The ancient creature's consciousness animated a figure formed of the very darkness, a shadow-form that acted as proxy for his own physical being.

She inclined her head to the shape as she would have greeted an actual person. "I am pleased that we meet at last, Zarathustra."

"You presume much, to commit violence in my demesne and dictate demands to my vassal." The words were a sourceless whisper from the darkness.

Constancia made the barest gesture, recognizing

Zarathustra's command of the region. "I attend to a matter most pressing. Delays of dealing with mortals and underlings is not a simple matter of inconvenience, but could result in disaster to all our kind."

"Grand words, and seldom have you indulged in such a degree of hyperbole." While the two had never met prior to this night, they had maintained a correspondence for centuries. It was not a bond based on friendship, however, but on enlightened self-interest. "Still, I cannot let such action go unpunished, even from someone of your stature."

"You know that punishment would have no meaning to either of us, lord of shadows," Constancia said with some irritation. "But if you feel the need to bolster the spirits of your people, I offer one of my initiates for punishment."

"The dark one, Qalhara. She was the agent of conflict."

"Her destruction would be far out of proportion for the transgression."

"Nonetheless—"

"Desist, Zarathustra. If you presume to take action against Qalhara, you would most certainly face retribution from the Lamia sisterhood. In addition, you will be stripped of the anonymity you treasure so greatly. Forget not my influence among our kind. It would be a simple matter to spread word of your existence, to reveal who is the true Cainite ruler of Antioch-Tripoli."

The figure paced without sound of movement and the room grew darker still. The shadows spoke again at last: "Two of your ghouls, then. One for each offense committed against my rule—public slaughter and the slight of my vassal."

Constancia made a show of considering the counteroffer, though her decision was already made. She preferred to keep all four ghouls in case of future difficulty, but if losing two now would move things along that much faster, so be it. All mortals passed from life; it mattered little to Constancia if two of her trusted initiates fell to death now or later. "Very well. Choose as you desire when our business is completed."

The room brightened somewhat. With Zarathustra's wounded pride addressed, much of the shadows slipped back to the standing figure. "And what business is of such import that you would demand personal audience?"

"I must gain transport to Egypt at once. None come to this land without your notice. I am confident that you can direct me to someone familiar with our kind who would provide suitably safe passage."

"This is but the simplest of tasks that mere kine could resolve!" Zarathustra exclaimed, the room plunging to full darkness with the surge of his outrage. "Yet you accost me with it?!"

Constancia raised one slender hand. "The matter is such that I do not have the luxury of waiting night upon night while my retainers negotiate with yours for the necessary arrangement. Again, I stress that the situation is of a most pressing nature."

"So you say," the shadows grumbled. Suspicion and petulance saturated Zarathustra's words. "Very well. There is one who sails for Egypt even now. He is of the blood—though trust him at your own risk, for he is a Follower of Set."

Half-remembered connections sparked in Constancia's memory. "You speak of Ankhesenaten, do you not?"

"The same. Though in these lands, he is known as Andreas."

Constancia had witnessed the unseen threads of fate manifest in so-called coincidence time and again, but it grew no less surprising for all that. She knew of the Setite Ankhesenaten, though only in references from others with whom she communicated regularly. He was further removed from Caine than she was—though his kind, as their clan name suggested, claimed lineage only to the ancient Set, the dark god of Egyptian myth. Being from such a younger generation made Ankhesenaten's blood far weaker than Constancia's own, and he lacked the millennia of unlife she had endured. Still, he had done well enough despite this. He had been among the undead for many centuries, establishing himself as a merchant of fair reputation. Ankhesenaten was said to be distinctly disarming and approachable; he had even developed a habit of using loose variations on his name suitable for different regions he frequented. Thus, the Setite went by "Andrew" in the Holy Roman Empire, "Andreas" in Byzantium, and "Ahsan" in Palestine. To hear the name Andreas so soon after facing Alexia Theusa was curious, certainly, though Constancia did not suspect the Egyptian vampire was Alexia's love reborn. Rather, it suggested that Constancia was still on a proper course. "Andreas of Egypt. Yes, he should suit my needs admirably."

"Then I will not keep you." A meeting of equals this was, but Zarathustra had no interest in prolonging contact with any-one whom he did not trust implicitly—which was to say, no one.

"There is one last detail, Zarathustra. Day fast approaches. I would ensure that this Andreas does not leave before I may request passage."

"Very well. I will send a messenger to Saint Symeon, requesting he delay till your arrival. But no more than that." The shadow figure dispersed, leaving the high priestess alone in the small chamber. Zarathustra spoke one last time from the fading dark: "But do not presume any favors beyond that, priestess, or I will reconsider our arrangement."

Chapter Thirteen

Principality of Antioch
24 August, 1204

The Crypt of Shadows was installed underneath a small keep to the south of Antioch. It was one of many places that Zarathustra used to meet with underlings and visitors. Darkness hung heavy from its deep groined archways and encroached upon the few torches that lit the subterranean chambers. The gloom projected a restless hunger that made even Constancia uneasy. The sensation was vaguely similar to the roiling souls in the Well of Bones, but it lacked the ghosts' desperate humanity. The darkness here was a force without conscience or discipline, kept in check only through the will of its master, Zarathustra.

The vizier Zakariah led Constancia and her retinue into the crypts' central chamber, a large oval room with a high ceiling obscured by smoke and shadow. Though he was nowhere to be seen, Zarathustra's presence could be felt. A resonant tension filled the air like an impending storm. Other shapes lurked in the hungry darkness ringing the chamber, though even with Constancia's acute senses it was impossible to tell if they were Zarathustra's progeny or willful pieces of shadow. She took some comfort, even amusement, in the uncomfortable flicker of Zakariah's aura. Though a loyal servant of ancient Zarathustra, the vizier had been Embraced as a Child of Haqim. *The living darkness is as alien to him as it is to me.*

The Assamite did a valiant job of keeping his unease in check, at least. In a tone verging on boredom, he said, "You have been found guilty of offense to the True Prince of Antioch-Tripoli, His

Most Vaunted Darkness, Grandchilde of Lasombra, the Master of Shadows Zarathustra. Do you accept your punishment willingly and without reservation?"

"We submit to the authority of Zarathustra," Constancia replied. She spared a look to her initiates. The four men stood in a clump, eyeing one another uncomfortably. They'd learned of the intended punishment less than an hour before. It was left unsaid what exact fate would befall two of them, but there was little doubt that it would end in death. To their credit, the ghouls had accepted the pronouncement without protest... though also without enthusiasm. Each initiate understood that their lives had changed forever with their induction into Clan Cappadocian. The ways of vampires were not the ways of mortal men. Any consequences would be borne with the knowledge that each man had chosen the course that led here. As adherents of the Road of Bones, the initiates could find comfort in knowing that their souls would move into the next stage of the cycle once their mortal lives ended.

Even so, the initiates would probably find far more comfort in being the ones spared the Lasombra's punishment.

Four figures stepped from the shadows. Though garbed in cloaks as black as the surrounding darkness, they were flesh and blood. They approached the Cappadocian ghouls and subjected each to a cursory inspection. After some minutes, during which the initiates struggled to keep their fear from escalating to outright panic, the figures split into pairs and approached two of the men. Hamarta and Dhanep looked to Constancia, but she had nothing to offer them. The choice was made.

The two ghouls walked with the slow shuffle of the condemned as the figures led them forward. Brusque gestures indicated that the men were to step upon the wide stone plinth at the chamber's center. When Hamarta and Dhanep were in place, the four robed Lasombra took up positions corresponding to the points of the compass and raised their arms in supplication.

"We present an offering of those who have sinned against you," proclaimed one. "Judge its worth, Great Zarathustra."

Roused by the words, shreds of darkness whirled about the room like a cloud of bats. Akil and Palladius shrank back while

Qalhara made ready to fend off a possible attack. Constancia eyed the door through which they'd entered, but it was lost in the gloom. The shadows swarmed the fitfully burning torches, plunging everything into darkness for a long, terrifying minute. When the light returned, it revealed Hamarta and Dhanep suspended above the plinth inside an arcane construct. Formed from the very shadows, the intricate design arrested the eye and chilled the soul. Sharp barbed probes sunk into their flesh, triggering screams muffled by gags of solid darkness. The men struggled without success against the many shackles, bands and spikes as the flecks of shadow swirled around them in a whirlwind.

Only brief flashes of the men were visible amid the tumult, but it was impossible to ignore their rising shrieks. A haze suddenly clouded Constancia's sight. She blinked; wiping at her eyes, her hand came away red. *The shadows,* she realized. *Hamarta and Dhanep suffer so many fine cuts that their blood sprays out in a mist!*

The many small wounds and other violations the initiates suffered kept them in agony without killing them outright. Finally, long after it seemed possible that Hamarta and Dhanep could still be alive, their cries faded to silence. The shadow swarm dispersed, revealing a shredded obscenity on the plinth. The sight overcame the surviving initiates' last shreds of control. Palladius fainted dead away, while Akil retched uncontrollably.

"The offering is acceptable," Zarathustra said from the surrounding shadows. "Your offense is forgiven, Constancia. I bid you travel from my realm with all due speed. And when you return to your monastery, I suggest that you choose an alternative route. I cannot vouch that I will be as accommodating, should you pass this way again."

Constancia rode toward the docks of Saint Symeon with Qalhara at her side. Her two remaining initiates, Akil and Palladius, followed, leading a quartet of spare horses. The mission's urgent pace gave the men little time for reflection, but Constancia could sense that the fate of their comrades weighed heavily on their minds. *They would do well to take the lesson to heart,* she thought.

Such circumstances may well arise again before this journey is ended.

The Setite Ankhesenaten's merchant ship was easy enough to pick out as they drew near. Large, yet with elegant lines that suggested the craft was capable of great speed on the open sea, *Golden Virtue* was the center of much activity. Sailors scrambled with practiced ease aboard the ship and along the quay, making final preparations for departure.

Two men with shaved heads and Egyptian features, though dressed in the manner of Byzantines, noticed the Cappadocians' approach. The pair turned from overseeing the crew to greet Constancia as she reined to a halt. The more muscular of the two stepped up to take the horse's bridle, allowing Constancia to dismount more easily.

"Please be welcome, High Priestess," the thin one said in Greek. His sharp features hinted at a shrewd intellect, while his smile was open and inviting. He dipped one knee briefly once Constancia stood on the wooden planks. "I am called Andreas. How might I assist you?"

Constancia greeted him with a nod. "I am pleased to see that the messenger reached you in time. Thank you for delaying your departure."

"No thanks are necessary. We would not have left port even had I not received word from Antioch." He smiled, turning his hands palms-out in a shrug. "This is the final stop of many visits to ports along the Mediterranean coast. We arrived here from Tarsus but the day before last. Only now are we getting underway."

"And your next destination?"

"Alexandria. The markets of Khem clamor for the goods that we have gathered from the east."

Khem; the Black Land. What the ancient Egyptians called their homeland. The word was not so old for Constancia, and she found some pleasure in hearing it after so long. "It happens that I have a great need to reach Egypt also. I would seek passage aboard your craft."

With another shrug of the hands, Ankhesenaten looked over the Cappadocians. "You carry little enough, you four. I expect I could find room. But your mounts... that could prove a problem."

"Then do not trouble yourself with finding a solution. We will secure stabling for them here, to await our return." Constancia was as concerned about the horses as she had been about offering Hamarta and Dhanep to Zarathustra's gruesome punishment. Which is to say, their existence was measured against the necessity of her search for the errant Giovanni. "It should be a simple enough matter to find suitable transport upon our arrival."

"Then there is the matter of your companion. She is one of the Lamia, yes?"

Constancia nodded.

"I have never had the pleasure of such company before, but one hears stories, you understand. They say the Lamia carry the plague." He paused and offered a small nod to the *Golden Virtue.* "Disease aboard a ship is a dangerous thing."

"Qalhara will refrain from feeding aboard your vessel, but I would request we stop en route to acquire some sustenance for her."

Qalhara bristled at the conversation, but knew it was all for the good. Lilith's gift of the humors came with a price for the Lamia, a virulent disease that spread to all the mortals they fed from. Qalhara tended to drain her victims dry, if only to prevent an unfortunate outbreak.

"Very well. We can purchase slaves in Cyprus, most likely." Curiosity was evident in Ankhesenaten's eyes, but he did not give it voice. Instead, he gestured to the man holding Constancia's horse. "Goreb can help your men arrange for the animals. Leaving us to discuss the small matter of a fee."

"Has there been any change to their behavior, Akil?"

"No, mistress. The serpent's men continue to ask after the purpose of our journey, but in subtle ways."

"That is the method of those who follow Set," Constancia said. "Whether Cainite or mortal, each excels at spinning speech to his advantage. With the trickery of words, he can make the unwary believe they have found a steadfast friend or trusted ally, even as the serpent sinks its fangs."

Akil and Palladius nodded, promising they would remember this caution. Qalhara made no response. She came from

Nubia, to the south of Egypt. She was familiar with the behavior of Setites, and even if her mistress's words were something over an over-dramatization, they would keep the initiates on guard.

Constancia was silent for a time, weighing her options. The Cappadocians had paid for passage aboard *Golden Virtue*, but they were under no obligation to divulge anything beyond their desired destination. Even so, she could not ignore the convenient coincidence that Ankhesenaten was available to ferry her at the very moment she needed passage. Nor could she dismiss that he was intimately familiar with the land of Egypt. Nor, indeed, could she forget that one of his chosen appellations matched the name of the renegade Alexia Theusa's long-lost love. After millennia as a seer, Constancia knew well that coincidences were but omens in plain clothing. To dismiss Ankhesenaten as a mere chauffeur would be to ignore the chance of establishing a useful ally or revealing a possible enemy. Whatever Ankhesenaten's involvement—a matter of some frustration, as Constancia had not gleaned anything useful from the oracles as yet—the Cappadocians would learn nothing by remaining secluded in their cabin for the duration of the trip.

"I have confidence in your restraint," she said, "but the Followers of Set are wily and persistent. They are sure to learn something of our plans despite your best efforts, unless we provide them with answers that will stop them from looking any further. I shall request audience with 'Andreas.' I shall sate his curiosity and glean something useful in turn."

Ankhesenaten's cabin was surprisingly spacious, given the otherwise cramped circumstances common aboard ships. It was to be expected, for Constancia understood that Setites indulged in luxury as much as Cappadocians subscribed to asceticism. At least Ankhesenaten was not as grossly decadent as others of his kind. The cabin was opulent without overwhelming the senses—or good taste.

He gestured for Constancia to be seated, then positioned himself across from her—close enough to be intimate but not so close as to be improper. "If the weather holds, we should reach Alexandria within another week."

"I understand that you are most curious about my journey." Constancia was not much for small talk.

"I admit to a curious nature, Mistress Constancia. But I would not dream of intruding upon matters which are yours alone to know."

Constancia registered his use of "dream," and wondered again at the manipulations of destiny. "Much do I appreciate this courtesy. I have spent each night aboard your vessel contemplating how we are come to meet, and if a reason exists beyond simple chance that has brought us together." Ankhesenaten was a perfect study in polite interest. "And what conclusion have you reached?"

Rather than answer him directly, Constancia said, "Our people have been at odds for many centuries, yours and mine. We Cappadocians seek the answers to death's mysteries, yet you Followers of Set guard with jealousy the land that holds unimaginable revelations."

"We merely protect that which is ours by right and heritage," Ankhesenaten replied, some heat showing through his suave veneer. "You—"

"Pray, let me continue. I have no fault with your desire to maintain influence over Egypt. It has long been my belief that much of what the ancients learned in bygone times is best left undisturbed beneath the sand. I have found that, like living creatures, some knowledge must eventually pass from function into oblivion. It is the way of all things." Constancia allowed a smile at the Setite's puzzlement. She was branching into the realm of the esoteric. "Yet there are those of my clan who would defy not only the order of things, but also your sovereignty of Egypt."

"Ah." Ankhesenaten's eyes shone with understanding. "The Lazarenes."

"Yes. Tell me, Andreas—"

"Please; we are soon enough returned to Khem. Call me Ankhesenaten."

Constancia acknowledged the correction with a slight raise of one hand. "Ankhesenaten. Tell me, what do you know of Lazarus's childer?"

"Little enough. Death-worshipers—Cappadocians like yourself—who trespass in our lands and steal our secrets."

"Accurate enough, though not even your clan possesses the secret they desire above all else." She noticed Ankhesenaten's thin lips twitch at the Followers of Set being labeled a "clan." The serpents denied any connection to Caine and the trappings that came with such ties. He let it pass, however, more interested in where Constancia was headed.

"I expect," she continued, "that you are familiar with who holds such secrets, are you not?"

Ankhesenaten gave her his complete attention. "Unless I misinterpret, you speak of the resurrected."

"Our kind is frozen in a moment of limbo—caught between life and death. A part of each, but belonging to neither. We do not break from the cycle; we are but paused for an unknown time within the course of its turning." Cold anger seeped into her voice. "It is not our place, nor the place of any other, to force change upon the cycle of life and death. Yet there are those who dare to do so. As you say: the resurrected. They would defy the cycle, forcing souls to life before their time is due."

"We speak of this another way, but I understand your point."

Constancia was certain he did. The resurrected—sometimes called mummies because their corpses were embalmed with *mumiyah*, or bitumen, in the ancient manner—were said to be the Setites' greatest foes. Just as the dark god Set had battled his brother Osiris, so now did the Followers of Set struggle against the reborn children of the god of life and death? She had sometimes wondered if the merchants who sold medicinal powders made from crushing the bitumen-infused corpses of the resurrected's more mundane cousins were not agents of an especially inventive Setite.

Regardless, the creatures were most rare indeed. Even with Constancia's centuries of research, she knew of mummies only through legend and rumor. What she had learned spoke of mysterious beings of great power—greatest of all being true immortality, a means to defy death entirely. "Then you understand also that there are Cappadocians who have long sought to learn the secrets of resurrection, though to do so defies the will of God and Cappadocius."

"What a curious thing," Ankhesenaten said. His lips offered the barest flicker of a smile, but his eyes were deadly serious. Mummies were far from a humorous topic among his kind. "Is that not just what your clanmate Lazarus has been hoping to discover? Why does your progenitor not punish such an affront?"

"It is of no moment to you why Cappadocius makes the choices that he does. All you need know is that I now take steps to deal with Lazarus and his childer."

The serpent's smile widened, a flicker of delight touching his eyes this time. "Fascinating. I wish you every success."

"I would be that much closer to achieving it if you would lend me your aid."

"I am flattered that you would find my humble skills useful, Mistress Constancia. Beyond ensuring that you arrive in Alexandria safe and whole, however, I could not imagine how I might assist someone of your power and influence."

"Then I shall spell it plainly. You have traveled extensively, plying your merchant trade. I need one such as yourself to act as a guide through Egypt. It would not do for other Setites to misinterpret my intentions, and I lack the time and temperament to explain myself each step of the way. In addition, it might serve you well within your order to have a hand in addressing such a troublesome thorn in its side."

"Mistress Constancia," Ankhesenaten said after he made a show of considering the offer. "I confess I enjoy your company. For that reason alone, I should be most grateful to offer my aid."

"So he believes only that we seek Lazarus, mistress?"

From Palladius's tone, Constancia sensed another question behind that one. "Do not fear to be straightforward with me, Palladius. What is your concern?"

"I… I would not imagine questioning you, mistress…" The initiate shuffled with discomfort under the high priestess's keen gaze. There was a creak of wood as Qalhara tightened her grip on the short javelin she was cleaning. Palladius blanched at the glare Qalhara directed his way. With a quaver in his voice, the ghoul got to the point: "Would the serpent be fooled that our small group would be sent to deal with the heretics?"

"I am certain he was not fooled for a moment, which is as I intended. He *is* flush with curiosity, however, and hopes to learn my true purpose as he assists me. The Setites are masters of seduction, it is true, but temptation is likewise their greatest vulnerability. As long as Ankhesenaten remains curious of my larger plans, he will aid me without reservation."

Palladius nodded with vigor and made haste to excuse himself. Constancia had no need to sense the flare of the ghoul's aura to know that he was as surprised at being able to question the high priestess as he was that she'd indulged him in a reply.

Once the initiate closed the cabin door behind him, Qalhara set aside the throwing spear and faced Constancia. "You play a dangerous game, mistress. It would be safer to gather a larger force and destroy Lazarus. Then we shall avoid both of the futures that you witnessed."

"We have gone over this more than once," Constancia replied, not without some gentleness. "There is no time to recruit anyone else. Cainites told of what I have seen would question and consider it from all angles. It is the nature of our kind. But we are lost if we indulge in such pondering. You are steadfast, and for that I am grateful. But even the initiates would question my decision if they were not bound to loyalty by draughts of my blood.

"And, even if we could sway others, now is not the time to face Lazarus. His blood is extremely potent, and Caine only knows what dark powers he has discovered during his centuries in the desert wastes."

"But he does not have me in his arsenal, as you do."

"True. But skilled though you are, Qalhara, Lazarus is sure to have any number of childer who will flock to his command. No, facing him directly is folly. We are better served catching up to the Giovanni first."

"And what if the Giovanni finds the Lazarenes before we catch him?"

Constancia's parchment-thin skin showed every detail as

the muscles of her jaw clenched. "We must make certain that does not happen."

Qalhara stood at the prow of *Golden Virtue,* her thoughts in conflict. She was perhaps the only being in existence whom Constancia trusted. In turn, Qalhara offered her mistress unreserved loyalty. But she was uneasy with Constancia's plan. Certainly the high priestess was far more learned in the interpretation of oracles than Qalhara; but the oracle was of such a sweeping, portentous scale, should it not undergo more intensive study than the few nights that Constancia had devoted to it?

Events had gone far beyond that point, though, and it was clear that Constancia would not be persuaded to change her mind. Qalhara might well have to act on her own, despite what her mistress commanded. She disliked even considering the idea, but she'd done it before. After realizing, centuries ago, that visions did not equal omniscience, the Lamia had taken steps to protect the high priestess without her knowledge. One Cappadocian and individuals from two other vampire clans had been rendered to dust at Qalhara's hands—their reward for planning against the Oracle of the Bones. She was certain that she'd made the proper choice in each case, but keeping such deeds secret from her mistress nonetheless felt like a kind of betrayal. *Yet if Constancia is misguided now, am I not obligated to protect her from herself?*

These ruminations continued their ceaseless cycle, as they had since she learned of Constancia's true motives for their journey. Yet Qalhara grew no closer to a resolution. In an effort to shake off her frustration, she looked upon the dark ribbon to the south that was Egypt. They would not reach Alexandria until late the next day, so this shadowy predawn glimpse was all she would get of the continent that was long ago her home. When next the Lamia awoke, she would stand on its shores.

Six hundred years. It has been six hundred years since I have seen the land of my birth.

Though the Nile Delta was still far from the land of Nubia, Qalhara could feel a connection to the place stirring deep within her. She had followed the Nile from lower Nubia—Wawat—through the length of Egypt, ending here at the sea. *This was the last sight of my old life, my mortal life. And now here I am, returned.*

Was there a deeper meaning to this? Qalhara had served Constancia long enough to understand there were layers to all events and actions, connections that were seldom apparent to untrained perceptions. Perhaps a link could even be found between the recollections of her past and the present dilemma. But so much time had passed. It was all but lost to her now.

A memory arose then, defiant of her all-but-forgotten past. The event that literally changed her existence. As with most who found their way to Clan Cappadocian, it began with death.

A corpse, skin stretched transparent as the gases of decay threatened to burst from within, eyes empty divots of gore from the hungry beaks of birds, maggots and beetles feasting upon the putrid flesh—this was Qalhara's first exposure to death. A child in the jungles of northern Nubia, she had stumbled across the body of her cousin, gone missing the week before. His legendary clumsiness had spelled his doom, for Kutasha had fallen into a shallow ravine and been impaled through the throat by a branch. He hung there still, a thick mass of flies fighting for a taste of the blood that had spattered from his neck down his body. Little Qalhara was unprepared for the gruesome discovery, having sneaked into the gully during a game of hunter-and-prey with her brothers.

Horrified and fascinated, Qalhara had poked at the dangling Kutasha with a length of branch. The stick burst the distended belly, releasing noxious fumes and the soup of her cousin's insides. The nimble girl barely recoiled in time, the putrescent mass splattering at her feet. Qalhara vomited in reflex till there was nothing left to bring up. She continued to heave and gasp for some minutes even after she staggered away to a fresher spot.

Yet her curiosity proved greater than her horror. The body awakened something within her, a primal fascination that led her to keep Kutasha's fate a secret. She returned over the passing weeks to watch her cousin's march of decay. When there was little more than well-picked bone, long fallen from the deadly branch, Qalhara felt an emptiness inside. There was more to learn of this, she was certain, but she could not find the path of enlightenment through the jungle of ignorance. Kutasha had shown her all he could. Sorrow gripped Qalhara, for she wished to understand more about this mystery of death, how the body transformed as death advanced, what caused these changes, what happened to the person who dwelled in the flesh—

What power death had, to accomplish such wonders! Qalhara stayed late, oblivious to the setting sun, and to the subtle change of sounds as the jungle acknowledged the arrival of the ultimate predator. Roused at last by an instinctive thrill of danger, Qalhara turned. She saw a woman, pale as the maggots that had feasted upon her cousin. The woman looked upon Qalhara and smiled, teeth sharp and white in the night.

"I knew that someone visited this place, studying this corpse, but I did not know if you would stay long enough that we might meet," the woman said. Her words had an exotic lilt, but Qalhara had no trouble understanding them. The woman extended her hand and continued with a smile, "Come. There is so much more to learn."

Despite the initial thrill of panic, Qalhara felt calm. She went with the woman that night—Indira, who taught her the mysteries of death and the secrets of Lilith, first as mentor and then as sire….

Qalhara startled from the memory. Having touched upon the thought a moment ago, she pondered it now in fresh light: She had left Africa as a mortal, but returned now as one of the undead. There was meaning to be found in this, she was certain. Perhaps even a solution to her concern about this mission to Egypt.

Just as the thought started to coalesce, cries erupted from the deck. A scuffle, shouts of warning and pain, and an inhuman shriek. Qalhara reacted on instinct. Her weapons were belowdecks, but she was threat enough armed with only her hands and her wits. She dashed back, but had gotten only a few paces when a pale shape darted over the rail. Qalhara got only the briefest of glimpses, for the form arced into the water to vanish with a splash.

Outcries continued on the ship in a cacophony of confusion. She parsed the sounds easily enough to understand that whatever danger existed had gone with the strange pale blur. Qalhara would not lower her guard until she was certain her mistress was safe, but Constancia then emerged from belowdecks. As composed as always, the high priestess asked for an explanation.

Qalhara shook her head. "I heard shouts and saw something go into the water; a figure of some sort. Beyond that, I cannot say."

"Something from the waters," the Setite Ankhesenaten called out from the rail. He looked as composed as Constancia, though one of his crew slumped at his feet. The man was covered in blood from vicious gashes to his throat and chest. "Creatures emerge from time to time, attacking unwary sailors."

Qalhara fought down the surge of hunger at the sight of all the blood. The last of the three Turkish slaves purchased in Limassol was long gone. Turning her attention to Constancia for direction, the Lamia saw her mistress looking at the murdered sailor with keen interest. "A vicious, desperate creature," Constancia said, "considering the wounds inflicted."

"It is one of the hazards of sea travel. We should be safe enough, now that the crew is alerted." Ankhesenaten gestured for two crewmen to address the body. "The sun rises shortly. It is best that you go below, Mistress Constancia."

Qalhara remained in place as Constancia went down the hatch and the crew returned to its duties. A *sea monster; strange indeed.*

Odd though it was, she had seen many bizarre things in her long unlife. The Lasombra ceremony flashed through her memory; then her thoughts moved on, back to the tatters of her contemplation just before the sailor was attacked. But the thought had dispersed like fog burning in the sun before it could form fully. Qalhara gnashed her teeth, irritated. Constancia would have seen the pattern in an instant, she was sure, even with the inopportune commotion.

The answer was still there. It lurked in the shadows of her mind. But Qalhara would not find it with the cold reason of a Cappadocian. She would have to hunt it with guile and stealth, with the grim cunning of a Lamia.

Part Three: Cairo

Chapter Fourteen

Alexandria
2 September, 1204

Markus Musa Giovanni's journey to Egypt was not filled with the revelations he had hoped. He had expected to glean further secrets from the clay fragment recovered from the Lamia's ashes. During the nights aboard the ship he'd contracted for the journey—a small Venetian merchant craft hired for an exorbitant sum from the fleet gathering for the Egyptian Crusade—Markus pored over the Lilith shard. He took pains to avoid touching the fragment directly, despite the thrill of attraction he felt from the thing. Having seen how it had warped the Lamia and destroyed one of his own ghostly servitors, Markus was not eager to fall under its influence. Despite weeks spent applying his prodigious intellect and his understanding of the arcane, he found nothing of use. Admitting defeat at last, he had sewn the fragment inside a leather pouch and resigned himself to using more straightforward means to track down the lair of the Lazarenes.

Unfortunately, doing so would take more time—time that he did not have. His journey from Constantinople had been fast, but the threat of the building Egyptian Crusade hung heavy. He wanted to be well on his way toward the Sargon Codex's hidden home before Egypt was thrown into turmoil by the crusaders' arrival. Especially if, in fact, Sir Hugh of Clairvaux was gathering his forces to come after the artifact itself. Markus would have a hard enough time liberating the tiling from wherever the Lazarenes had hidden it. He did not look forward to facing battle-hardened warriors with the Codex in his possession.

Since the ship had arrived in daylight, Falsinar and Beltramose were responsible for contacting the merchant Alessandro Sforza. Markus had heard of the man only by reputation. A mortal ghoul of one of Markus's Giovanni cousins, he had been sent to Egypt to act as the family's contact in the trading city of Cairo. With his aid, Markus's ghouls had found secure lodging for their master and then set about learning the local gossip. They shared their findings with Markus that night. News of a possible crusade against Egypt was a favorite topic, easily overshadowing talk of the Nile's annual flood, which would reach the delta in a few short months.

"I should not be surprised that news of the crusade arrived here before us," Markus said. "There are always faster ships, and the Assamites are said to be able to send messages across great distances. Still, it is all the more urgent now that we find the trail of the Sargon Codex. What of this Sforza?"

"Pleasant enough and with a solid reputation in the area," Falsinar replied.

Beltramose nodded his support. "He has been helpful so far without prying about our purpose here. And he seems well versed in the importance of discretion."

"Good. He is our best starting point. I will speak with him shortly to see what he has heard about the Lazarenes." Beltramose confirmed that Alessandro was agreeable to a visit at any time of the night. He looked around the vaulted chamber that was set aside for their quarters. "But what of your, ah, *other* servants?"

"I have sent them to investigate, but there is no guarantee what they will find. They are as new to this land as we are." A thrill coursed down his spine, equal parts exhilaration and unease. He was acutely aware that they were in a land not just foreign, but alien. Egypt was a place of ancient mysteries, a place in which powerful creatures dwelled—creatures who had no great love for outsiders. And he was here alone, far from the protection of his family or his clan. Markus was confident in his powers, but he lacked a reliable local network to help keep him safe or to aid in finding the Codex. All he had were a pair of ghouls, five recalcitrant wraiths, and whatever they could glean from the locals. Perhaps it might be worth the risk to hold the Lilith shard. A brief touch, just enough to gain a sense of the larger Codex…

No! I must not listen to the shard's whispers! He pinched his nose between finger and thumb and shrugged off the sensation as best he could. "Come; I would speak with Alessandro Sforza immediately."

Markus discovered that their quarters formed one wing of a small estate built in the Muslim style. It was an older structure, crafted with some skill. Alessandro was doing well to afford such a place. Falsinar and Beltramose led Markus across a central courtyard to the opposing wing. A waiting servant took them immediately to a large sitting room and announced that Alessandro would join them momentarily.

The man who came in a minute later was of average build and wore a caftan in the local style over clothing of a stylish Venetian cut. He offered Markus a warm greeting, but dispensed with polite banter when it was clear that his visitor was filled with urgency.

Pleased with Alessandro's astuteness, Markus launched into his reasons for being in Egypt. Leaving out any mention of ancient artifacts and crazed Lamias, he described his interest in finding the Followers of Lazarus. "Tell me, Alessandro, do the Lazarenes sound at all familiar?"

"I am sorry, *Signore,*" Alessandro said. He had a too-wide mouth and a habit of accompanying his conversations with vigorous gestures. Friends and those with whom he did business learned to put away any delicate items when Alessandro came by. "They do sound curious, though. I should think that, soon enough, misguided souls worship even the most obscure Biblical figures."

Markus didn't bother to explain that the Lazarus he spoke of was not exactly the figure from the Bible. "Would that I might indulge in a theological discussion, but circumstances deny me the opportunity for leisure."

Alessandro offered such a hearty shrug that his caftan almost fell from his shoulders. "Of course, *Signore.* I wish that I had even a crumb of useful information."

Markus waved away the apology, though the concern in his belly was not so understanding. Even a man as well-informed as Alessandro could not know everything. The Lazarenes were hardly renowned outside Clan Cappadocian; it was no surprise that a mortal—even one who dealt with the undead—was not aware of them. The merchant might provide other useful details, though. "What of Cappadocians? Has there been any mention of such individuals?"

"I have heard the name. In my dealings with your family, of course, but perhaps once or twice from others in this region. It is my understanding that Cappadocians are not very welcome in Egypt, though I cannot say why." *The Setites guard the Egyptians' secrets of death with great jealousy. And the infiltration of that heretic Lazarus into this place has not made them any more inclined to aid our studies.* Aloud, Markus asked, "Nothing beyond that?"

"Nothing of any significance, *Signore.*" Another shrug stirred the merchant's clothing in a brief flurry. "I am most happy to help the Giovanni, but you may learn more by speaking with one of your own kind."

"I had not thought there were any Giovanni in Alexandria at this time."

"That is true enough, but I do not speak of your family, exactly." Alessandro made a sweeping gesture at the room's far wall. "You will find a sizable congregation of Cainites in the great city of Cairo. They are quite a mix—Latins, Saracens, and other religions even more obscure than your Lazarus-worshippers. Cairo is unique in many ways, yes? But surely someone there will have the knowledge that you seek."

"I can but hope."

Markus reached Cairo just over a week after his meeting with Alessandro. The place was as impressive as he had heard. The streets bustled with activity even in the dead of night. Countless varieties of exotic dress, language, and nationality could be witnessed simply by standing in one spot for a few minutes. It was especially jarring to see the mix of Latin and Muslim, given his recent exposure to the rhetoric of crusade.

He soon confirmed that the vampiric population was subject to a similar dichotomy, though with an intriguing twist. The Cainite who ruled over his fellows in Cairo was a Roman by the name of Antonius. He was of Clan Ventrue—vampires as suited to leadership as the Cappadocians were to the study of death—and had held sway as sultan for centuries. That he shared a name with another Ventrue of note was no coincidence. The sultan was the progeny of the same Antonius who had long been companion to Michael and the Dracon in Constantinople. Markus found it intriguing that a Latin and a Christian such as Antonius the Younger could maintain control among a predominantly Muslim vampiric population.

Then again, Antonius's rule might not be as secure as appearances first suggested. In the two nights that followed his arrival from Alexandria, Markus learned that the Followers of Set controlled almost every aspect of merchant activity in Cairo and the surrounding territories. Given Cairo's position as a major trading center, it suggested that Antonius ruled in name only. The true power among the undead rested in the hands of the merchant Setites.

It was a familiar arrangement to Markus—the Giovanni played much the same game with the Lasombra vampires who claimed Venice—and were they any other vampires, these merchants would have been a great help to his investigation. But even with a letter of introduction from Alessandro Sforza, Markus doubted he would get little help from the Followers of Set. It was frustrating since, being undead as well as involved in commerce, they were otherwise exactly the type he preferred to deal with. Markus did not need to hide behind a veil of mortality with fellow vampires, couching his questions in innuendo. He could state his purpose in a way that another Cainite would understand, saving a great deal of time and energy. And merchants were well informed due to their extensive travels. The Setites were certain to be quite knowledgeable, given their ties to trade throughout the Mediterranean and Arabia. They were not unlike the Giovanni in this respect, skilled at making deals and as honorable as anyone in matters of business—which was to say, they had no inherent loyalty to anything but making the best sale possible.

The similarities did not go much beyond that, however. Setites were renowned for their insidiously scheming natures. Fellow Cappadocians had told the Giovanni that the serpents' true interests went far past matters of trade. The Setites hoped to lure the curious into arrangements to compromise the very soul. This was no mere hyperbole where the powers of the undead were concerned.

Add to that the friction between Cappadocians and Setites, and any dealings with the Followers of Set were sure to be a perilous affair for Markus. Having no desire to put himself at the mercy of the duplicitous serpents, he would investigate an alternative path first.

The creature with flesh the color of ashes fixed his guest with a polite gaze. "We have not received one of Clan Cappadocian in some time. What brings you to the demesne of Sultan Antonius, the heart of the empire of Salah al-Din?"

Markus accepted the implied welcome with a nod, pausing a moment as he once more pondered the many oddities that encompassed Cairo. Take these words of Jubal, advisor to Antonius, lord of Cairo's vampires. The mortal emperor Salah al-Din had established the *madrasah* system of education, opened the royal enclosure of al-Qahirah to public access, and built the imposing structure of the Citadel that defended the city from all transgressors. Perhaps of greatest significance, the champion of the Muslim people had retaken much of Palestine from the crusaders in the waning years of the last century. Just a portion of many notable accomplishments, to be certain. But Salah al-Din had died a decade ago. Even so, the mortal warrior-king's legacy was significant enough that he was spoken of with the same reverence as that given a living ruler, and not just by Cairo's mortal population. Jubal lent equal respect to the name Salah al-Din as he did to Antonius, whom he had served for generations.

"I must apologize on behalf of my clan, Jubal. Much as we are fascinated by the land of Egypt, past and present, we face little welcome from certain of its residents."

The other vampire bowed his hairless head, which was the

color of potash and capped with a simple turban of rich silk. "I have heard rumors now and again that some source of friction kept the Cappadocians away. It pains me to know this to be true."

"Would that I could change things with a word. But, alas, though circumstances may change, I do not expect that it will happen this night." Rumors, indeed. Markus had been in Egypt not even two weeks and he had seen ample evidence of the sway the Setites held here. Jubal could not help but know that the serpents denied the death-obsessed Cappadocians entry to a land steeped in the mysteries of the afterlife. "I have no quarrel with the Followers of Set. Alas, I suspect that they will be no more inclined to aid my journey if I explained this."

"And what journey is that?"

This was the difficult part. Markus needed to find the Sargon Codex, but he could not just spit that out. The artifact was sure to be of great interest to any vampire clan, even whatever obscure one had sired the odd-looking Jubal. Markus was confident that the Codex was in the care of one of the renegade Lazarene cults who dug the sands of Egypt for secrets and who had given rise to much of the animosity that existed between Cappadocians and Setites. The question then became, did Jubal know that the Cappadocians considered their Lazarene cousins heretics? If so, Markus could not simply say he was looking up an old friend from Mount Erciyes. Best to learn as much as Jubal knew before committing to an explanation. "Are you familiar with a sect known as the Lazarenes?"

"Followers of Lazarus, given the name," Jubal said. He quirked one brow, a natural enough gesture made strange due to the lack of hair on his dry skin. "Again, I have heard rumors, but I would not presume to take them as truth."

"I shall not feel insulted, if that is what worries you."

"Very well. I have heard that the Lazarenes are a branch of your clan; scholars of death also. I… well, I had heard that there was a schism of sorts, some time ago."

"A schism, yes." Markus affected a shrug, suggesting it was merely one of those embarrassments that happen from time to time. "As I told your representative prior to our meeting, I came to Cairo on matters of trade for the Giovanni. But I hoped, as long as I was here, that I might also attempt a... rapprochement with my erstwhile clanmates."

Jubal's features were polite as ever, but his swirling aura revealed that he thought Markus's interest went quite a bit deeper. Always the diplomat, he said simply, "Too many of our kind indulge in secrecy and conflict. It is heartening to see someone seek to transcend differences."

Markus nodded, as if he savored the wisdom of Jubal's words. "So have you encountered any of the Followers of Lazarus in Cairo, then?"

"I have not. And, as chief advisor to Sultan Antonius, it is my proud duty to greet all those who visit this city. I know very little of them beyond what I have just said. I think the Lazarenes dwell far from inhabited places, though I could not say why."

This was true enough of most Cappadocians. "The solitude aids in our studies. Well. I must admit to disappointment. If one such as yourself has no knowledge of where I might find my brethren, I could not think where to look next."

"I am most sorry that I could not lend you assistance in this matter. Ah! But I might aid you in another area. Your... Giovanni business. You are looking for new avenues of trade, yes? The Bahariya Oasis is home to many fine goods that would surely find ready buyers in the Latin territories."

"Really? I have not heard of it. Where would I find this oasis?"

"It is a key stop in a trade-caravan route that ranges through the western desert. Inquire at the bazaar; you should have no trouble finding a caravan heading that way."

"I thank you for that piece of information. At least my journey will not have been a complete loss."

Jubal stood, his lips parting in an odd smile that displayed many small, sharp teeth. "I am most glad that I was able to help in some small way, Markus Musa Giovanni. Your brief visit was a delight that I shall enjoy for nights to come."

"It was a pleasure meeting you as well, Jubal," Markus replied. He stood to bow, towering over the gray-skinned vampire. "Thank you again for your aid."

"It was nothing, I assure you. May Allah keep you well and grant you good speed in your travels."

"You are sure we will find the Lazarenes at this... what was it called, again?"

"Bahariya Oasis." Markus rubbed a broad hand across his beard. "And yes—as sure as I can be, all things considered. Jubal was as reserved in manner as he was cautious in words. But for his aura, I would have thought nothing of his advice beyond its surface import."

Falsinar waved a hand, granting his master's keen insight. "And what is an 'oasis,' then?"

"Underground wellsprings create a place of greenery in the midst of the desert. I made some initial inquiries. It appears that Bahariya is, indeed, a major settlement along a caravan route that has seen use since the time of the pharaohs."

"Is there anything else that you need to attend to in this city, then," Beltramose asked, "or shall we arrange to join the next caravan?"

"I shall see what the shades have learned from their investigations in the city, but I feel that we are on the proper course."

"*Signore?*"

"Make the arrangements, Beltramose."

"By Christ and Caine!"

"What, Beltramose? Are you injured?"

"A fatal blow to my dignity, Falsinar. Did you not see? That beast spat on me!"

"Ah. So it did. Did not Alessandro explain that camels are prone to such action?"

"How spiteful. And I did nothing to it."

"There are customs in this land we know nothing about. Perhaps you insulted the beast without knowing."

"It is a *camel*, Falsinar."

"Perceptive as always, good Beltramose."

"I shall not rise to your transparent attempts to bait me. I have grown beyond such childishness."

"How enlightened of you, my friend. Then let us return to

our master's resting place, that we may... Beltramose? My steadfast companion. I must ask a most delicate question."

"I shall bring my full faculties to bear in answering it, loyal
Falsinar."

"Then I hope to receive a coherent answer. Here is my query:
Did you wipe yon camel's vile expectorant upon my back?"

"I am shocked that you would think me capable. Now
come. We must be present when *Signore* rises, to tell him of our
success."

"Of course. Lead on, Beltramose."

"Why, thank... no, I could not possibly. After *you*, Falsinar."

"I insist."

"Perhaps if we share the honor and walk side by side?"

"Verily, you possess the wisdom of Solomon."

"You flatter me, Falsinar."

Usama ibn Wasir waited with the pensive jitters of an addict. In
truth, he was simply a high-strung sort. Add to that his eagerness to convey this latest information to his master and the wizened caravan factor was close to having a fit.

He cursed the languid, lowering sun, urging the coming
night to arrive forthwith. The chamber in which he paced was
already shrouded in shadow. A lattice over the single small window, the only source of light, displayed a hundred golden dia-
monds that tracked across the opposite wall. The beams faded
at last, and Usama hurried to light a pair of lamps. The tinted
glass of the shades provided a pale green illumination, creating the feel of being beneath the surface of a murky pond. This
often unsettled other visitors to the chamber, but for Usama it
provided a semblance of calm. With the lighting of the lamps, it
would be but a few more minutes until the Great One appeared.

And indeed but a short while later, Usama turned in his
pacing to find that he was no longer alone. Each time the caravan factor came to this place, he was greeted in the same fashion: The Great One arrived as if stepping from the very air.
Usama almost caused himself injury in his eagerness to genu-
flect before the dark master.

"Great One, your humble servant debases himself before

you! Truly, I am a wretch, unworthy of being in the glory of your presence!"

"Yes, yes, Usama. We have been over this before, and you will find no disagreement passing my lips." The voice was a silky caress, calm with a hint of humor and command in equal measure. "What news do you bring me this night?"

"I have this day made arrangements for a Latin merchant to join a caravan to the Bahariya Oasis!"

"I would find this surprising, were it not your job to perform that very task. I take it there is something interesting about this merchant?"

"Yes, Great One. Please accept my apologies!" Usama pounded his forehead against the rug's intricate embroidery, partly out of love for the creature before him, partly out of frustration that he was making a garble of his news. He took a deep breath. The faint odor of must and exotic spices that exuded from his master lent him focus. "It was a collection of small clues, the sort of thing I would dismiss had you not urged me to look for them."

"So tell me of these clues."

"First, I did not deal with the merchant himself, but with his subordinates. These two spoke in the language of the Venetians—which I learned from servants of yours far more worthy than myself. It has proven a most useful tongue, that I may command arrangements that my rivals cannot—and pass my findings along to you in each instance."

"You are a most loyal and clever servant, Usama. Pray continue. The night passes with the speed of a camel fleeing his owner."

"Many pardons, Great One! These men, they desired to join the next caravan on the oasis route. I told them of one that will depart in three days, and they were most eager to place themselves among its number. They also requested an enclosed cart—their trade goods, they claimed, would not stand prolonged exposure to the elements."

The creature opposite Usama had listened with bored tolerance up to this point. Rich cloth shifted in a heavy rustle and jewelry fashioned from precious metals clinked together as he leaned over the caravan factor. Bright gold, slitted eyes regarded the mortal with interest. "Curious that they did not have a wagon of their own. And enclosed?"

"They were very clear on that point, master. I recalled your words on the subject. So after agreeing upon a price I followed them to see what more I could learn."

"And what did you discover?"

"I overheard them, Great One. They spoke of returning to their patron when night fell, to tell him of their success!"

"Did they, now? That is most interesting. And where does their patron bide?"

"I cannot say, Great One! Pity me; my old bones were not sufficient to keep pace. I lost them in the crush of the bazaar!" Shame gripped Usama. "There is no excuse for my failure!"

A flicker of irritation disrupted the creature's smooth countenance. "Do not upset yourself, Usama. You have performed adequately. I may not know where the Latin is now, but I know where he will be."

"The Dark God Set blesses you with a vision of the future, Great One!"

"No, Usama," the other replied with an effort at patience. "You just told me they arranged transport with the Bahariya caravan."

"Of course, Lord! I am but the least shadow of wit in the face of your brilliance!"

"I shall not argue with you on that score either, Usama. Tell me, what name did the Latins give to their patron?"

Usama gobbled air as his mind scrambled to recall. "It was Giovanni, Great One. They called him Giovanni!"

A cold smile split impossibly wide across the lean face of the Follower of Set who went by the simple name Bek. "Did they, now? How interesting. You have done well in the service of the Dark God, Usama. Very well indeed."

Markus turned away from the last wisps that had once comprised the purgatorial shade of Hartmut. The Genoan sailor had had the bad fortune to contract the plague in Constantinople and the worse fortune to have his bones collected by a certain

Venetian necromancer in need of spectral slaves, who cared nothing for letting them reach the rewards of the afterlife. The ghostly flotsam faded into nothingness.

"What happened to him?" Markus demanded, staying calm only with effort. His three remaining wraiths simply cowered in silence. This journey was difficult enough without the shades causing further complications. At first, they had made minor but notable gestures of defiance after Vesta was destroyed. Nothing of great concern—being slow to fulfill their orders or supplying vague answers to his questions—but such willfulness could not go unpunished. He was too preoccupied with his investigations to take more than basic disciplinary efforts, which had had less impact since they reached Egypt. In fact, the night after arriving in Alexandria, Infantino—easily the strongest of the wraiths—had almost broken free of his control. And all the spirits had become more restless, even panicked, in the two weeks since. Neither entreaty nor interrogation could pry an adequate explanation from them. As best he could understand it, the Egyptian spirit world was far stranger and more frightening than anything they had yet encountered. Markus felt a creeping unease from this land, but he didn't see why the ghosts' reactions were so much more pronounced.

And now this. In the nights leading up to the caravan's departure, Markus had had Infantino stay close to warn of anyone who might have unpleasant designs toward him. The other ghosts were to check into the merchants traveling in the caravan and see what more they could learn about the Bahariya Oasis itself. He formed them into pairs—Hartmut and Rina, Viator and Domnola—hoping that safety in numbers would calm their agitation somewhat.

Hartmut and Rina had not returned on the night before the caravan was to leave, so Markus performed a summoning ritual. He had already known that Hartmut would come back alone, for the necklace that was Rina's anchor no longer emitted the telltale echo of her soul. He hadn't expected Hartmut to be in such bad shape, though. The ghost was nothing more than ethereal tatters which dispersed within a few minutes of his return.

"He spoke too quietly for me to understand, but I know you could hear him. Tell me what you know—tell me what destroyed them!" He put all his authority behind each word, but to no avail. "Do you think that you need not fear me any longer? Whatever happened to Hartmut and Rina, at least they have the comfort of oblivion now. I can make you suffer for centuries in your pathetic condition. Now answer me!"

Infantino roused himself enough to mutter something about the ancient dead.

"Other ghosts did this? I might do well to impress spirits of such power into my service." The three wraiths erupted in panicked spasms. Markus thought they might even attack him—not that it would do any good. Wraiths made excellent spies, but they could do little against physical beings. "Calm yourselves! What is it about the ghosts of this land that you fear so much?"

The wraiths merely flickered in silence.

Though neither the oldest nor the most powerful member of his family, he was nonetheless skilled at the necromantic arts. Yet, even with further interrogation, he could not discover the source of the ghosts' trepidation, and they were unwilling or unable to explain it themselves.

Markus paced in frustration. *We profess to be the masters of necromancy, yet we know so little about the realm of spirits!*

A quick rapping on the door forestalled further thoughts. Falsinar poked his head in the chamber. "Pardon, *Signore*, but it shall be dawn soon. We should secure you in the wagon and hasten to the caravan site."

"Yes, thank you. I shall be ready in a moment."

Markus cast a cold gaze at his ghosts after Falsinar left. "You have kept your secrets for now. Very well. I will find a way to expose them soon enough—though, when I do, you may pray for the comparatively peaceful destruction that your three compatriots suffered."

Chapter Fifteen

Cairo
18 September, 1204

It took an effort for the High Priestess Constancia to keep her temper in check. "What do you mean, you do not know where he is? Is it not your role to ensure that all Cainites who come to Cairo pay their respects to the sultan's court?"

"That is so, Mistress Constancia," replied Jubal. "But your words strike at the heart of the matter. Markus Musa Giovanni has left Cairo."

"But surely you know where he has gone."

"I cannot say with certainty." Jubal's expression was the same polite deference he had shown Constancia from the moment she had first set foot in the opulent receiving hall deep in the citadel of Salah al-Din. "At most, I may tell you what road he took from the city. Where he has gone from there is unknown to me."

Constancia cast her cold gaze upon him, the Beast roiling within her anew when she realized she would have to make a formal request for the information. *I have no time for such courtly pettiness!*

"Very well, most learned and sagacious Jubal. I ask with all humility that you reveal to me what path Markus Giovanni took from Cairo."

"I am given to understand that he journeys to the Bahariya Oasis."

At Constancia's inquiring glance, Ankhesenaten spoke up. "Bahariya is the first and greatest of a handful of oases that form a trading circuit through the western desert. Almost three weeks' travel if the weather is kind, I would say. Longer by caravan."

Constancia wished to learn more about the place, but it would require asking questions she would rather Jubal not hear. "And do you know when he left for this oasis, Jubal?"

"Three, perhaps four nights past. I could send a slave to the bazaar to find the caravan factor with whom he made arrangements, if you wish. I should learn more details within a night or two. In the interim, I could arrange an audience with Sultan Antonius. He is sure to be eager to hear of recent events to the north."

"I must decline your kind offer and invitation," Constancia demurred. She had made a decision, and with it regained her mantle of calm. "I predict that we shall have left Cairo ourselves by that time."

Jubal bowed his head in regretful understanding. "Perhaps when you pass this way again, then."

"Perhaps. Who may say what the future shall bring?"

Ankhesenaten's estate was an impressive affair built of fine marble in a style reminiscent of ancient Egypt rather than more current Muslim sensibilities. The rooms were large, with high ceilings and dramatic views of the surrounding countryside just north of Cairo. Low couches and piles of pillows comprised much of the furniture, while the walls were adorned with colorful frescoes and the floors were covered in dazzling tiled designs. Despite—or perhaps because of—the luxury inside, Constancia spent almost all her time in the large estate's courtyard, which had nothing more than a few palm trees and a fountain as decoration.

It was there that she faced Ankhesenaten, her need for answers overshadowing much of her self-control. Patience was a watchword for ancients such as she, but ever since her departure from the isolation of Mount Erciyes, she'd been compelled to act, feeling as unsettled as a vampire only a few years into unlife. Constancia did not enjoy the sensation. Still, she had hoped to reach Alexandria before the Giovanni. A few mundane inquiries had revealed that Markus was most likely in Cairo already. They had rushed south, only to find that they had missed him again. She hadn't felt panic before; it was unlikely that any Lazarenes would be found in large cities. But Markus's trail was headed in a new direction, toward the type of wilderness her clanmates—heretics or no—often preferred as a setting for their rituals. Her chance would soon be gone.

She stood in an unadorned gown, as still as the marble fountain that formed the centerpiece of the courtyard. Yet she radiated a palpable tension that gave even ever-present Qalhara pause. "What do you know of this Bahariya Oasis? What lies there of interest to a Cainite?"

Ankhesenaten watched the ripples in the fountain as water trickled from the mouths of the serpents that ringed its edge. "Your pardon, Mistress Constancia," he said at last, his attention still on the water. "I have pledged my services as guide. But I fear I am unable to fulfill my role to satisfaction."

"You claim you know nothing of import about the oasis?"

The Setite faced Constancia, hands clasped behind his back. "I cannot aid you because I lack knowledge that would help me accomplish my duties in your service. A fortnight past, aboard my vessel, you claimed that you planned action against the Lazarenes who pollute Khem. Yet since our arrival in Alexandria, your inquiries have been directed toward this Markus Giovanni. As I have understood it, the Giovanni are Venetian merchants who are known to dabble in sorcerous pursuits. Yet you suggested in speaking with Jubal that he is… what is the phrase Latins use? 'Of the blood'? Well, then. How does this Giovanni of the blood relate to your renegade Lazarenes?"

"That is none of your concern, serpent." The high priestess turned the force of over two thousand years of unlife fully upon Ankhesenaten. "We arranged for a service, one which you may perform well enough without knowing the full details of my purpose. You go beyond those bounds at peril to your existence."

"I… take your words to heart." Though clearly shaken, Ankhesenaten did his best not to back down. With visible effort, he continued, "And I caution you to do likewise with mine.

Aged and powerful though you are, know that neither you nor your attendants would see Mount Erciyes again should I suffer destruction while in your service."

"You are but a whelp. Who are you to put forth a threat to me?"

"I am a loyal servant of Set, once and future lord of Khem. And you have been granted passage through this land in my care. My brethren know of this arrangement, just as they will know without delay should I fall to some foul misdeed. A whelp I may be in your eyes, but do you and your trained Lamia possess power sufficient to defy the entire Walid Set?" Though they conversed in Greek, the serpent used the Arabic term for his brood, underling that Constancia was on foreign soil, not he.

The two were still for a long march of seconds, each struggling with the surge of emotion brought on by the rise of the Beast. They were not alone in maintaining the barest restraint against outright violence. Qalhara stood silent to one side, motionless, yet ready to move in an instant to protect her mistress. The Setite's bodyguard, Goreb, was similarly prepared. After ten seconds that lasted a century, Constancia turned away. She forced a human sigh through her atrophied lungs— the first in several mortal lifetimes—and began a measured pace around the serpentine fountain. "You are familiar with what certain of the blood call the Dream, are you not? Good. I am not surprised. It has inflamed the desire of many of our kind, even those of you who claim origins separate from Caine. You know, then, that Constantinople was agreed to be the closest embodiment of the Dream. With Constantinople fallen and Michael destroyed, Latin and Greek Cainites have been thrown into a frenzy of confusion. Even now, they clamor for someone to champion the Dream as Michael once did. They hunger for a city to replace Constantinople's glory—hunger for it with a passion rivaled only by the ever-present thirst for blood."

The quiet cadence of Constancia's commentary soothed Ankhesenaten's heated temper. The recent altercation was set aside—though not forgotten—as he became intrigued by her words. "Go on."

"I have seen the threads of fate that tie the present to the future. Two choices exist. In one, the Dream lives on; while in the other it is sent into the realm of memory."

"Ah." Ankhesenaten tapped a finger and watched the new pattern of ripples disperse across the water's surface. "Then this Giovanni threatens the Dream's future in some way with his plans to find the Lazarenes. And you come here to stop him and save it."

"You are almost correct, Ankhesenaten. But I do not act to sustain the Dream. I plan to see that it dies."

Moonlight cast a cool sheen upon the Setite's bald skull as he lifted his head. Constancia stood on the other side of the fountain, her own gaze directed up at the night sky. Ankhesenaten's golden eyes flickered back and forth in consideration. "Hmm. Then let us ponder how this looks when viewed from the other direction. This Giovanni hopes to ally with the Lazarenes in an effort to renew the Dream?"

"Something of that nature." Constancia was not certain exactly why Markus Giovanni had come to Egypt, in fact. The oracles did not address that detail, only that he would encounter Lazarus if she did not intercede in time. She had heard little more than passing details of Markus Giovanni prior to recent nights, so his appearance in the visions was a surprise. Yet where the oracles fell short, she applied reason. Alexia Theusa's outburst in Mount Erciyes confirmed a suspicion that Constancia had long held, that Alexia was herself a heretic. The preeminent Cappadocian in Constantinople, it stood to reason that she would have either converted or manipulated her local clanmates, including this Markus Giovanni. In all likelihood, she'd sent him south to Egypt while she headed to Mount Erciyes. Beyond that, Constancia was not willing to speculate. She would learn the truth soon enough when she caught up with the Giovanni—and then she would set him on a new path.

Constancia set these thoughts aside; they were of no relevance to the role that Ankhesenaten must play. He need only be persuaded that the success of Constancia's cause was of paramount importance. "You may wonder why I move with such haste to see that this does not transpire."

"I have returned to that question with some frequency."

"Next to us Cappadocians, your kind should best understand the import of what I tell you now: If I do not intercept Markus Giovanni in time, he will somehow give the heretic Lazarus the opportunity to place himself as the penultimate power in all creation—hoping to supplant God Himself, and even to cast aside your dark lord, Set. And not only will Lazarus attempt this...

"He will succeed."

"What is it, Qalhara?"

Tire Lamia raised her tattooed brow. "I have said nothing."

"Your silences say more for you than ten thousand words from the most skilled orator." Constancia returned to contemplating the stars that shone outside her chamber window. "And do not forget that I have some small skill in reading auras."

"Very well, mistress. It is surprise. I had not thought it possible to seduce one of the serpents."

"Is that how you view my handling of Ankhesenaten? I told him no lies. Nor did I promise anything that is beyond my power to accomplish."

"No, you did not. You were far more subtle, mistress." Constancia looked over her shoulder, lines of amusement creasing the spare planes of her face. "I sense disapproval."

Qalhara left her reply unvoiced.

"Yes? Well. You are aware of the choice I had to make, Qalhara. The cycle will be forever shattered and all existence thrown to madness if Lazarus achieves apotheosis. Yet defying the event will result in the end of the Cappadocians. There is no third road we may choose. And even then, it is not much of a choice. For if Lazarus wins godhead, our clan—and all that is—shall be subjected to such change that its survival will be meaningless."

Though still silent, Qalhara flexed her jaw as though chewing her words to manageable size. At last, she returned Constancia's gaze. "So you have said, mistress. And I reply now as I have every other time: With stakes such as these, should we not have amassed greater forces than just ourselves and a pair of ghouls?"

"Do not forget our loyal guide." Seeing Qalhara was not in the mood for levity, Constancia gave her bodyguard her full attention. "The future is balanced most precariously, and we have never been a well-organized clan. It would have taken far too long to gain consensus, let alone gather a sizable force. And even with but you and 1, traveling as rapidly as we have, still I feel that time grows dangerously short."

Qalhara's shoulders slumped a fraction. She, also, felt the press of time. But still, something was being overlooked. Some detail that would set aside her lingering doubt. She had almost grasped it the last night aboard *Golden Virtue.* If not for the interruption of the pale shape that had plunged into the dark sea… Qalhara shook off the thought. Being distracted by such contemplations would dull her edge, making her useless as Constancia's protector.

"I feel your concern," the high priestess said. "Would that matters were otherwise. As they are not, we must deal with them accordingly. With Ankhesenaten assured that grave cataclysm will strike his treasured land if he fails to aid us, we have surmounted the final impediment to success."

A crease formed between Qalhara's brows. "Are you not premature, mistress? We have not yet caught this Markus."

"Granted. But that will change soon enough. We shall be hours from Cairo by dawn, once Ankhesenaten finishes arranging for our travel." Constancia paused, her ivory teeth shining softly in the moonlight, "And, truly, Qalhara. Do you think it possible that a lone Giovanni could pose a difficulty for us?"

Ankhesenaten adjusted the sleeve of his indigo robe after he rapped on the heavy door. A small panel opened in the wood, revealing rich olive skin and a pair of suspicious dark brown eyes under black brows. Ankhesenaten nodded and said a phrase in a tongue already old when the tomb of the first pyramid was dug. The panel closed as quickly as it had opened and the door sprang wide an instant later.

With motion as fluid as water, Ankhesenaten slipped into the courtyard. Goreb was but a step behind, as silent and constant as his shadow. The thickset ghoul who admitted them threw the heavy iron bolts and made certain that the door was secure. He then grunted at Ankhesenaten and resumed his guarding stance, looking as immovable as the Sphinx. Ankhesenaten turned his attention to the interior of the estate. Perhaps a dozen people trafficked through the courtyard, slaves and attendants addressing various tasks for their master. The activity maintained the same steady pace no matter what the hour of the day or night. Those who drank of Set's dark gift might rest while Ra's chariot traversed the sky, but their servants could not afford the luxury.

Ankhesenaten had just enough time to appreciate the bustle around him when a voluptuous woman, clad in silken veils and adorned with a wealth of cunningly fashioned bracelets and baubles, entered from the far side of the courtyard. He recognized her from previous visits as Ghaliya, a most capable and treasured slave.

"May the Dark God watch over you," she said, nodding to the two visitors. Ankhesenaten returned the greeting and indicated he wished to be brought to her master without delay. Fluttering eyelids tinted with kohl, Ghaliya led them along a columned passage. She stopped before an entryway strung with glittering strands of beads. Then, with a bow, she was gone. Goreb stood, ever watchful, at the threshold, while Ankhesenaten entered through the beaded curtain.

The large chamber was strewn with many carpets and pillows made of silk. Rich hangings covered the walls, and tastefully placed oil lamps cast a welcoming light throughout the room. In the center, reclining in intimacy with a youth whose gender Ankhesenaten could not determine, was the Setite spice merchant Bek.

Though exceedingly opulent, the chamber seemed a dingy hovel compared to the peacock that was Bek. Embroidery upon embroidery covered every inch of his robes, beneath which peeked silks in a riot of colors. Ankhesenaten was not sure if he had ever seen some of the hues Bek sported, even in his most exotic travels. Gold and silver glittered from the man's fingers and wrists, while precious gems dripped from his ears and hung about his neck. There were entire kingdoms that contained less wealth than that the great Setite trader wore about his person. As if to compensate for the obscene riches he wore, Bek had a strikingly spare build that moved with a sinuous grace.

"My brother!" Bek cried out. He shooed away the youth and struggled to his feet amid the pillows' treacherous footing. Arms thrown wide, he drew Ankhesenaten in a hearty embrace. "It has been too long. Please, sit! Do you thirst? All that I have is yours. You have but to command and it will be brought before the words have passed from the air."

"I am unworthy of the honor that you show me," Ankhesenaten replied.

"How can that be? You are faint from hunger; that must be it. Come, I will bring you a girl just going through her first changes. Or would you like a man, hearty and at the peak of health? I could not bear to rise another night if I let you starve a moment longer."

Ankhesenaten could not help but smile at Bek's effusive good humor and expansive manners. "Truly, I cannot. I come on a matter of urgency that does not allow even a moment's relaxation in your fine home."

"My heart breaks to learn that our time shall be so short." Bek's voice was as jovial as before, but a cunning gleam arose in his eyes. Each vampire pursued efforts on behalf of the Walid Set—both merchant practices and the more subtle seductions of the Dark God. Bek was always eager to strike a blow for the faithful, whether in a purely commercial sense or in the larger realm of the spiritual. "Still, let no one say that Bek is not sensitive to the needs of his guests. Tell me, in what way may I aid you this night?"

"I have heard that a certain Venetian merchant, one Markus Giovanni, travels with a caravan bound for the Bahariya Oasis."

"Ah, yes. Of the Clan of Death," Bek stated.

"Just so." Ankhesenaten was somewhat put out. Bek operated from the comfortable confines of his Cairo home, while Ankhesenaten ranged far and wide performing his trade. He had hoped that an addition to Clan Cappadocian would be fresh news for Bek, as it had been for him, but his fellow Setite had found out from another source. Ankhesenaten took it in stride.

He saw more of the world than the Cairene merchant did, but this did not always grant him a greater wealth of knowledge. Bek garnered much useful information thanks to his vast network of spies and business contacts. It was all the more impressive as he had entered the innermost circle of the Walid Set a mere three centuries before. That he was aware that members of the Giovanni trading family had come to the attention of the Cappadocians was another example of the man's savvy.

"I come to you because of the responsibilities placed in your most capable hands," Ankhesenaten continued as his brief disappointment passed. Bek's duties to the Walid Set encompassed more than the obvious. Beyond increasing the clan's involvement in the spice trade, he was charged to see that undead from other lands did not grow their own trade in Egypt. "Considering your efforts to undermine Cainite trade, I felt certain that you would know the movements of their kind in our homeland."

Bek made a languid gesture. "It pleases me that my humble efforts on behalf of the Walid Set have not gone unnoticed."

"My brother, did you offer this Giovanni some assistance in finding transport along the Bahariya route?"

"What is your interest in the Cappadocian, if I may inquire?" Bek's voice was as smooth as before, but now contained a note of caution. It was, as yet, unclear where Ankhesenaten was headed with his questions. Bek didn't want to say something that might jeopardize his own position among the Followers of Set.

"Under other circumstances, the Cappadocian and what you plan for him would be of no concern to me. In fact, I would bring you nothing but praise for your efforts. However, these circumstances are most unique. I have need of this Cainite. Please, my brother, tell me of your plans."

"Very well. I saw a chance to end new Cainite expansion before it even established itself, while also dealing one of my local rivals a blow. I dispatched word to some of our brethren in the western desert. They will recruit brigands known to me, and meet with the caravan along its route toward Bahariya." There was a light jangle of precious metal as Bek spread wide his arms, indicating the fate of the entire caravan was in little doubt.

Ankhesenaten worked to keep his anger in check. If Markus died, he would have no chance of uncovering the Lazarenes or building a useful relationship with the Oracle of Bones. He'd not have Bek rob him of that. "It would be most unfortunate for the Walid Set if Markus Giovanni were destroyed prematurely."

Bek showed more irritation than concern. "The caravan is gone four nights already, and I dispatched word to the assassins that same evening. There is no telling when the two groups will meet."

Ankhesenaten smiled without a hint of warmth. "Surely a figure of your skill and influence could contact our brethren before they reach the caravan."

"Even one such as I has his limitations. I may certainly send word, but who is to say whether it will reach them in time?"

"You had best hope that it does so." Ankhesenaten's brittle smile was all that held back the tide of his anger. He had assumed, coming here, that Bek would be happy to entertain his request. It was now clear that the spice merchant had achieved sufficient stature within the clan to try challenging his elders. "I do not exaggerate when I speak of the urgency involved in this matter. Markus Giovanni must be captured, not destroyed. He may have knowledge of great use to the Walid Set—knowledge that must not reach Bahariya Oasis."

Bek pursed his lips, his eyes in idle contemplation of a nearby tapestry. "If the need is truly as dire as you suggest, I can make every attempt to communicate your wishes to the assassins. It will require spreading word throughout our brethren, of course."

The implied threat was clear. Bek did not believe these claims entirely. Personal desires rather than concern for the Walid Set could be motivating Ankhesenaten's demands. Should this prove the case, Bek would have established ample witnesses in their fellow Setites. Ankhesenaten wasn't worried. He had learned enough from Constancia—even after discounting the hyperbole intended to sway him—to understand the extent of the danger they faced. It helped that he could apply further context gleaned from the wandering madwoman he'd encountered in Tarsus. "I commend you on your thoroughness, my brother, and I wish to aid you in any way that I can. Indeed, a thought strikes me now. If you were to make available some of your finest mounts, I might speed after the caravan and deliver word to the assassins myself."

"But of course. I may arrange something for tomorrow evening, I am certain."

"My brother, you sell yourself short. I am certain you can assemble everything I need within the hour."

Chapter Sixteen

Road to Bahariya Oasis
30 September, 1204

The caravan trail was first laid down in the time of the pharaohs. Though dynasties—indeed, even entire civilizations—had been forgotten in the time that followed, the route remained. Recent years had even seen traffic through the western desert grow as trade flourished under the reign of Salah al-Din. Though that great Muslim ruler had died ten years before, still the trade route endured. As far as Markus Giovanni knew, the caravan trail would remain for another three millennia more, and he could only hope to prove as enduring as it.

He had a great deal of time to ponder such things, considering his accommodations along the journey to the Bahariya Oasis. He had decided to keep himself hidden from the rest of the caravan. He couldn't very well appear around the camp fires each night without also providing a plausible reason he was never seen during the day. Instead, Markus spent almost the entire journey inside the enclosed wagon that Falsinar and Beltramose had procured. He passed his days in slumber and his nights in study—whether interrogating his ghostly servants or poring over the clay fragment long ago removed from the legendary Sargon Codex and placed in the care of Alexia Theusa. Unfortunately, he made little headway with either pursuit.

Markus emerged only in the ebb of night to feed on various members of the caravan. He drank little blood from any single mortal, instead taking a small amount from a handful of people. The piecemeal approach required more effort, but draining one person after another of all their blood would create undesirable complications. The victims of his feeding slept fitfully and were fatigued the next day, but such things were not unusual in the harsh climate of the great western desert. Just as importantly, Markus kept himself at the peak of his strength. Christ and Caine only knew what dangers might present themselves along the way, and Markus was determined that he would not be caught lacking.

It was not a very relaxed trip, but Markus was comforted with the knowledge that it was only temporary—and that time was no longer the factor it had been. The night before the caravan left Cairo while Markus waited for his ghosts to return, Falsinar and Beltramose had learned that the Egyptian Crusade was ended before a single ship had even left the Golden Horn. Travelers coming to Cairo from Alexandria had spread tales of the impending invasion, causing more than a little concern among the Egyptian populace. But ships reaching Alexandria not a week later than Markus's own arrival had unloaded most welcome news, which made its way in haste to Cairo and further into Muslim lands. The leader of the Egyptian Crusade, Sir Hugh of Clairvaux, was destroyed. Details of what had happened varied with the teller. Some claimed assassination, others revolt in the ranks, others a deadly curse. Markus supposed the truth lay equally among all the choices, and whatever the cause, the result was the same. Sir Hugh had amassed the crusade through the sheer power of his influence. With him gone, no one of sufficient charisma remained to lead. Already, troops were dispersing to pursue other, more personal, affairs.

Without the threat of impending invasion, Markus could take whatever time he needed to track down the Sargon Codex. He had debated sending new word to Venice and waiting in Cairo for additional aid from his family. But now that he was in Egypt, and with the plans for the caravan already made, Markus could deny his curiosity and thirst for knowledge no longer.

A light rap sounded outside the wagon. Markus's keen senses had registered his retainers' familiar footsteps before they reached the wagon, so he slid open the bolt without hesitation. Falsinar and Beltramose started clambering inside. Like every other night thus far, they took their rest within the wagon. The night was a few hours on; Markus could see that most of the camp was settled in for sleep already.

"Good evening, *Signore*," Beltramose said as he slipped his lean frame through the door. "There is little enough to report. This day has been much like every other for the past fortnight."

"The dunes grow larger and it becomes impossible to keep the sand from finding the most uncomfortable places to lodge between clothing and skin," Falsinar agreed, "but otherwise we have seen nothing of note. What say the shades?"

Markus shook his head. "Since Hartmut and Rina were lost in Cairo, they are almost useless. I have interrogated them thoroughly, but I can find no source for their fears other than that this land strikes them as exceedingly alien and dangerous. Only Infantino may be coaxed from my side, and he returns with stories of strange figures and frightening creatures that populate the realm of the dead. Even my skills have been hard-pressed to glean from him any useful information about our course or our destination."

"I must admit," Beltramose offered, "that knowing the restless dead fear this land does not improve my sleep."

"You need not worry. Whatever they fear can no more affect the physical realm than can the ghosts themselves. A few frights, perhaps; nothing more."

The ghouls appeared mollified and they settled down to sleep. Markus only wished he were as confident as he made himself out to be.

"Gaaah!"

"Beltramose, if you please! I had just succumbed to the embrace of Morpheus."

"Blame our master's shades for my outburst. One of them just passed through me. The pest lingers even now like a chill wind!"

"Passing strange, my friend. I had not thought the ghosts willing to leave Master Giovanni's side."

"And yet I shiver uncontrollably. I am too tired for such games. I must find our master and demand he call off his pet."

"He feeds among the camp. Perhaps it would be best to await his return, that you do not reveal—"

"*Hssst!* Silence, Falsinar. I see movement with sinister intent."

"How can you tell such a thing in the dead of night?"

"The luck of the moment. Come; peer through the crack of the door. The spot a few yards to the right of that dune, you see? Where the caravan made its latrine when we stopped for the night."

"I see nothing."

"Yes, but a moment before, one of the caravan guards stood where you see nothing."

"So he moved on."

"Helped along by a form that rose up from the very sands and wielded a pair of wickedly curved blades. A chance reflection from one of the fires on the metal drew my eye at the perfect moment."

"Lack of sleep and the pestering of ghosts has addled your perceptions, my friend."

"Perhaps. Then again, perhaps our master ordered one of the shades to warn us of danger in the only way it—ahhh. Yes! No sooner did I speak the words than the chill has left me."

"I do hope, good Beltramose, that this isn't an elaborate prank meant to rob me of my precious sleep."

"By all means return to bed, Falsinar. I take no responsibility if you wake up dead, however."

"Hmm. Perhaps I might gird myself and help you take a further look. Merely to prove you agitate yourself for no reason, of course."

"Of course. You are a saint, to endure my... uh, Falsinar?"

"What is it now?"

"Perhaps my nerves continue to play tricks, but I would swear that the creaking and the sand trickling down suggests there is someone on the roof of our cozy wagon."

"How curious. Well, perhaps the two figures I spy approaching with drawn weapons mean to deal with our visitor."

"Really? Do you think it possible?"

"Beltramose. We willingly entered into the service of a

creature under God's own curse, in the hope that we benefit from the scraps of wealth and power that our dark master might see fit to toss our way. Circumstance does not tend to favor ones such as we."

Markus was glad he continued to force Infantino to check the perimeter each night, despite the effort it required. The ghost had returned, more focused than he had been for weeks, with dire news. Infantino didn't know the exact number of attackers, but at least two Cainites were among the total. Since they were deep in the desert of Egypt, Markus had little doubt that they were Setites.

Already the serpents and their mortal lackeys stole past the perimeter of the caravan, dispatching sentries and slumbering merchants with grim efficiency. Markus was not so naïve as to assume this was mere bad luck. Cairo had the veneer of civilization, of undead existing in a strained but nonetheless sustained harmony. The murderous Setites this night were proof that the gossamer umbrella of truce did not extend to the surrounding desert. He was their target; the rest of the caravan was an incidental sacrifice.

The serpents shall find fulfilling their task a challenge, Markus vowed.

He would fight back with the full strength of the powers at his command. In hasty preparation for conflict, he gorged on blood. It thundered through his veins, quickening his long-dead limbs to action. It swept through his mind in a haze of red, leaving a firestorm of frantic thought in its wake. He'd filled himself so full that his arteries were taut cables snaking across his body. His veins trembled with each heartbeat. His mouth was a crimson slash, teeth pink with bloody spittle. His beard was a stiff tangle of drying gore. More blood spilled with his urgent feeding to stain his gray tunic to ebony.

The four men who shambled around Markus were likewise spattered. He had slain the merchants in haste, eager to take their blood. He then dripped a portion of the vitae upon his victims, raising them to a twisted semblance of life. These creatures were weak and pathetic compared to the savage corpse knights Markus had created in Constantinople months before. He lacked the time to perform that complex ceremony this time, as the rest of the encampment was even now rousing with alarm. Still, these corpse servants would at least hinder any efforts the Setites might make against him.

There was irony, true enough. The serpents had already slain the caravan sentries and the Lord only knew how many slumbering merchants. Were he a true master of the arts of death, Markus could have summoned up these fresh corpses from wherever they had fallen. Ancient Cappadocians were said to bring forth legions of the dead in an instant, the things bursting from resting places long forgotten beneath the earth. Markus was no weakling, but he must content himself with those bodies he could touch directly with the power of his blood. It cost him little enough to create these servants, at least. He remained flushed with strength from the sheer volume of blood he had ingested. His might would be sufficient to—

A rush of air was the only warning of the attack. Suddenly, Markus saw a cloaked figure with a heavy sword chop into the rearmost corpse. The strike made a wet sound and the attacker simply vanished before the reanimated servant fell to the hard-packed sand with an almost relieved groan.

"Stand fast!" Markus ordered the remaining corpses as he turned with blades drawn. He faced only the desert night—or so it seemed at first. Like the Nosferatu and the Assamites, the damnable Setites knew the secret art of obfuscation. This attacker hoped to addle his mind into thinking no one was there until it was too late. But Markus's awareness transcended the mortal realm. His consciousness was too disciplined to be so easily tricked by the mind of another. His coustille struck with such force that the Setite staggered back. The serpent shuddered to visibility, all concealment lost. The attacker's guise was that of a reptile, glossy black with whorls of color. Slitted gold eyes glared from an alien visage. A wide, lipless mouth yawned open to display opposing pairs of long, needle-sharp teeth. Though twisted by dark powers into something monstrous, enough remained human that Markus could see that the thing was female.

She called out something in ancient Egyptian—a language Markus had not yet had the opportunity to learn—and took a more defensive stance. Her scimitar was longer than either his coustille or his dagger, but his large size gave him a formidable reach compared to that of her own slender reptilian arms. He had no idea of her fighting skill, but her yell suggested that she'd called for the support of others.

Showing her a blood-tinged grin, Markus pressed his advantage. "Flank her," he directed, then stepped back. The Setite responded with upset yells and some impressive swordplay, swinging the scimitar in a series of maneuvers meant to keep the corpses at bay. She had no idea that the things had no skill in battle, but her ignorance would end soon enough.

The Setite displayed certain qualities of a snake, but she was still made of flesh and bone—substances that fell under the command of a Cappadocian. Markus employed that control now, drawing upon the raging power of the blood to send a whisper of death to the serpentine woman. He mouthed an old Venetian curse to focus the mind (other Cappadocians used other tricks, he knew) and smiled as the rigidity of the dead fell upon his foe. Her muscles and joints tightened and froze, locking her in mid-swing. Off-balance, the serpent fell to the sand. The thin screams that tore from the locked muscles of the Setite's throat proved a minor distraction as Markus hacked her head off. The blade of the all-purpose coustille was just short enough to make the task a messy one.

Thinking it was best to avoid going toe-to-toe with any other Setites, he liberated a bow of curious design and a quiver of arrows from the rapidly decaying remains. *A few well-placed shots should give even an invisible serpent pause.*

After reanimating his fallen servant, he continued with his grisly retinue in tow toward the wagon. Having been exposed to the way the Followers of Set clouded the mind, Markus was sensitive to similar attempts at invisibility. Fleeing through the growing tumult of camp, his corpse servants trailing after, he saw two more of the shadowy forms. The creatures struck terrified merchants from the darkness even as their mortal allies fought in more conventional fashion. Markus left them to their fate. The death of a few traders mattered little in the larger scheme, and their struggles would cover his retreat.

Flames bloomed a few-score yards ahead. Markus shrank back on instinct, his inner Beast quailing at the sight of fire. A merchant rushed up in that moment, though whether to attack or beg aid was unclear. The man faced Markus—his huge blood-ied form, his visage a fanged mask of primal fear, with a quartet of shambling, bloodless things trailing behind—and fled even more quickly than he'd approached. His cries of a monster lead-ing the dead were soon swallowed in the surrounding din, but they were sufficient to return Markus to his senses.

Luck has carried me this far. I pray that it sustains me a few min-utes longer.

Rounding a half-fallen tent, he saw that the flames arose from his wagon. His preternatural senses caught the faltering shrieks as those trapped inside succumbed to the conflagration. Two figures stood silhouetted before the pyre, admiring their handiwork. Steeling himself against the terror of flame, Markus marshaled his creations and advanced.

"You invite disaster upon yourselves," he declared, "stand-ing oblivious to your surroundings like this."

Falsinar and Beltramose spun around, weapons already to hand by the time recognition struck. The men shared another brief start as they registered the corpse servants with their lord.

"You are quite correct, *Signore,*" Falsinar replied, regain-ing his composure first. He pointed his falchion at the wagon, which was now fully engulfed in flame. "We allowed this to distract us."

Beltramose somehow combined expressions of chagrin and extreme watchfulness as he began scanning around them. "We had only just found our way clear, *Signore.* Another moment and we would have begun looking for you."

"Hmm. And from your chortling just before, I take it you are responsible for destroying a perfectly serviceable wagon?"

"Not out of whimsy, I can assure you!"

"No. So how is it you gentlemen stand here, hale and whole, while others are consumed in yon pyre?"

"I must credit Beltramose with the inspiration, *Signore,*"

Falsinar said as he made a more casual scan of the perimeter than did his compatriot. "We were surrounded—a creature atop the wagon and two of his minions coming for the door. Then Beltramose suggested we might use the hatch we had fashioned in the floor for your less conspicuous comings and goings."

"We were only just through when… something burst in the door," Beltramose continued. "I could see nothing in the darkness, but it grabbed my ankle in an iron grip. I had no room to draw my sword, so I had to content myself with my knife. I struck a lucky blow, and the creature snatched its hand away so fast that it tore the blade from my grasp."

The men shared a grin, and Falsinar took up the tale again. "As chance would have it, the pair of men rushed forward to aid their master. Beltramose spiked the trap door while I slipped from under the wagon in time to shove the rearmost fellow inside the wagon."

"We had already spilled lamp oil in hopes of covering our retreat," Beltramose finished. "Still, there were some moments of touch and go when we were not certain we would set the wagon ablaze before its new occupants released themselves."

Markus could not help smiling along with his men, even though all their belongings were mixing to ash. One item in particular was foremost in his thoughts. "Inspired, gentlemen. While I am most gratified that you escaped certain death, I admit my dismay that we have lost the Lilith fragment."

"Be dismayed no longer, *Signore!*" Falsinar presented a small pouch. "I thought it might be of some use to you still, so I grabbed it while Beltramose opened the trap door."

"Most excellent. Let me stow this; then it is best we—"

"*Signore,*" Beltramose interjected, "if you are about to say it is best we depart before facing more of these heathen creatures, I must point out that we are too late." Having interrupted his own vigil to secure the pouch, he now saw a half-dozen robed figures advancing with bloodied weapons on display. They were of little enough concern, given the skill of Markus and his men. But he also registered the hazy, flickering forms of three Setites. "A trio of Cainites is among their number, gentlemen. They are cloaked from your sight, so I shall deal with them. I leave it to you to handle the mortals."

"I take it your shades are of no use to us here, *Signore*?" Falsinar asked.

"I might force one of them to manifest. Even those in service to the undead have fled in fear upon encountering a restless spirit. But even would I command them, I cannot sense where they lurk now. It shall just be us three in this battle."

Beltramose offered a tight smile. "Let us not forget our four new friends."

"Indeed. They shall serve a useful function, at least." It was unnerving to turn away from the wagon fire, with its flames so near. But while Markus could feel the heat, not having to look at the hungry flickering dance calmed him a great deal. *Pray it makes the Setites as uncomfortable as it did me; I shall need every advantage I can find.*

The enemy closed with confidence. They had twice the numbers of Markus and his men—including three Setites against a lone Cappadocian—and the burning wagon blocked any hope of retreat. Markus knew they must strike fast and hard or they would be overwhelmed. He commanded the corpses to move to one side with their arms wide, then unlimbered the bow he'd taken from the Setite. The Egyptians quickened their advance when they saw Markus ready the weapon, though they were barely a dozen strides from melee already. Markus drew back the bowstring with the confidence of frequent practice and shouted, "Kick up the sand!"

The approaching bandits didn't understand Venetian. Thinking it was a battle cry, some chuckled while others tossed curses in response. Markus ignored them for the moment, his attention on the corpse servants. The animated dead felt the import of his will and began kicking fine, spattering clouds of sand. Handfuls hit solid nothingness where a pair of Setites neared from the flank. The sand did little to show their position for more than the barest heartbeat at a time, but it was enough to send them scampering back in surprise. They knew now that Markus could see them; they would not be so lax again.

The third serpent, likewise shrouded to fool the mind, was coming from an opposite approach. He craned his head to see what was happening with his brethren. The first arrow drove through the Setite's chest, just missing the heart and punching through his back. The wound would have been traumatic to a mortal, but was little more than an inconvenience to the undead. The second arrow was more effective. It smashed into the vampire's face, hitting under the brow ridge at just the right angle to shear off the tip. The barbed arrowhead turned the Setite's eye to jelly and tore into a good portion of his frontal lobe. The force of the arrows' impact knocked the vampire from his feet. He flickered to visibility while in midair and slammed to the ground in a cloud of sand. Though the Setite was not destroyed, it would be some time before he could restore his brain enough to do more than twitch spastically.

"That was a gift to us, gentlemen," Markus confided as he tossed the bow aside.

The six mortal bandits cried out in surprise, but did not abandon themselves to revenge as they rushed forward. Though no soldiers, they showed that they were old hands at battle. Yelling names and shorthand phrases to one another, they quickly maneuvered to surround Markus and his men.

Unprepared for their disciplined response, Markus ordered Falsinar and Beltramose to pull back even closer to the fire. The heat and crackle stirred terror in his bowels, but he would not succumb to fear. *I am Cappadocian; I am Giovanni. I shall not bring shame to my lineage in such a place as this!*

With his opportunity lost to engage the remaining Setites, Markus threw himself at their minions. Falsinar and Beltramose drew courage from their master's example. The battle was equal, though barely. Markus was almost ninety years a vampire, and had had another thirty before that as a mortal. Most of that had been spent in the study of death and spirits, but he had trained perhaps a decade all-told in the military arts. Though Falsinar and Beltramose had not been very career-minded back in their days as *condottieres*, this was through no fault of their martial skills. And the burning wagon offered significant tactical aid. Though its heat was oppressive, it kept them from being surrounded and its glare fast strained their attackers' eyes.

Although they held their own, Markus soon passed the

breaking point. They were outnumbered, it was true, but by simple mortals. The Setites remained out there, hacking at shambling corpses that could do no more than flinch ineffectually from their unseen attackers. "Enough!" Markus roared. "You cannot see them, you worthless husks! Just grab for them! Grab and do not let go, or I shall find the souls that once cowered in those pathetic skins and devise such torments for them that the Devil himself never contemplated!"

One of the raiders attempted a killing blow as Markus ranted. He twisted desperately, deflecting the blade to strike deep into his shoulder. The scimitar became stuck in bone; as the hapless bandit strove to free his weapon, Markus at last succumbed to the Beast.

Dagger and coustille thrust upward to skewer his attacker. He left the blades in his victim and turned for the next. Already coming to his companion's aid, the raider swung without hesitation. Markus lunged to one side, taking a glancing blow, and grasped the bandit's sword arm with one mammoth hand. The mortal's limb shriveled to a useless husk in an instant. The man fell back, his cries an equal mixture of terror and agony. Markus snatched up the bandit's fallen scimitar and slashed twice with hard strokes to silence the screams.

The remaining three Egyptians—Beltramose had felled the fourth a few moments before with a vicious cut across the abdomen—took a defensive stance. Markus and his men were wounded but unslowed, while the bandits were down to half their number. One looked around for aid from his masters.

The two Setites were near, but otherwise occupied. The sight might have been amusing if circumstances weren't so dire. The animated corpses were proving sufficient distraction that the pair had trouble concentrating to maintain their obfuscation. The vampires hacked and cut at the hapless things, which clutched at their clothing with clumsy hands. A lone cadaver had even scrambled onto a Setite's back. It did nothing more than hang there, but was determined enough to remain that the Follower of Set had yet to succeed in removing it.

Markus roared a challenge and lunged at the nearest bandit, determined to carve his way through to the Egyptian vampires.

The scimitar was clumsy in his hand, but the fury of his blows sent the raider scrambling backward, swinging his own sword in a desperate blur to deflect the attack. Falsinar dropped his opponent as the tide of battle turned, and rushed to support his master. Then the Setites finally chopped the corpse servants enough that they lost their last spark of animation, and likewise hurried to aid their remaining men.

The bandit fell before the combined attacks of Markus and Falsinar just as the pair of serpents came upon them. Falsinar retreated, as desperate against the Setite as the dead bandit had been against Markus seconds before. He was left to his own devices, though, as Markus faced a vampire his equal in size and rage, with the same scaled hide and sinuous movements as the woman he'd fought earlier. Neither enraged Cainite bothered with the finesse of mystic attacks, instead clashing with a harried series of sword blows.

The Setite scored a deep cut in Markus's side, and the pain shocked the Giovanni from his killing frenzy. He staggered and forced the wound to close, suffering another hit on his thigh as his foe followed up on the advantage. Markus reeled with the blow, his mind racing with newly recovered clarity. He had no doubt he was outmatched, and things promised to get far worse very quickly if he didn't change tactics immediately.

First he tried to throw the Setite off-stride by switching to an attack. It was nothing more than a feint, really, but it did the job. Markus followed up with an attempt to disarm his serpentine foe. It might have worked with his coustille, but the scimitar was not as willing in his hand. The blade rang against the hilt of the Setite's sword, throwing off the rhythm of both combatants. Markus staggered on the uneven sand and found himself inches from the serpent's alien visage. The gold eyes bored into his own and a strange lassitude seeped into his limbs. His current peril lost its immediacy; all that concerned him was the rich golden orbs. Markus felt his throat tighten, then realized it was the Setite's hand. A curiosity, but insufficient to tear his attention from the mesmerizing eyes…

Then a sharp, cold wind blew through his mind.

Infantino! The ghost had plunged through Markus, the

moment's frigid chill shocking him back to his senses. Panic and fury returned in full force, and he used it to draw deep upon the power of the blood. His thick hands grabbed the Setite's arm, holding the creature fast as he spat a thick wad of blood that spattered the serpent's face and shoulder. If he had whispered a hint of the grave's decay to the first Setite to lock her limbs, here he had spat out its full withering might. "Dust to dust," he croaked.

The Setite meanwhile uttered a garbled shriek. He wrenched himself away with the strength of desperation as his body crumbled and flaked to heavy ash on contact with the corrosive blood. Enough flesh dissolved to dust that his arm tore free of his body. It remained clutching Markus's throat for no more than an instant before it disintegrated in his grip. The Setite stumbled away, the power of unlife sustaining him though much of his upper body and the lower portion of his face had crumbled away. The other serpent, now handling Falsinar and Beltramose with an effort, spared a glance at his compatriot's screams. He broke off his attack and dashed to intercede as Markus moved for a finishing blow.

"Death is my realm," Markus growled through a fresh mouthful of blood. "Come, you both, and let me show you its secrets!"

The wounded Setite gasped something unintelligible. His companion looked upon the injury and then directed his reptilian eyes at Markus. With not a little hesitation, the serpent raised his scimitar.

"You doubt my power?" Markus said. "Another lesson, then." He indicated that Falsinar and Beltramose should remain as they were. Already standing over the hacked bodies of his erstwhile corpse servants, he spewed blood upon the cadavers. As before, they stirred in a matter of seconds. Four bodies arose to stand between Markus and the Setites, their countless wounds forgotten in the power of Cappadocian magic.

Another, more urgent croak came from the injured serpent. His compatriot nodded. Retreating with sword held defensively, the creature lent a supportive arm to his fellow Setite. He said nothing, but his golden eyes promised Markus revenge in some future night. Then the pair faded to nothing and slipped off into the desert darkness.

"Run if you will," Markus called after them. "You cannot hide from me! Indeed, your very servants shall spell your doom!"

Markus went around to the fallen raiders with stiff-legged strides, scattering more of his blood upon them. They arose as the dead merchants had, cadavers empowered with Markus's will. "Go forth. Find your former masters. Hound them day and night. Make certain they never forget the price paid for crossing Markus Musa Giovanni!"

Ten corpses lurched into the night. Shortly all was silent but for the crackle of the burning wagon and the faint sounds of the few surviving merchants bemoaning their tragedy.

The two ghouls took their cue from their master's stolid form. Falsinar staggered to the wounded Setite—who, even with his mind half gone, was struggling to remove the broken arrow from his brain—and hacked the creature's head off. Beltramose strove to remain vigilant against further attack, despite his injuries and exhaustion. Then Markus sagged, dropping to his knees in the bloody sand.

"They are gone," he croaked. "The corpses will wander for a few more days before my power leaves them. They can do nothing, but it should frighten these heathens long enough for us to reach the oasis."

"Good… very good," Falsinar replied after exchanging an unnerved glance with Beltramose. "But you, *Signore*. How do you fare?"

Markus raised his shaggy, blood-flecked countenance. "I am as you—wounded, tired, and finished with this blasted land and everything in it. I will be restored, and I will give you of my blood that your wounds may knit as well. But to do so I need fresh sustenance."

The ghouls looked at one another, Beltramose fingering his neck.

"The merchants, gentlemen. Bring me all who remain. They will see us through to our destination, though not in the manner they had intended."

They reached Bahariya Oasis but two nights later, guided by the lone merchant who had not fallen to the raiders' swords or to Markus's thirst. Habib was assured that, as payment for his services, he would receive the five horses and two camels that had survived the Setites' raid and were now their transportation. No fool, Habib knew he would be lucky to receive the gift of his own life, and he brought the huge foreign monster to the home of his cousin. Cowed by horror, Habib admitted he stayed there when the caravan made its stop in El Bawiti, the largest settlement in the oasis region. It would now be home to Markus and his men during their brief stay in the region.

At least, Markus hoped that it would be brief. The battle in the desert had removed any doubt that he was in the land of the enemy. Even should he encounter the Lazarenes, he doubted he could rely on them for assistance. They were proud of their heresies against the Clan of Death; they pursued their studies here in defiance to the wishes of Cappadocius himself. What interest would ones such as they have in offering succor to a Cappadocian? And their hostility was guaranteed if he demanded from them the Sargon Codex. The best Markus could hope for was academic curiosity in an offering of knowledge from Giovanni studies. Enough to gain entry to their lair and there seize the Codex.

That part of the plan still required some working out. While Markus had no qualms with causing injury to the Lazarenes in the name of his family and his clan, it was folly to think that he could depart unmolested with the Sargon Codex under one arm. He was confident answers would present themselves once he got a look at the Lazarene haven.

"This is the place?" Markus asked in accented Arabic. Habib responded with a weary nod. The dwelling was typical for the settlement, low and built from clay bricks. Two, perhaps three rooms with a weathered door and a couple of tiny windows. Markus dismounted, adjusting the robes he had taken from a merchant's belongings to replace his own torn and blood-soaked garments. With a jerk of his chin to indicate that Habib should join him, Markus offered the reins of his horse to Falsinar.

"We are here, gentlemen," Markus informed them in Italian. "As there is no corral that I can see, we shall draw undue attention to ourselves if we keep our menagerie here also. I caught the pungent odor of a stables when we first entered this quaint settlement. Take the animals there and return to me."

"But we do not speak the local tongue," Falsinar replied. "How are we to make arrangements?"

"If you cannot explain yourself with coins, use one of the beasts as barter. I shall express our desires to Habib's cousin in the meanwhile."

Upon their return an hour later, Falsinar and Beltramose saw that there was no cousin to be found. Habib looked more dazed than ever, though whether it was from confusion as to where his cousin might be or from some other source was unclear. Markus let the man crouch in the corner of the main room, staring blankly at the dust and dirt covering the floor.

"I must apologize on behalf of our hosts," Markus told his retainers. "As best I understand it, Habib's relatives had forgotten that the caravan would be coming. Dear cousin and his family are not even here, and they have left their home in quite a filthy state. Still, it shall be adequate for a few nights. It is not the most secure, but it will protect me during the day and should be unremarkable enough if anyone with an interest seeks to find us."

Falsinar and Beltramose accepted their master's words without comment. Markus had invited them into other dwellings whose residents were gone for some reason or another. All seemed to suffer from poor housekeeping, though, as a layer of fine dust covered most surfaces. The men had learned not to look too closely at either the dust or the explanation Markus supplied for the convenient vacancy. They did take pains to clean thoroughly any surface upon which they ate or slept, however.

It was an effort to do so now, exhausted as they were from their travels. Markus had given them a fresh draught of his blood after the battle, sufficient to heal even their most grievous wounds. Cappadocians might not be among the strongest or swiftest of the undead, but they were possibly the hardiest. The vampiric blood likewise gave the two ghouls an inhuman level of stamina, sufficient to remain alert through the last few harried days and nights of travel. But Falsinar and Beltramose were nonetheless mortal. Exhaustion expressed itself in their every movement, but most tellingly in the lack of the chatter that was at other times a constant between them.

Markus was not oblivious to this. "It is but a few more hours to sunrise, gentlemen. Stay vigilant until then. We should be secure enough. You may spell one another on watch through the day and regain your strength. Tomorrow night, I shall begin my search for the Lazarene temple."

"Yes, *Signore*," Falsinar said. "By your leave, I shall begin my search now for the latrine."

This brought a chuckle to the three Italians, but Habib remained oblivious. As Falsinar stepped from the home to hunt down an outhouse, Markus stooped to check on the merchant. "He might benefit from a brief taste of the blood as well," he said after a moment of poking and prodding. "It could behoove us to have local who is loyal to our interests...."

His sharp ears caught the soft crunch of boots on hard-packed earth, but he at first dismissed it as Falsinar returning. The man had only just left, however—and besides, Falsinar could not be approaching from three different directions—

"Beltramose! To arms!" Markus roared. He spun around, snatching the coustille from its scabbard just as the squat door burst inward. Behind his master, Beltramose scrambled for his long sword as vampires poured through the doorway.

Part Four: Bahariya Oasis

Chapter Seventeen

Road to Bahariya Oasis
2 October, 1204

"An entire caravan slaughtered," Ankhesenaten observed with more than a little curiosity. He pointed with his chin to a collection of large mounds, well advanced in decay after only a few days in the desert heat. "Even the animals put to the blade, by the looks of it."

Constancia pursed her lips, surveying the massacre. Seeing death, even on such a large scale, bothered the high priestess no more now than it had any of the countless other times she had encountered it. It was the clear lack of appreciation for the transition from life to death that displeased her. "This was no effort of simple bandits. I expect such a collection of horses and camels would fetch a grand price at market, would it not?"

"Oh, certainly. Far too valuable to waste in such careless fashion. Unless the bandits felt they could not take care of them all as they made for their destination."

"Far less effort to simply leave the beasts to fend for themselves." Constancia nudged her camel forward to look over the rest of the carnage. To her mild surprise, the normally contrary beast complied without protest. "Neither animals nor goods were the goal, here. I believe we may make a reasonable guess as to what—or whom—was. Ah. Yes, this should do."

"You have found something?" Ankhesenaten's mount was not cooperating, so he swatted it with his crop until it kneeled for him to dismount.

Constancia had already slipped down from her camel. She

ignored the Setite as she paced an area of windblown sand to one side of the camp. Her mind was instead focused on what the environment might divulge. Still, a portion of thought returned to the same topic that had hounded her night after night since they had taken this trail. She had come with utmost speed from Cairo, the camels making good time despite their periodic displays of willfulness. Qalhara and the initiates Akil and Palladius understood well Constancia's imperative to intercept Markus Giovanni as soon as possible. Ankhesenaten had likewise been persuaded. The Follower of Set had discarded the amenities he normally enjoyed on trips, traveling as light as Constancia with but his bodyguard Goreb in attendance. Yet even pushing the mounts to the limits of patience and endurance—the former exceeded far more quickly than the latter—and stopping only for the necessity of avoiding the sun, they still had not overtaken Markus Giovanni. They had drawn ever nearer, at least—indeed, this was the closest yet that they had come—but it mattered little enough how close they got if still they failed.

Then, at last, she caught the tantalizing residue of an aura she had only sensed in visions. Her awareness straining to utmost alertness, Constancia redoubled her investigation to find where the residue was strongest.

Ankhesenaten strolled over, long face alight with interest. "What is it?"

"Do not disturb her." Qalhara's voice was as low and dry as the breeze that played with the end of the Setite's robe.

Startled despite himself, he recovered just as quickly and offered the Lamia warrior an ingenuous smile. "I had not heard you approach."

Qalhara nodded. Having learned over the past months of travel with Ankhesenaten that he would ply her with all manner of questions until he gleaned the barest morsel of information, she decided to spare them both the ordeal. "Mistress Constancia looks for the place most likely to explain what happened here."

"Aside from the obvious, you mean. Yes; well. She is so accomplished at her art that she can see any place in time, then?"

"Worry not, Follower of Set," Qalhara replied. "She has not attained true omniscience yet."

Ankhesenaten opened his mouth to debate the qualifier she had used, but Qalhara raised an ebon hand to demand silence.

Constancia had made markings in the sand as she paced. She now stood in the center of a crude but effective arcane circle. It was poor substitute for the focused energies of the Hall of the Dead, but it would be sufficient for the task at hand. Channeling the ancient and refined power that suffused her, the Oracle of Bones cast back for the secrets from a few nights before.

The breeze faded to weak, fitful gusts, then stilled entirely. The camels moved into a clump, their simple minds seeking reassurance from the subtle tension radiating out of the pale, slight and unliving woman. Though motionless as a statue left from the time of the pharaohs, the intensity of Constancia's stillness gripped the others' attention just as it unnerved the animals. Even taciturn Goreb grew distracted from monitoring the surrounding landscape.

Constancia returned to herself at last, and tilted her head to direct a sharp look at Ankhesenaten. "My clanmate has garnered the attention of a great many besides ourselves."

"You have learned what transpired here, then?"

"It is of little enough consequence." She waved away the issue and headed for the camels, which seemed torn between taking flight and submitting to her dominance. "Markus Giovanni survived an assault here but two nights ago."

"Had the caravan not been attacked, it would still be a night or so from Bahariya." Ankhesenaten spoke almost as if to himself. He cast a look around, then nodded Goreb toward their mounts. In a louder tone, he said, "As it is, riding hard, one could reach it in four, perhaps even three nights. If that is still where he travels…?"

"I have no belief to the contrary."

With nimble grace, Ankhesenaten mounted the camel Goreb made to kneel. "Then we had best move with haste of our own. For if your concerns are accurate, there is no telling the mischief that may transpire if this man reaches Bahariya before us."

Despite seeing the lights flickering in the desert night but a few miles distant, Constancia was not in a pleasant mood. Riding one of the laconic camels that Ankhesenaten had appropriated for their travel was the least of her irritations. She was entirely focused on her increasingly troublesome clanmate, Markus Musa Giovanni.

They had pushed themselves as hard as was possible. Yet there was no doubt that Markus had arrived in Bahariya before them, perhaps by even a full night. That meant nothing in and of itself, of course. Constancia's visions made no reference to the oasis explicitly. But her instincts, honed over centuries, said that the chances of deflecting Markus from an encounter with the Lazarenes grew smaller the longer he spent here. The heretics might crave isolation just as their conventional Cappadocian brethren did, but Constancia sensed that the Lazarenes would be drawn to this spot of green in the middle of nothingness. Like more renowned—and more conspicuous—sites like the Great Pyramids or the Temple of Horus, this place had intimate knowledge of death. The ambience was subtle but unmistakable.

"What more is there to this oasis?" she asked.

Ankhesenaten offered her a puzzled look. "Pardon?"

She gestured with an arm that was almost translucent in the moonlight. "This oasis, and its surrounding plains. Simple enough to the eye, but there is history here. History of a kind unique to the land of Khem."

"Ah. You speak of the study of death? You Cappadocians do appear to think of little else. It is before my time, but I recall something about governors in the latter days of the empire who attained significant authority here. By then, influence from other cultures made the practice of mummification open to more than the pharaohs and... others of whom I will not speak here." The Setite paused to spit blood-tinged phlegm onto the sand. "Soon enough, not only nobles, but any who could afford it, were mummified upon death and laid to rest. But the procedure lacked many of the important old details. The priests in this region, as I understand it, made an effort to recapture some of the purity of the old process. Perhaps even to develop new methods."

"I can well imagine such a thing appealing to a nest of Lazarenes."

Sensing something more forthcoming than usual in Constancia's demeanor, Ankhesenaten chanced a question of his own. "How widespread are they, then? The Lazarenes."

"There are enough." Cold fire flickered behind Constancia's eyes. Just as it seemed she would say no more, the high priestess continued in a low, contemplative tone, as if speaking to herself. "I cannot say with accuracy, despite the effort of visions. Searching for so long, but finding so little. Had they a single lair, we should have tracked them down long ago. They scatter, singly and in small groups, pursuing their heresies through the long nights…. But, in the end, how many? Few, thankfully. Lazarus was always selective of those whom he drew in, and of those upon whom he would bestow the dark gift. Some lurk in this place, it is certain. But not all. And Lazarus? Those rare times I have pierced his veil of protection, I have seen him wandering. No barrier daunts him in striving for the secrets of resurrection…."

Constancia snapped from her reverie. Ankhesenaten wondered if she had strayed to the edges of a vision, but the question curdled in his throat as the full force of the ancient Cappadocian's attention fell upon him. "So, those who practiced the rites of mummification here had no ties to your ancient enemy?"

Ankhesenaten clenched his jaw. They had spoken before of the resurrected. Mummies who followed the greatest of them all, Horus—himself the offspring of the oppressor Osiris and his sorceress-whore Isis. That conflict was at the heart of almost every activity the Walid Set pursued, in one way or another. "I showed you courtesy in discussing such sacred matters once before, but further details are not for profane ears."

"I need not know details. I simply wonder if the Lazarenes might have—"

There came a yell and the dull sound of steel striking flesh. Qalhara was already rushing over, Goreb not far behind. They found Palladius, one of the initiates, struggling to regain his feet after having fallen off his camel. The beast stood still, directing a large, annoyed eye at its rider. Palladius pointed past the camel. "Something came for me, just off the trail! I struck at it, but..."

Qalhara and Goreb dismounted and circled from opposite sides. Goreb uttered a cry and lashed out at the thing just now rising from the sand, Palladius's sword stuck in its shoulder. Goreb's scimitar cleaved through the arm grasping for the intrusive blade. Qalhara caught the dismembered hand reflexively as it tumbled through the air. She almost tossed it aside, then paused to take a closer look.

"Hold," Qalhara commanded. She turned to Constancia, who dismounted to accept the offered extremity. Goreb made to strike again, but a subtle motion from Ankhesenaten was sufficient to restrain him. The creature, for its part, scrambled with even less grace to remove the sword imbedded in its flesh.

"Dead but a few nights," Constancia judged after considering the hand. She strolled over to the corpse, which stilled its antics as she drew near. "Yet it remains quite lively. The question, then: Who created you? Our wayward Markus Giovanni? Or have you wandered from some Lazarene hole?"

The animated corpse said nothing. It lacked the spark of true life and force of will to form words—to do anything of its own volition, in fact. Nonetheless sensitive to Constancia's necrotic power, it remained still as she circled it.

"From his style of dress," Ankhesenaten said tentatively, "I would guess he... it... came from the caravan."

Constancia allowed the slightest nod. "Given the manner of death and the state of decay, I would agree. A boon for us, then. For it may show us where its creator will be found."

She raised a hand. A single ruby drop welled up in her palm and began a slow journey over the heel of her hand toward her wrist. Constancia's palms bore cuts made centuries before, bloodless creases that she chose not to heal. They allowed her to summon the blood necessary for death magic without the crude application of knife to flesh. Constancia placed her open palm on the corpse's forehead. The cadaver went rigid. Its body, already well along in rot, decayed at an increasing rate. The others watched in varying degrees of curiosity and disgust as flesh sloughed off in sticky clumps; as rotted organs spilled forth and curdled to sludge; as muscle and ligament snapped from bone and dried to stringy fragments. Within a minute, all that remained was a brittle skeleton. Then it, too, began to crumble, a brief shower of thick dusk that left nothing but a few powdery fragments of skull in the palm of Constancia's hand.

"It was, indeed, a creature of Markus's fashioning," she said as she wiped the residue from her hand. "Amusing. It was commanded to harry those who attacked the caravan."

"Amusing?"

Constancia favored Ankhesenaten with a flicker of a smile. "That was a crude servant, empowered with but the least amount of Cappadocian magic. Though it might wander this desert for a handful of nights, it was not a true threat to anyone."

The Setite accepted the claim with a dubious nod. "And what has that revealed about its creator?"

"Aside from a certain droll wit? Much indeed. I sense his aura. Young, but potent. We can follow his trail more directly now, with no need to distract ourselves with querying locals for every morsel of information.

"We are close. Very close indeed."

They reached Bahariya Oasis with few hours left before sunrise. It was an expansive place, comprised of a few key settlements. They rode into El Bawiti, the largest of them all. The governors to ancient pharaohs had dwelled here, and the bulk of trade passed through here, from those ancient times down to the present. Hundreds made their homes here, perhaps even thousands. Constancia saw only a portion of the place, but the low shapes extending into the desert night hinted at numerous dwellings. In this late hour, the number of lights flickering could be counted on one hand. The stillness of slumber permeated the settlement like a fog.

"We should look for a place to pitch our tent," Ankhesenaten said. "Dawn comes soon."

Constancia shook her head. She might have agreed, had they not encountered the corpse. In a place this size, in the deepest part of the night, they would have had no opportunity to begin a search for Markus till the next evening. Now, however, she could follow the residue left in the wake of Markus Giovanni's passage. There was sufficient time left to find him before the sun rose.

The fragmented shimmer of Markus's aura led them to a small dwelling in a run-down part of the settlement. Constancia tensed in her saddle in anticipation. Her mount was feeling contrary again and refused to kneel for her to dismount. Eagerness broke free of her normal reserve and the high priestess leaped to the ground like the girl she had been countless centuries before. She was still a dozen paces from the rude home when she sensed other spiritual residues—the subtle chill of mortal lives snuffed out. Caution returned, and she waved Qalhara over. "Death visited here, I would say but one night past."

Qalhara was already taut with alertness. She stepped in front of her mistress and looked the dwelling over, as well as the other homes scattered around the small square in which they stood. Sensing no immediate danger, she nodded. The two women came to the door together, Akil and Palladius keeping a wary eye on their surroundings. Ankhesenaten and Goreb stayed by the camels, content to let the Cappadocians handle things for the moment.

Up close, Constancia saw fresh cuts on the old wooden door. Scratches and other signs of abuse were evident on the clay brick of the building itself. She shared a look with Qalhara. These pieces of evidence did not bode well, but neither Cainite sensed any imminent threat. Constancia cast about for Markus's aura again, but the area was a muddle of perhaps a half dozen conflicting auras. She was certain he had been here, and not long ago at that. As to whether he was still within this home, she could not say. Dawdling outside would not reveal the answer. With a twitch of one slender finger, she indicated Qalhara should announce their arrival.

Qalhara had raised her hand to knock when her preternaturally acute hearing caught a faint scrabbling from the opposite side of the dwelling. She moved on instinct, drawing a spear from the scabbard on her back and dashing around the side. There, struggling through a small window, was a gangly man in Latin dress. He had a thatch of dark, curly hair and a prominent blade of a nose.

He did not notice the Lamia at first, focused as he was on freeing his sword belt from something inside the hovel. Then his head jerked to one side—the opposite direction from where Qalhara stood—and he uttered a harsh whisper in Italian. "I see nothing! You had best not be trying to make me look ridicu—what? The other direction?"

Constancia and a curious Ankhesenaten stepped around the corner behind Qalhara just as the man craned his head toward them with a grunt of effort. The point of Qalhara's spear was but an inch from the tip of his distinctive nose, and the Lamia's expression made it clear she felt no hesitation in making use of it.

"Oh, hell," Beltramose said.

Chapter Eighteen

Bahariya Oasis
6 October, 1204

The thin man sat against one wall, a collection of twitches and tics. He kept looking around, starting every so often and muttering under his breath. The significant bruise that discolored his temple suggested the source of his addled condition, but Constancia hardly noticed his antics. She was more interested in his missing master, and on matching all that he had just told her with what she had previously known and suspected.

The first oracle, all those months ago in Mount Erciyes, had spoken of her clan's destruction, of the death of Cappadocius himself. She was now all but certain this would transpire at the hands of Lazarus. She was troubled by this, despite her understanding of the cycle of life and death. When the time came for the founder to truly die at long last, it must be allowed to happen no matter who the agent of that destruction might be. To do anything other would be to tamper with the cycle itself.

And there lay the greater danger. For if Markus Giovanni fell to the Lazarenes' influence, their heretical leader would have no need to usurp Clan Cappadocian. Lazarus would instead attempt apotheosis—worse, he would achieve it. Cainites by the score would flock to him in the belief that he embodied a new Dream. And embody it he would, in his own way. But it would be a Dream warped by power unknown to any other than the Creator Himself. The world would be transformed, the cycle broken.

She had figured that Markus Giovanni was sent to

Constantinople to meet with someone who could help establish a pact between the Giovanni and the Lazarenes—namely the heretic Alexia Theusa. Whatever the Giovanni family's reasons for doing so, she assumed that Lazarus would attempt to achieve godhood armed with some unique knowledge culled from the Venetian sorcerers. It had troubled the high priestess to think that the necromancers might hold such secrets.

But if this mortal thrall, Beltramose, was to be believed—and there was no way he could hide the truth from the High Priestess of Bones—then Markus Giovanni had not come to Egypt at the direction of Alexia Theusa. Quite the contrary, in fact. Constancia still did not trust the necromancers Cappadocius had brought into the clan—the Giovanni were too ambitious by far for that—but it was some comfort to know that they did not seek to join forces with the Lazarenes.

The shock was learning of the real source to it all: the Sargon Codex. That it rested in the Lazarenes' hands, and that Lazarus would use it to achieve the Godhead. Given that, the Giovanni's courage was commendable, coming all this way alone to liberate the codex. But he was mad to think he might succeed. It was a marvel he had gotten this far. Or was it? The codex was said to be the blueprint for apotheosis. Amid his scattered ramblings, Beltramose claimed his master held the key to completing the codex, a splinter stolen from Alexia Theusa. *Have Lazarus's powers grown so great that he can manipulate events from afar, thereby fulfilling his own prophecy?*

It was possible. But whatever influence Lazarus had applied, Constancia would not stand by and allow his twisted desires to be realized. Godhood must not be reached; the Dream must die. Alas, no longer would simply redirecting Markus Giovanni's course accomplish this. She would have to liberate both Markus and the Sargon Codex. Herself, and with only a single Lamia warrior, two mortal initiates, an untrustworthy Follower of Set, and his bodyguard. Her mouth quirked the slightest amount.

"Mistress?"

"I was measuring our assets, Qalhara."

"You mean to go after the Giovanni, then."

The smile grew. "I must admit, I wish now that you had

been more persuasive in urging me to rouse Mount Erciyes to action."

"As do I. But you are right. Better that we strive now than arrive with an army too late." Qalhara turned away. She had been more contemplative than usual since they had begun this journey. She had voiced much of what bothered her, but some last detail still lurked in the depths of her mind. But Qalhara did not utter it now. Instead, she said, "What does puzzle me, mistress, is why they left that one alive."

Constancia glanced at the neurotic, mumbling Beltramose. "Look at him, Qalhara. What good is he to anyone?"

"A most terrible nightmare grips me, Falsinar.

"You doubt me? Look at yourself, then, my friend. What cruel jest do you attempt, appearing before me in such a fashion?

"...Ah. You see? And cast your gaze about this crude chamber. The only women I see are beautiful, but in the most frightening fashion. Gray and drawn as death, that one. And black and dreadful as the night, the other. What does that say of me? Am I doomed to die unloved, with no progeny to carry on my family's proud name?

"Yes, well, 'twas more a rhetorical question, Falsinar. But let us not dwell overlong on my romantic woes. See now, another of the damnable serpents who accost us throughout our journey in this accursed land. He seems normal enough, that one. But look—he is hairless as a reptile, and his eyes? Cold as the most deadly asp.

"...Yes, I agree, his clothing is rather dashing and of fine quality. But I do not concern myself with matters of wardrobe now. My sanity is of greater import.

"Ho! So say I? Well, your lack of sympathy is noted.

"So you have said already, my friend. But I refuse to believe it. No, it is but a nightmare, the result of undercooked mutton and too little sleep. I shall awaken soon enough, and you will see...."

Chapter Nineteen

Temple of the Lazarenes
6 October, 1204

Markus Giovanni awoke to darkness. The pervasive, absolute blackness defeated even his preternatural sight. One such as he, however, did not rely on sight alone. Using the remainder of his acute senses, he began exploring his prison.

The cell was small, a mere three paces on a side. But even with his formidable size, stretching his thick arms up and jumping as high as he could, he could not find a ceiling. This was not the first puzzle that the place presented him. In feeling out the chamber's dimensions, Markus could find no door. The four walls were blocks fitted together with cunning skill, with not even a hint of secret panel or bricked-up opening. It might even have been airtight, for all he knew. He drew a few experimental breaths, but that proved nothing. He would have to sustain that for some time before he ran out of air. And what would that prove? He had no real need to breathe. Best to spend his time in more productive fashion.

He began a second investigation of the walls, this time with the same exacting detail he had applied to the catacombs under the Church of the Holy Apostles. Despite intense effort to remain calm, he was close to frenzied rage by the time he finished with the third wall. He reared up, snarling his anger at an uncaring universe—and saw a smattering of distant lights far above. Stars. They edged just past a darkness marginally more solid than the night sky. It was the upper wall of his prison. Though Markus had difficulty reckoning the distance with the handful of stars as his sole point of reference, he estimated the cell's opening was at least one hundred feet up.

"Clever," Markus said, the discovery restoring him to calm.

"It is, is it not?" a voice replied. It had the smooth confidence of ultimate authority, yet it was neither gloating nor self-important. "A simple solution to a most vexing problem."

Markus barely concealed his surprise. His senses had not offered him the slightest hint that anyone else was near. He made conversation gamely as he tried to find where his visitor hid. "The most secure, yet manageable, means to imprison a Cainite, you mean."

"You are as quick with your wits as I was led to believe, Markus Musa Giovanni."

"It is obvious enough, given my circumstances." Markus supposed he shouldn't be surprised that his captor knew his identity. Those who had ambushed him in Bahariya had known exactly what they were doing. He'd been subdued in moments, struck by the same rigor that he'd inflicted upon the Setite woman. As such, he had a good idea of those who had imprisoned him. The question foremost on his mind was whether he had been maneuvered to this position even before leaving Constantinople, or if it was more a matter of the Lazarenes seizing a convenient opportunity.

"The latter," the voice replied. "Ah; do not be so startled. Your thoughts fairly cry out. I find it refreshing. The thoughts of most are a ramble of disconnected fragments. Yours, in contrast, are clear and well formed, like a vase of crystal. Be proud, childe. You have a most powerful mind, albeit an undisciplined one."

Markus found no reassurance in the words, though he bridled at being called undisciplined. Even in his time as a mortal, his brilliance had been as worthy of note as was his size.

"I speak not of intelligence, childe. Creatures roam this desert with the wits of a vole. Yet their minds have the strength to shatter mountains to powder. Perhaps that is how the great desert was first formed." The voice allowed itself a chuckle. "No, not intelligence, but discipline. It is the same as with the arts you have studied. You applied yourself with diligence and have accomplished great things. It can be the same with the mind. But we are not here for a lesson, are we, Markus Musa Giovanni?"

"I would imagine not; though I am unclear as to what agenda does lie at hand." He could make out more detail as the moon edged further overhead, but there was little enough to see aside from the featureless walls. Whoever the stranger was, he remained hidden in the night. Somewhere above Markus, certainly. He thought he could make out a slightly darker patch midway up one wall. *A window, perhaps, from which the Lazarenes can gaze upon their new pet?*

"There is no need for bitterness, childe. We are on the verge of great discovery."

Two more voices murmured their agreement, a Greek chorus to the lone speaker. *How many of them lurk above me, watching me like some specimen?*

"Your arrival could not have been timed better had I planned it," the speaker continued. "I debated for some months whether to call for the final piece of Sargon's puzzle. I had mastered the secrets of the codex; all that remained was the final reference, extracted long ago in preparation of my studies. Then I discovered that it was already on its way, carried by one of my own estranged brethren."

Markus sagged against a wall as he finally realized who the stranger was. Thoughts flooded his mind, and he held to the thread of conversation only with effort. "So you… you hope to achieve apotheosis."

The other voices repeated the word, an eager whisper that echoed through the shaft. "The Sargon Codex holds the potential to do many things, but that is the greatest of them."

"And you removed the Lilith fragment intentionally?"

"It was too much a temptation otherwise, having the complete codex before me. I would have courted disaster by using it without the utmost understanding of its potential." Another quiet, self-deprecating laugh. "After all, though time is of little import to our kind, the thrill of discovery can overcome even the most reasoned approach. Do you not agree?"

In other circumstances, they might have been a pair of scholars debating before their contemporaries. Markus wondered if this was intentional, the banter there to give him time to consider the full significance of his situation. At least it gave him the chance to regain his composure. "But you would have to know what the portion said when you chipped it away. Your temptation would not be kept in check."

"You disappoint me. Surely you have felt the power trapped within the fragment itself?"

"Yes. Yes, I have." Markus thought back to the rush of limitless vitality. "So it is not just a matter of a missing word, but of a component."

"Indeed, the codex is a perfect summation of Chaldean mysticism. Each word is critical, but so is the texture of the stone, the exact positioning of one character in relation to the others. It is as much architecture as it is text."

"So removing the Lilith fragment would be akin to the removing the keystone of an archway," Markus said, becoming excited by the problem-solving nature of the conversation despite himself. "You could still understand the entire pattern of the codex, but it couldn't bear weight."

"A rough metaphor, but workable. I worked with the most trusted of my brethren. Learned in Chaldean mysticism, he volunteered to peruse its contents and remove a key component. His censoring had to mar the meaning of the remaining contents as little as possible, while nonetheless leaving doubt as to how it related to the whole."

"Quite a challenge, I should think. And how could you be certain your volunteer would not try to master the codex instead?"

"I have done so myself only after decades of research. He had but a few months." Amusement was clear in the voice. "And, lest the temptation grip him in the future, I destroyed him afterward."

The other voices confirmed their brother's fate and their master's wisdom.

"And why do you reveal so much to me?"

"Simple enough. I would that you are informed fully before you choose."

Markus stared up the shaft. "What choice lies before me, Lazarus?"

The Methuselah laughed as if at an old friend's anecdote. "You have been incisive thus far, Markus Musa Giovanni. Is the choice not clear? You must decide whether to join me, or be destroyed."

A familiar scent drew Markus's attention. His hypersensitive nose caught the tang of fresh blood, but underneath... "Falsinar?"

No words came in reply, but the scrape of boots and the coarse rustle of fabric confirmed that someone was above him. It was not Lazarus or his pair of sycophants. That ancient creature and his lackeys moved so silently that it wasn't clear when they'd even left, although the cajoling had ceased some hours before. *For all that I know, they lurk up there still.*

In contrast, Falsinar had been in his service long enough that the man's movements, even his smell, were as familiar as his own. Though no one responded to his repeated calls, he grew certain that his retainer was somewhere above him. Just what Falsinar was doing remained a puzzle until Markus heard the bell-like tone of metal on stone, followed by a thick liquid gurgle. The scent of blood was powerful and immediate. He cast about when the first trickles of vitae spattered on the ground. It came from a vertical groove he had noticed in his earlier investigation. Wider than the other abutments between blocks, it proved to be a channel down which blood now flowed. The fluid was still warm, taken just a few minutes before from its host—a large animal of some sort, given the strong odor.

Despite gorging himself on merchants and beasts in recent nights, Markus was overcome with thirst. He crouched, lapping with greedy tongue at the stuff. Only after the edge was taken from his need did Markus wonder if the blood might be drugged—or worse. Just as he kept his ghouls bound to him through draughts of blood, so too could one Cainite force loyalty upon another. It typically required multiple feedings, but who knew what innovations these heretics had developed during their time in the desert? He flung himself back from the trickling stream, wiping at his beard in dismay.

"Worry not," Lazarus's voice informed him. "There is

nothing more than a camel's essence in that vitae. And spices to slow the rate at which it congeals, of course. You are still your own man—perhaps more so now than ever, away from the chains of family and clan."

"If that is so, why am I in this pit?" Markus spat back, the anger of the Beast giving him strength to challenge a Methuselah.

"Silence!" one member of the Greek chorus declared. "How dare you show such disrespect to our master!"

"No, Andel. Allow him to vent." But Lazarus's next words showed none of the humor from before. "Your outrage is misplaced, childe. You came to steal from us. Had not your resourcefulness and potential impressed me, your ashes would be mixing with the desert sands even now. You are free to choose your fate—but do not presume that you are free *before* you make that choice. Should you join my cause, you will be raised from the depths of that pit as Christ was lifted unto heaven. Should you remain bound to the ways of the past, you will see the sun one last time when it shines down the length of this stone shaft."

"Then my choice is made. I pledge myself this very moment."

Levity returned as the Lazarenes shared a laugh. "It is not so simple," said the one called Andel. "You must desire with heart as well as mind to enter the fold. A decision made merely to avoid destruction would have no weight."

Markus laughed in return, though without mirth. "Yet I am to decide before dawn? I can feel lethargy overtake me even now. You would have me find the truth in my heart in the next hour?"

"Epiphanies have struck in less time," Lazarus observed. "But no, I do not expect a decision this night. You will be safe enough from the coming daylight. But you shall remain in this cell until your give me your answer, freely and without reservation."

Then Markus heard only footsteps as Falsinar retreated from the edge of the shaft. He imagined that the ghoul followed the silent Lazarenes. *Was he offered the same choice that lies before me? And Beltramose also? Do they both side with the Lazarenes now?*

Though he called after the heretics and his servant until his throat was raw, Markus received no answers.

A strange ache filled Markus. It was similar to the hunger for blood, but it was his mind that burst with desire, not his body.

The shard.

A chill swept through him at the thought, a thrill of fear and longing combined. He had touched the thing but once, had carried it a thousand leagues without succumbing to its lure. Why now, when it no longer hung from the pouch at his belt?

Without warning, tatters of memory surged through his mind like flotsam on an angry wave and crashed against the shore of reason. He staggered, his heavy frame smacking against the unyielding wall. When his senses cleared, he discovered himself sprawled in an undignified heap. Pinkish drool made a tacky mess of his beard and he realized he was muttering nonsense.

I am acting like a novice, Markus berated himself, scrambling for composure. He had thought the shard's previous mutterings were due to its being so close to his person. But now it seemed that range had nothing to do with it. Indeed, distance had not mattered once Sir Hugh had fallen under the Lamia's thrall. *Am I as weak-willed as that Templar? No! I am a Giovanni and a Cappadocian. I am a man of reason and intellect. A piece of pottery cannot control me!*

The cold longing abated, the swirl of memory receded. He stood, wiping his mouth as a smile parted his lips. "Not such an undisciplined mind after all; eh, Lazarus?"

Yet Markus did not believe his own bravado. He had repelled the shard's song, but the disquieting tickle in the back of his mind suggested that his victory was only temporary. He was infected by the Lilith fragment.

How long before I suffer the same fate as the Templar and the Lamia? How long before I am a mindless pawn? Or... am I already?

Markus felt a chill of a different sort as he wondered if it was truly his own choice to search for the Sargon Codex. What kind of folly was it to think he could brave the dangers of Egypt, penetrate a Lazarene stronghold and escape with such a potent artifact? Was he nothing more than a courier?

But the shard is returned, the codex is made whole. Why does it still call to me?

As if in response, a new surge of sensation threatened to overwhelm him. Markus forced it back, blood-sweat breaking across his brow with the effort. "Are you not yet done with me? What service would you have me perform from my prison?"

He knew then that it was not simply the shard, but the entire codex, that called to him. It yearned for his release. It wanted him free, to join with it again in a permanent union—a transcendent embrace far greater than his transformation from mortal to undead.

And, though he quaked to his disused bowels at the idea, a part of him yearned for it with equal passion.

The creature called Lazarus stood before the Sargon Codex with infinite stillness of body and spirit. Andel and Osia stood by the chamber door, watching in awe as their master finished returning the Lilith fragment to its rightful place.

His followers had recovered various texts of the ancient Egyptians, among them rituals that could fuse minerals into a single piece. But Lazarus had used a simple mortar to bond the pieces together. Directing arcane efforts upon the codex would invite disaster upon whomever was foolish enough to try—and could spell its destruction as well. For, despite the spiritual energy that suffused it, the Sargon Codex was still a fragile piece of clay made thousands of years before the birth of Christ. It endured hardship better than some mundane bit of craft work, but it could still suffer damage, even destruction. As such, Lazarus took pains to touch the tablet only when necessary, and he was careful about channeling his vampiric arts near it. He had striven for too long to lose the codex to some thoughtless mishap.

Even the removal of a piece had been decided after great deliberation. He had wondered through the years if it was a wise choice. What if the fragment could not be recovered, or secured back in its place? Thankfully, such worries were no longer necessary. The codex was whole again. The artifact radiated a sublime tension that Lazarus sensed only due to intimate familiarity. It was like nothing so much as a call—a summons, if you will.

Lazarus resisted the lure with a resolve grown from millennia of self-discipline. The codex was a portal to transcendence that begged to be used, but he would do so under circumstances of his own choosing. He had not survived so long by acting rashly. He would risk apotheosis in a few weeks at the earliest, only after he checked every detail of his findings one last time.

"Soon," Lazarus said; his followers took up the word in echo. "The long wait shall be over soon."

Markus expected to be consumed by the sun. The exchange with Lazarus had surely been some perverse cat and mouse, meant to leave him in an agony of hope until his final death. In the unease after the Lilith shard's call, part of him welcomed destruction. *Better to die my own man than endure as the puppet of some alien agency.*

But just as salmon tones spread across the circle of sky far above, he heard the grinding of metal gears. A slab of blackness consumed the growing light at a slow and deliberate rate. Straining his will against the lethargy of dawn, he stayed conscious long enough to watch the thick stone slide all the way across the opening.

He awakened the next night as he usually did, perhaps an hour after darkness fell. He'd slumbered so deeply that he hadn't heard the stone being retracted with the setting of the sun. He lay still, certain that there was some presence in the shaft above. But there was only the circle of night. Then he realized what was distracting him—a murmur at the base of his skull. *The codex.* He shook off the call as best he could by focusing on finding some means to escape.

First, he channeled the blood to heal what minor injuries he'd suffered in his capture. This left a gnawing, though manageable, hunger. He welcomed it, using the dull ache as a buffer against the yearning that the shard stirred within him.

Next, Markus tried to summon his ghostly servants. He knew of a way he might escape from this place, but he would need their help even to attempt the ritual. The problem was, he lacked the charms of binding that enslaved the spirits to his service. Like their mainstream Cappadocian brethren, his captors had no expertise with ghosts. It remained, as yet, a specialty of the Giovanni family. Even so, the Lazarenes were not so ignorant that they didn't recognize arcane implements. They'd stripped from him anything of apparent use, from his weapons and the Lilith shard to the bone necklaces and pouches of powdered organs. He still had a chance of contacting the ghosts without any charms, as long as the wraiths were nearby. Controlling them would be that much more difficult, but he was out of alternatives.

He sent his call through the beyond, but there was nothing. They were either destroyed or gone past the range of his control. *Wait... Infantino?*

Markus strained to bring the tantalizing wisp into focus. It came slowly, drawn by the command of his will. Then a voice called out, startling him from his trance.

"I see you took my words to heart," Lazarus said. "Your thoughts are more disciplined this night."

Markus peered up the shaft, though he was still unable to sense anything of the Methuselah beyond his voice. "I learn quickly."

"So it would seem. And, likewise, there is much that we could learn from you."

"You flatter me."

"Not at all. The Giovanni study a most interesting art that might benefit us greatly."

Mention of his family sparked an idea. His desire for knowledge was genuine enough. There might be a way to agree to Lazarus's terms while also achieving the goal that had brought him to Egypt in the first place. "I confess that your offer appeals to me. But how can I be certain that I will be more than a simple slave in your thrall?"

"Were that my desire, I could control you as easily as a puppet."

Markus felt a shiver at the matter-of-fact tone. "Very well. But you spoke of my family. Would you not prefer the aid of all Giovanni, rather than just myself?"

"Speak plainly, childe. What is it that you want?"

"Let us continue our dialogue man to man, not captor to prisoner." Markus focused upon the truth of his feelings, forcing the underlying scheme into the depths of his mind. "Let me see with my own eyes what you promise, and I will give the offer my utmost consideration. Further, should I accept your offer, I will recommend to my patriarch that the Giovanni family likewise pledge their aid."

A muttered dialogue ranged in the dark above. Markus missed much of it, but he sensed that those who attended Lazarus cautioned against freeing him. It continued for a few minutes until a curt word from the Methuselah brought silence.

"Very well," Lazarus called down. "It is reasonable that we speak as men of intellect, whatever may follow."

He sensed Falsinar approach just like the night before, as well as another whose movements were not familiar. The faint clang of metal and the creak of leather and hemp echoed down the shaft. An angular silhouette soon swung into space and started lowering a cleverly designed harness. It was a tight fit for Markus's sizable girth, but he jammed himself into the arrangement of straps with alacrity. Within moments he was hoisted to the opening midway up the wall.

A simple corridor extended away in darkness. Two figures stood just before him, with three more further down the tunnel. The nearer ones turned a winch that pulled Markus from the depths. Though dressed in desert robes, Falsinar's stocky form was easy to recognize. Then Markus realized that Falsinar lacked any appreciable aura, and his face was a blank mask. His earlier silence became clear. Falsinar was no more. Death magic had charged the ghoul's corpse with vitality to create an animated servant. The other man was a stranger, but it was obvious that he, too, was nothing more than a morbid automaton.

Markus had no time to contemplate his erstwhile retainer's fate, for the other figures stepped forward. Each was clad in gray robes, raised hoods making it impossible to make out any features in the meager light that struggled down the shaft. The one to the left was tallest, while the one to the right had a slender build evident even under the robe's hanging folds. Neither demanded his attention like the figure in the center. Though concealed in the robe, Lazarus had an aura of such potency that Markus had to avert his gaze. Markus was physically larger, but the Methuselah radiated such age and power that he felt like a clumsy child.

"Walk with us, Markus Musa Giovanni," Lazarus said. "Let us see if we can come to terms."

The codex was a faint but constant distraction in Markus's thoughts. He gained a sense of where it lay as he walked with the Lazarenes—helpful, since intellectual curiosity was only a small part of his request to be freed from his prison.

Unfortunately, its insistent call combined with the Methuselah's overwhelming presence made it difficult to keep up his end of the conversation, let alone look at his surroundings. He did his best, taking in the narrow corridors, the hints of worn hieroglyphs and the occasional opening into another chamber, but it became a jumble in his memory. More distinct were the few other inhabitants they encountered. Dressed in the simple robes most Cappadocians preferred, the Lazarenes showed their master far more deference than Markus had thus far, and like him, they uniformly averted their gaze. He counted only a handful of Cainites aside from the three who guided him; far more numerous were animated corpses like Falsinar. Markus didn't bother with the distraction of trying to count them, but he was comfortable estimating their number at almost two dozen.

"You seem uneasy," Lazarus said as the other sycophant, Osia, led them down a short hall. A series of doors opened onto identical chambers appointed with a cot and a simple wooden chair. They stopped at the last door, the corridor's narrow confines bringing them all uncomfortably close. "It would be a shame if your plea were nothing more than a ruse."

Markus covered his panic as best he could by admitting a goodly portion of the truth. "It... it is not every night that I meet one of your veneration. Being in the bottom of a pit with destruction imminent lent me courage. Now, I fear making a misstep."

"Do not presume that you have avoided destruction yet, childe," Lazarus chided. He stepped into the room, gesturing that the others wait in the hall. "There are few whom I can claim as equals. But surely you have encountered enough elders at Mount Erciyes that you may display more composure."

"I have never been," Markus said as he followed the ancient. He sensed disapproval and concern from the other Lazarenes, but they left without protest when their master flicked his wrist. Only Falsinar remained, the other corpse servant having long since wandered off on some other errand.

"No? Pity. It is a most enlightening place. Its many vaults and libraries hold revelations of great interest to any who study death."

"I had thought you fled from Erciyes long ago. Yet you speak of it with familiarity."

"I am familiar enough with the place and those who dwell there. Others call me outcast and heretic, but that does not keep me from anywhere that benefits my studies. The Mount is far less secure than you might suspect. Yes, I have visited more than once. I have absorbed every scrap of knowledge to be found in its many passages, adding it to my own understandings." Lazarus bowed his head in a strangely pensive pose. "It is most impressive, what our kind have learned through the centuries. We can pry secrets from the dead and command their remains, but we only ever studied the echoes of the soul left in the corpse. Even I assumed the truly vital elements of the soul were beyond our reach once separated from the flesh and taken beyond the firmament. Ironic, do you not agree—for the echoes in the corpse are linked to the immortal soul, are they not?"

Markus was fascinated despite himself. "That is what I believe."

"Exactly! What you believe; what the Giovanni believe. Was that the motivation for your family's study of necromancy? Or did it form as a result of it? No matter; what is important is that your studies drew Cappadocius's attention. You have become part of the clan… but the rest of our kind remain unschooled in the ways of the spirit. Was it not my sire's wish that you share this knowledge?"

"Not all share the desires of Cappadocius." Markus and his fellow Giovanni weren't exactly eager to divulge the workings of spirit sorcery. They were cautious about where they placed their trust. Yet Augustus, patriarch of the Giovanni family and Markus's grandsire among the undead, had been prepared to share their knowledge of necromancy in return for the honor of being inducted as equals in the clan. But the trust gained from that act was lost when he saw that many were uneasy with the Giovanni and their black arts. The Giovanni were not the heretical pariahs the Lazarenes were, but neither were they welcomed as fully as Markus had once told his retainers. Secrets were kept from them—the rare art of divination, the innermost workings of Mount Erciyes, and more besides. The Cappadocians might thaw in time, but the Giovanni were resolute that their secrets would remain just that—theirs alone—until then.

"Others shun you," the Methuselah observed. "Some even claim you are as heretical as myself. Shocking, is it not? Such ignorance from those who should be open to possibility."

"So you propose that we join in our respective heresies?" Markus scraped up a trace of humor. "Some Cappadocians may mistrust us, but that is a far cry from our sharing the same label."

"And what is my heresy, childe? Is it not a matter of arbitrary interpretation? The Cappadocians espouse the Road of Bones. Existence follows a set cycle of life and death. Where is the heresy in quickening that process? It does not break the cycle; it simply accelerates it. Indeed, is not our circumstance the true heresy?"

"Vampirism is but a pause in the turning," Markus asserted, though his tone betrayed his uncertainty. "Resurrection usurps the most fundamental of God's gifts."

Lazarus laughed. "Hardly a logical approach. I submit that the Curse of Caine usurps the cycle. The Lord punished Caine for defying His plan in slaying Abel. Though afflicted with vampirism, Caine continued his defiance. He made others like him, others who stand outside the cycle. And what has God done in response? Nothing!"

Markus's reply was garbled as doubt sprouted amid his

convictions. The cycle was considered inviolate, the domain of God alone. *But by whose claim? It is what we are told, as part of the clan. Are my beliefs no more than Cappadocian dogma, learned along with the ways of unlife and death magic?*

"I am no different from any other Cappadocian," Lazarus was saying, "no different from the father of us all." Markus trembled in outrage and confusion. He knew the mind of Cappadocius no better than he did that of God, but Lazarus's words smacked of heresy nonetheless. "You presume much, Lazarus. He would have made it known long ago if he condoned your actions."

"You think that he has not? Perhaps not in the manner of the literal-minded. But never, in those rare times he returns fully to this world, has he denounced me." Cold laughter shook the deep hood. "And, of course, I can find his blessing in the Sargon Codex."

"Because you sought it as he did? Similar actions do not equal shared intent."

"Not because he sought the codex, childe. *Because he wrote it.*"

Chapter Twenty

North of Bahariya Oasis
7 October, 1204

"Rather unremarkable, as temples go," Ankhesenaten observed.

Constancia ignored his sarcasm, her attention on the next rise. The rocky outcrop was the only significant landmark for miles, but she would have assumed it held nothing of interest if Markus Giovanni's aura hadn't led directly to it. "It is safe to assume that the Lazarenes have fashioned an underground lair. Sensible, given the terrain and their desire for secrecy."

"Well, yes," the Setite replied, not bothering to conceal his irritation. They had been together long enough that neither wasted effort in trying to overlook their conflicting personalities. "So, shall we go announce ourselves?"

Constancia offered a minute shake of her head and quirked a thin eyebrow at Qalhara. It was clear that a frontal assault was out of the question, but she left it to the Lamia to suggest their next step. Qalhara was a better strategist than she.

"I believe it is their main entry," Qalhara said. "It looks unimpressive, but see how the rocks create a strong defensive position? No; there must be other passages."

"We would find them in time, but time is not a luxury we have. Do the Setites have a means to seek out hidden openings?"

"Of course! It is the first gift our Dark God bestowed upon us." Ankhesenaten's laughter did not reach his golden eyes. His tone grew quiet as he continued. "Come now. You spoke of calamity should your wayward Cappadocian fall into the

Lazarenes' clutches. Well, they carried him off two nights past, and yet the world remains unchanged. I think that I may have been duped into aiding you in what is nothing more than a minor squabble. Why should I offer any further assistance?"

Constancia dug her fingers into the hard-packed desert sand, her not-insignificant patience strained with the trials of the past few months. "Believe what you like, serpent. But consider this before you go: Regardless of whether the peril exists, I offer you the chance to strike at a Lazarene temple. That would stand you in good stead with your people, would it not?"

"A chance at walking into my own destruction, more like," Ankhesenaten grumbled. "I pledged to offer you safe passage in our land, but I have no interest in suicide."

"Then I release you from your pledge."

The Setite quirked his lips in mild surprise. "Understand that you shall no longer have my protection, should you encounter any of my brethren."

Constancia raised a hand, brushing away his caution. "More pressing matters concern me."

Ankhesenaten looked from Cappadocian to Lamia, then glanced at his bodyguard. "Very well, High Priestess. Know that I bear you no malice, but I cannot guarantee the outcome of our next meeting."

A smile touched Constancia's mouth, but she didn't challenge his bravado. She and Qalhara watched the Setites slip back down the slope and depart on their camels. "There is potential in that one, if he does not fall victim to his ego."

"Imperious crone," Ankhesenaten said with good humor as they rode south. "We have learned an important lesson, Goreb. The Walid Set are not the only ones skilled at manipulation. I admit, I was cowed by her power, swayed by her stature. I know better now. And I know something else, do I not?"

Goreb looked over, puzzlement barely making a dent in his stolid features.

"I know the location of a Lazarene temple, Goreb. High Priestess Constancia may search for her secret entrances and her wayward Giovanni for as long as she likes. I shall gather

a force of Walid Set to wipe that nest of corpse lovers from the
very face of Khem!"

"If only we had sufficient forces—" They had returned barely
before dawn the night before, but Qalhara picked up the argu-
ment as if they had never spent a day in slumber.

"Is that all that worries you?" Constancia spun, her parchment-thin skin even paler than usual, ice-blue eyes filled with
the specter of disaster. "This place is thick with centuries' worth
of burials, of these Egyptians' so-called mummifications. I
sense the bodies resting beneath the sand like a field sown with
death. I can reap that crop in moments—an army of the dead at
my command! But it avails us nothing if we are too late to stop
Lazarus from claiming the Giovanni."

"Summon your army, then." Qalhara said, her own blood
rising with concern. The stress of the visions, of the choice her
mistress had made, was taking its toll. She'd never seen the high
priestess so manic. "They might lack the power of Cainites, but
give me one hundred corpse knights and I shall overwhelm any
who presume to stand against us!"

"Bottleneck."

The two women turned in surprise. They had comman-
deered a home on the outskirts of the oasis, more secure than
the place where they had discovered Markus Giovanni's ghoul.
And it was he who spoke now. Beltramose had been cast aside
when his master was abducted, knocked unconscious by a for-
tunate blow and left collapsed in a corner. He'd been addled,
barely aware of his surroundings, ever since they found him.
But the bewildered expression he'd worn for the past two nights
was gone, replaced with one of nervous resolve.

"What did you say?"

Beltramose shook his head. "Not me. Falsinar. He says that
sending a large force through the temple's main entry would
create a bottleneck. Only a few could hold you off while the rest
escaped with Markus."

The Lamia warrior showed him rows of sharp teeth. "What
do you know of—"

"Qalhara." Constancia had recovered much of her

composure, and looked at the ghoul with keen interest. "I had not noticed before. This man has two auras."

"How can that be?"

"Of course. A soul clings to him, like a drowning man to a piece of flotsam. Most curious."

"Then this… Falsinar? It is a spirit?"

"The Giovanni studied necromancy before Cappadocius brought them into the fold. It would seem that this mortal has some skill in the art, to have such a pet."

Beltramose shrank into the corner as if he could burrow away from Constancia's scrutiny. "What? Falsinar is nothing of the sort."

"That blow has softened his brain, mistress."

Constancia looked the ghoul over carefully, poking him a few times as she made her evaluation. "Perhaps. I care not how he perceives the thing; all that matters is that the spirit seems to have some knowledge of the Lazarene temple."

"Yes!" Beltramose cried. "He does!"

"Does he know of an entrance other than the one by the rocks?"

"How should I—what is it, Falsinar? Have you not been listening? That is why they are here. Then do it, and give me some peace for a moment!"

The women shared a puzzled look. "What was that about?"

Beltramose slumped in exhaustion. "He wondered if it would help free our master if he checked."

Constancia watched as a smoky wisp detached from the ghoul and flitted out of the building. "Most curious indeed."

Falsinar could hardly move, so paralyzing was his fear. But he had no choice; he must venture into the desert again if he hoped to see his master freed, if he hoped to escape this nightmare.

The journey was as harrowing as the first time he had crossed—a plain rent with fissures that exuded noxious fumes, banshees tearing across its surface to stir up sand clouds that tore right through him, the shadowy flicker and echoing moan of things in the vastness—

No, this time was, if anything, worse than before. At least

then he had not understood his circumstance. The memory of that night was still an open wound in his thoughts. Rubbed raw by the current terror, it overwhelmed him now with the remembrance of his death:

He was searching for a latrine, of all things. Then a whisper of movement and a mountain fell on his head. He awakened to a nightmare, a chamber at once cramped and of infinite dimensions. Candles flickered in a dance that promised madness if he looked too long, and a figure robed in darkness stood over him—dripping blood on his face!

He bolted, sparing the strange room one last look as he fled. The figure hadn't moved... and neither had Falsinar's body. He saw himself on the stone slab, his head tilted at a curious angle. His mind reeled, unable to encompass what he saw. When he next had a conscious thought, he was standing next to a clump of large rocks on a blasted desert plain. He had vague memories of dim chambers and winding tunnels, of a handful of robed figures and many more shambling forms. A pall hung over everything, cobwebs that obscured his sight no matter how much he brushed at his face.

As his senses returned, Falsinar realized that he'd passed a group carrying Markus. His master was held rigid by some unseen force as decayed things carted him along like a piece of luggage. Falsinar wanted to rush to his master's side, but he feared venturing back into that terrible place. Yet the world outside was no more comforting. He stood on a cracked desert plain over which heavy, dark clouds rumbled and cracked with lightning. Despair gripped him and he felt the creep of nothingness at the edge of his senses.

A thought seized him then, chasing back the darkness and filling him with strength of purpose. Beltramose!

Falsinar barely remembered crossing the desert. Its very emptiness was horrifying. A hungry wind raged across it like some mammoth unseen beast. Things lurked just out of sight all around him, ready to strike at any moment. The washed-out light suggested a kind of day, but it was impossible to tell with the thick clouds mossing above him. They seemed driven by some malevolent will, spewing zephyrs of stinging darkness at him. Green bolts of lightning cracked ever closer as he ran, shattering his nerves and filling his nose with an acrid stench.

Only the thought of his steadfast companion gave him the strength to struggle on. He didn't even know where he was going, except that he was certain that Beltramose drew closer with each step. He came upon the oasis at last, but it was nothing like he remembered it. The palm trees were dead and splintered fingers clawing at the angry sky. The grass was a sickly gray and looked sharp enough to pierce the skin. The buildings were indistinct, but for some that were scorched black or tumbled to ruins. Worst of all, creatures lurked amid the desolation. He never got a good look at them, nor did he ever want to. The brief glimpses were enough to send screams tearing at his throat.

Falsinar forced himself to silence and crept toward the hovel he'd left a lifetime ago. Beltramose was inside, sprawled in one corner with his long sword pulled halfway out of its scabbard. He feared the worst until he saw the telltale rise and fall of his friend's chest. With aery of relief, Falsinar rushed to his friend's side.

"You idiot," a cold voice spat.

Falsinar whirled, snatching for the falchion that was no longer at his belt. Two men and a woman stood on the other side of the room. He hadn't noticed them before, so concerned was he for Beltramose. The three stood out from the hazy surroundings with startling clarity. The speaker was hardly a man, but a tall boy of perhaps fourteen years with strangely florid skin and sunken, fevered eyes. The other man, a heavy set Turk of middle age, had a dozen vicious wounds gaping open on his flesh. It was difficult to tell the woman's age, for much of her face and upper body looked as if pulped by a fall from a great height. Each moved in strange fits and starts, as if time was not constant in this place. Disturbing as all this was, Falsinar sensed something familiar about the three creatures.

"You would have been free," the youth continued, "but instead of passing on, you come running back for your friend. You've had it now."

"You do not scare me," Falsinar replied, though the squeak in his voice suggested otherwise.

The trio's laughter was like insects skittering over flagstones. The woman shuffled forward, pointing a ruined arm at him. "It is not us *you need fear, Falsinar. If the things that infest this land do not get you, our 'beloved master' shall."*

"What… what are you talking about? Who are you?"

"You do not recognize us, after all the time we have spent together?" The youth affected dismay. *"Your old friends Infantino, Viator, and Domnola?"*

Falsinar shook his head even as he sensed the truth of the boy's words. *He had never met the people whose souls Markus ensnared. Yet these three were no strangers. They had all spent years in service to the Giovanni, they in the spirit realm, he in the physical world. Falsinar had grown to know their feel without ever realizing it.* But if I can see them—

"Ah! Understanding strikes," *Infantino chortled.* "Yes, my friend. You are like us now, a soul cursed to suffer in this hell on earth."

"I cannot… I was only just—"

"Yes, yes. At least your end was quick. I would rather that than the lingering agony of disease."

Numb understanding swept through him. "Why?"

"It is different for each of us," *the big Turk rumbled.*

Infantino nodded. "Easier for you maybe, since the veil between worlds is so thin here. Only our esteemed master could say for certain."

"Yes, Markus! Why are you not with him?"

"He has not called us—and he will not, if God spares us the slightest pity." *Infantino glared wild-eyed at the surrounding walls.* "Our fate is horrible enough without traversing any more of this Egypt."

"But if…"—if I am like you—"…if it is so dangerous, only Markus can protect us. We must seek him out!"

Viator stalked forward, and Falsinar noticed the big man's body was transparent in some places. "We will go, when the sun is highest. But not to him."

"Away from here," *Domnola confirmed.* "Escape this land together."
"

"It is a pitiable existence, but it is all we have," *Infantino said.* "And only as one can we hope to make it. Come, Falsinar. You are lost if you stay here."

Falsinar looked at the three wraiths, each wearing the gruesome evidence of their deaths for eternity. He could sense their desperation, a companion to his own feelings of agony and loss. He looked at the crumbling hovel and the injured form of Beltramose. Near enough to touch, but separated forever by a gossamer veil.

"No. I cannot leave my friend. He is all I have left."

"Then may God have mercy upon you, Falsinar. For you will find none in this place."

Chapter Twenty-One

Temple of the Lazarenes
7 October, 1204

Markus stood with mouth agape. "No... Byzar said that Cappadocius and Sargon were contemporaries—"

"Byzar? I had thought him destroyed long ago. Where did you encounter...? No; it may wait for another time." Lazarus struck a contemplative tone as he tapped his memories. "Remember, my sire adopted the name 'Cappadocius' in the wake of his Embrace. His mortal past was a mystery none pursued. He was eager to leave it forgotten, just as his progeny were eager to learn the secrets of death. A few of us, the first of his offspring, knew meager portions of the truth—enough that most felt the need to look no further. Aside from myself, only Byzar was sufficiently curious to investigate. He did not dig deeply enough, however."

Doubt and curiosity were worms in Markus's mind. He might not agree with all that Lazarus said, but the Methuselah's other observations were nonetheless well-reasoned enough that he could not dismiss this claim out of hand. In the end, the scholar within him won out. There was no harm in listening, after all. "And what is the larger truth?"

"Ah, if only I could have discovered it with such a simple question. Alas, I pieced it together only after long years of study." The loose robe swirled as Lazarus turned as if to get a better look into his memory. "Prior to his Embrace, venerable Cappadocius was a mortal visionary who went by the name Sargon. He endured revelations of transcendent wonder and agony, messages from God Himself that revealed truths never before experienced by man. Such was his wisdom that, even while in the throes of hallucination, Sargon transcribed what he witnessed."

"The codex," Markus muttered.

"It is impossible to keep objects of mystic significance from the awareness of Cainites. Sooner or later, they will sense their existence. So it was with Sargon's tablet of visions. Such was its import that Sargon used all his skill to keep it hidden until he could make greater sense of it. Even the powers of the undead were not sufficient to reveal its hiding place. But perhaps a greater treasure lay in the visionary himself. Sargon was Embraced, at least in part, so that Cainites might gain access to the divine secrets he had translated." Lazarus fell silent. There was but the sigh of the wind across the distant top of the shaft, then he continued. "The Curse of Caine did more than transform him into one of the undead. The creature who had been Sargon lost any clear remembrance of his prior visions… including knowledge of where he had secreted the codex. I have long pondered this irony, but even to this night I have no answer why this might be. The blood of Caine is potent indeed; perhaps it drowned Sargon's connection to the divine. Or it may be that the Lord Himself rendered judgment upon Sargon for taking the Embrace. Only He may say with certainty."

"And so Sargon was reborn as Cappadocius."

"Yes. And the irony of his creation hounded him through millennia. He has spent his immortality in a fruitless effort to recover his forgotten revelations."

Too many questions roiled about within Markus to give any one voice. He picked one at random. "But Cappadocius is reputed to have such skill with visions. If he is—was—Sargon, how could the codex remain hidden for so long?"

"There are no simple answers where oracles are concerned. Nor where the Lord is involved." There was a smile in Lazarus's voice. "Our own existence is testament enough to that, would you not agree? The answer lies in the divine, childe, and in manifestations of mortal faith that defy even the most powerful of our kind. Clever indeed was Sargon in the steps he took to conceal his tablet. It was thirty years after I found its hiding place before I hit upon a means to enter safely, and another five before I felt confident that I could remove it intact. It is no wonder that the great Cappadocius had never tracked it down, let alone recovered it. Consider it another irony; he was too close to see the clues."

"And now that you have the codex, you seek apotheosis. Toward what end?"

"You assume it is for power. No; I seek to answer the fundamental issues of existence once and for all," Lazarus said. "Sargon's tablet is the key to understanding God's plan—even of addressing the curse that afflicts all our kind."

"But..." Markus struggled to process it all. "Wait. What need do you have of me? The final piece of the Sargon Codex is in your hands. If you achieve godhood, of what importance am I?"

A surprisingly human sigh came from the robed figure. "Though apotheosis shall lay bare much that remains hidden, it is hubris to assume that I will enjoy total omniscience... at least for some time. My followers shall continue to be of great aid. And you, with your unique perspective on the realm of the spirit, shall be of particular use. Think of it, childe! Imagine knocking down the last barriers of ignorance, casting aside the last shackles of mortality that yet bind us. You search for the same answers as I. Look at what you have accomplished thus far. Look at the risks you have taken with but rumor and legend as your guide. Does it not excite you to know that ultimate discovery lies within your grasp?"

Markus could hardly deny that he felt a thrill. *Can it be so simple? Based on a few clever words, am I to ignore all that I have been told of the Lazarenes?*

He remained far from such a commitment. Even so, he had much to consider—not the least being how he still planned to carry out his unformed idea to spirit the Sargon Codex away from this place. "My apologies, Lazarus, but I am quite overwhelmed by all this. I beg solitude to consider all that you have said."

"Very well. It shall be dawn soon enough. Stay here for the

day; we shall return at midnight." Lazarus indicated the silent form of Falsinar. "I shall leave your retainer to watch over you. Do not think you can bend him to your will; he is my creature now."

Markus understood perfectly. Despite the improved quarters, he was still a prisoner.

The Methuselah moved to the door with fluid grace. "It is up to you to decide what you shall believe, Markus Musa Giovanni. But tarry not long in making your decision. The future will not wait."

Markus pondered his options until lethargy overtook him. The call of the codex remained with him through the day, buzzing in his head like a swarm of bees. Dreams of ancient memory harassed him during his slumber, and he awakened feeling an almost mortal fatigue.

He could endure this no longer—resisting the codex on the one hand and holding his own with Lazarus on the other. The time had come to make his escape. He had hoped to see some easy way to snatch up the Sargon Codex and make a break for freedom, but there were no easy solutions. While he sensed where the tablet rested, he couldn't begin to guess which passages led to an exit. He had hoped for fate to bless him with a convenient opportunity, but it appeared he would have to rely on his own skills.

With more than a little trepidation, he thought through the ritual he'd first considered the previous night. It was little more than theory extrapolated from his studies; he wouldn't even have contemplated it under other circumstances. Never had he actually tried to step into the spirit realm.

To succeed, he needed the aid of a powerful spirit. He had sensed Infantino before, but there was no guarantee that the ghost was still nearby. Knowing that Falsinar was dead suggested another option, but that assumed the ghoul's soul had even survived the trauma of death. If so, it would be the equivalent of a newborn in the spirit world: useful for basic tasks, but far from worthwhile for the ritual that Markus planned.

It would be dangerous, and it meant he couldn't even try to

take the codex. There was no telling what kind of reaction there would be if the artifact passed through the boundary between life and death. It pained him to leave the thing in the Lazarenes' hands, but the alternative was to remain. *And if I stay, soon enough I shall snap and become the codex's creature. Or Lazarus will sense its influence. Either way, it shall spell my end.*

It was far from a perfect plan. But at least it would be some while before Lazarus made his bid for godhood. If Markus was lucky, he could mobilize others of his family to wrest away the codex. Now that he felt its lure, it wouldn't matter where the Lazarenes took it. *Sooner or later, it shall be ours.*

To his surprise, when he called for the spirit, the response was immediate, almost as if Infantino was waiting for the summons. There was an odd quality to the shade, but there was no mistaking his vibrant energy. Relief washed over Markus. Without the amulets of binding, it would have been difficult to force the wraith to him. As it was, the slave would be easy enough to control once he drew near.

Markus spoke without preamble when the smoky aura flickered into sight. "We are short on time. I shall tear an opening in the shroud that separates our realms. You must focus your entire will upon me so that I may step through. Do you understand?"

A whispered echo came in affirmation, but Markus did not begin immediately. It was a desperate gamble. Markus had none of the tools he would normally use for such a ritual except his will and his blood. The barrier was quite thin in this land, but it did not follow the same rules as any physical substance. If he and Infantino lacked sufficient strength to breach the shroud, the backlash could destroy them. Infantino was already dead, so Markus didn't spare him much concern. But he was rather fond of his own hirsute form.

Lest Infantino get any rebellious ideas, Markus poked at the spirit with his will. The hazy aura shuddered like smoke in a gust of wind. He wasn't sure just how such prodding affected the wraiths, but he assumed it served a similar purpose as a riding crop to a horse's flank.

He stood in the center of the room and started muttering the Latin phrases that would draw him into a trance state. Calm came upon him quickly, and even the siren song of the codex faded almost to nothing. He felt the telltale tingling of his extremities and brought his left wrist to his mouth. His fangs tore into his cold flesh and the blood sprang forth through the wound at his command. With measured steps that matched the rhythm of his chant, Markus paced the room's tight confines. His wrist flicked blood in intricate patterns, creating a mosaic of red on the floor and portions of the walls. He'd fed well on the camel's blood, but the ritual threatened to drain him dry. The chant was his anchor, keeping him centered even as the hunger grew to a ravening thing that threatened to break free from its chain.

At last the pattern was complete. The tenor of the chant shifted, a whisper of death and of realms alien to anything pondered by sane minds. A sheet of frost crackled over everything in the room, and Markus shivered despite the hardiness of his undead flesh. The cold that stole over him was far beyond anything the mortal world could offer. His teeth chattered, threatening to throw off the pace of his chant. Pushing himself along through sheer momentum and stubbornness, at last the silvery shimmer of the veil between life and death became visible.

He reached out and grasped the barrier, which squirmed in his hands like some gigantic sea creature. Markus sensed more than saw Infantino mimicking his action on the other side. He kept up the chant through gritted teeth and tore at the shroud with all his strength. It bucked with such force that Markus was slammed into a wall. He held on doggedly and strained at the thing again. This time there was a ripping sound that sent splinters of molten glass through his innards, and a fetid wind blasted through from the underworld to shatter the cot against the ceiling.

He had only moments before the hole closed, and he barely had the strength to lever himself through in the face of the furious wind. He called to Infantino, but the ghost had been blown back as the rip opened and was only now struggling to his feet.

Markus had one foot through when the door burst open

with such force that it splintered against the wall. He glimpsed a number of robed figures jostling past Falsinar in the narrow hall and redoubled his efforts. A pair of arms latched around his waist just as he lunged the rest of the way through the gap. With Markus through, the ritual was complete. The tear in the shroud collapsed with a thunderclap, shearing in half the unfortunate who'd grabbed Markus.

The unfortunate Cainite shrieked in agony, the trauma already sending him into torpor. It was a massive injury, his lower abdomen and legs ripped away, but the blood of Cappadocius made for a hardy clan. The Lazarene might have survived under other circumstances, perhaps even regenerating his lost flesh after a century or so. But he was stuck in the spirit world with Markus, who was ravenous from his own blood loss and exertion. The reek of the Lazarene's gore splashed all over him sent Markus into a frenzy. Instinct overwhelmed reason, and he fell upon the injured Cainite with a deadly hunger.

Markus was saved from diablerie—cannibalizing the very essence of one of his own kind—when a curved blade plunged through his back. The pain was fierce, like a blow to his very soul, but it shocked him back to his senses. He cast aside the Lazarene and writhed to get free of the awful weapon's bite. The blade obliged, the barbs along its edge ripping through him in further agony. Calling out to Infantino, Markus spun to face his attacker.

"I am here, master," Infantino declared, his grin as wicked as the bloody weapon he wielded.

Already unnerved by the bloodlust that had overcome him and struggling to get his bearings in the vast desolation of the spirit world, Markus could do more than gape at the thing that had long been his ghostly slave.

The wraith looked, for the most part, as he had when Markus first found him a few years before—a tall youth dead from the ravages of fever. But his body now sported an appendage impossible to the human form. The blade that had stabbed Markus waved at the end of a many-jointed appendage which sprouted from Infantino's midsection, like some obscene umbilical cord. Its surface was hairless and hard, the carapace of a crab, and a hundred tiny teeth along its edge promised to saw at Markus with the same viciousness as the first blow. Infantino moved like a crab as well, scuttling sideways around Markus, forcing him to stumble in place as he tried to keep the ghost in view.

Markus struggled to master his shock. "How... dare you! I am your master!"

"No longer," came the reply. The wraith's eyes were the bulging orbs of a madman. "I can still feel the pull of your necklace—but they are yours no longer. The Lazarenes tossed them all in a cupboard for later study. I shall be destroyed long before then, however, just as Viator and Domnola have perished. Only I remain, and I have vowed that I shall be the last of your slaves!"

The blade lashed out again, but Markus's senses—strangely heightened in this alien place—registered the coming blow an instant before it moved. He threw himself to one side as the weapon stabbed into the ground. The wound was slowing him down, and it was no mundane injury easily healed with the power of the blood.

"You souls drift endlessly in this place, worthless and forgotten," he declared through a grimace. "I gave you purpose!"

"You kept us from finding peace! We grew to yearn for the embrace of oblivion, but your cursed bindings even kept us from that escape." Infantino raised his arms, and his fingers grew into talons of the same bizarre chitin as his slashing blade. "I came to watch your pathetic end in this place, but God at last smiled upon me. He has delivered you here, that I may exact vengeance upon you!" Infantino was not subject to the same demands as a physical form. The wraith twisted and writhed in his attack like nothing from the world of the living. Markus fell back from the attack, stumbling over the uneven floor. He struggled for some tactic, some means of escape, but Infantino gave him no time to think. Only the twisted layout that was the underworld reflection of the Lazarene temple provided any aid. The design differed from the true temple—he had emerged in a room much larger than his tiny cell—but the corridors were just as cramped. He fled through an opening, turning down side passages at random. The halls blunted the effectiveness of Infantino's sidling movement and slashing strikes, but Markus could not run forever. His body started feeling clumsy and sluggish, like the half-remembered instances of being drunk in his mortal life. The wicked blade cut his back to tatters as he stayed mere steps ahead of Infantino. He bounced off a wall, taking a chance turn that took him along a twisting, upward-angled passageway. The meandering course gave him a moment's relief from the stabbing blade, but Infantino's taunts remained loud in his ears.

Then the walls fell away. Vast space surrounded him, a cracked plain spreading to infinity under a bruised, lightning-tossed sky. Surprise conspired with pain and fatigue, sending him in a sprawl. He struggled to rise as Infantino burst from the hole in the ground.

The wraith paused, seeing his quarry kneeling before him. "How does it feel, my master? To know only fear and pain; to be herded like some beast? Now die, knowing that you have felt only a taste of what we have suffered!"

Infantino reared back to strike with blade and taloned hands. Then a shape darted from the rocks surrounding the hole and grappled him from behind. Infantino roared in frustration, his odd appendage whipping over his head to jab at his attacker.

Markus drew upon his waning strength and wrenched a stone from the chalky ground. Staggering forward, he threw himself amid Infantino's flailing hands. He brought the stone crashing into the wraith's skull in a series of heavy blows, even as the claws gouged awful rents in his own body. It became a battle of wills; victory would go to whichever of them could outlast the other.

Infantino fell at last, but only after the substance of his spirit was rendered to a viscous pulp.

Markus collapsed an instant later. Every cut that he suffered burned with a cold agony, and his body felt as if it were weighted with a dozen ship's anchors. His senses swam in delirium, but he struggled for consciousness long enough to learn who had come to his aid. The figure approached, stumbling also from the wounds it had suffered. He couldn't make out the face through his haze of pain, but he recognized the voice immediately.

"Signore?" Falsinar said. "Come; I will take you to safety."

Chapter Twenty-Two

Bahariya Oasis
15 October, 1204

Markus awoke from seven nights of torpor to the sound of strange voices. Though the situation was fast becoming routine, he appreciated it not at all.

At least I am not in some pit this time.

He was in some kind of farmhouse, in fact, built of clay bricks in the same style he had seen throughout this land. He had grown weary of Egypt, but he was most grateful to see anything at all after suffering the ravages of Infantino.

He felt a dull ache in every inch of his body that made even lying still uncomfortable. It meant his body was healing, at least, albeit far more slowly than it would have from wounds inflicted by a normal man or beast. It would be some time before he was entirely whole, but he was well enough this night to rise from the bed.

Or perhaps not, he thought as a wave of dizziness made him stumble with his first steps. *I need blood.*

Beltramose rushed into the chamber at the first sound of movement. "*Signore*! Are you certain that you are well enough to be up?"

"The weakness shall pass," Markus grunted, "but I must feed. *Now.*"

Beltramose bobbed his head and scampered from the sleeping chamber. The voices in the other room ceased their dialogue, and Markus heard his ghoul ask for a container of vitae.

The silence remained even after the lanky man returned, a stoppered clay flask in hand. "This is the same that has been fed to you this past week. Mistress Constancia said that it—"

"Who did you say?!"

Beltramose gestured with the flask. "A priestess of some sort. She was most vital in helping you cross back from the other side."

"'Of some sort'?" Markus couldn't help chuckling. "My friend, you reduce one of the eldest of my clan to a few simple words."

"Yes, well. She would speak with you, if you feel well enough."

"Are you her servant now, Beltramose? No; do not apologize. I am most curious to meet her as well. Give me just a few moments." He drank deeply from the flask, tasting strange flavors as the blood flowed over his tongue. He imagined that the fluid was subject to a Cappadocian ritual that hastened his healing. Or it could easily contain a philter to subject his will to another, just as he used the power of his own blood to maintain his ghouls' loyalty. But if that were so, ingesting the stuff for seven nights put him long past the point where he might resist such charms. *Best to enjoy the healing power of the blood. Time enough later to determine if I am again a pawn.*

Markus was not as unnerved to stand before the High Priestess of Bones as he had been with the heretic Lazarus. Granted, the circumstances were different, but he would have expected this meeting to be just as tense. Constancia was a creature of tremendous age, power and influence, and Markus's sire had told him that she was foremost among Cappadocius's advisors who had spoken against the Giovanni entering the clan. But Markus found her cool poise and obvious intellect appealing, even attractive. Constancia had the drawn features common to the clan, but her deathly pallor was less that of an aged corpse than of some idealized vision of death.

He was more apprehensive seeing the Lamia who stood protectively next to the high priestess. This scarified and tattooed creature with charcoal skin and a deadly glare was a far cry from the gray, emaciated thing that had once dwelled beneath Constantinople. Yet while he knew that that Lamia was driven mad by the Lilith shard, he doubted he would ever feel at ease among any of the sisterhood.

Still, it was the third figure that elicited an immediate, and most extreme, response in him. The slender, hairless vampire had a nuanced grace simply rising to his feet that Markus knew all too well from the brief yet violent encounter a few short weeks ago. "Do my eyes deceive me, High Priestess? Do you traffic with serpents?!"

"And a good evening to you, Markus Musa Giovanni," the Follower of Set replied in a mild tone.

"Do not presume to jest! Your brethren savaged an entire caravan in an effort to destroy me!"

"Yet I would venture that you acquitted yourself quite well."

The Beast surged inside him, quickening the newly ingested blood. He was not yet whole, but he would teach this thing the price of—

"Calm yourself." Constancia hardly raised her voice, but her tone cut through his rising frenzy like a crack on the ice of a frozen pond. "We have no time for this posturing."

"Quite," the serpent agreed. "I came to parley, not to be assaulted."

"Would that your fellows had been so civilized," Markus growled. A glance from Constancia made him draw in the reins of his anger even tighter. Struggling for calm, he said, "My apologies, Mistress Constancia. I am no better than an animal to rant with no understanding of how things stand."

She dipped her chin slightly. "Then allow me to enlighten you, for the world itself has become imperiled by your ignorance."

Markus found the rebuke harsh indeed, but the cold gleam in the Lamia's eyes warned against making protest. Constancia gestured and they all sat—the three of them upon the stools they were using when Markus entered the room, he making do with a corner of the cold hearth that took up one wall of the small dwelling. Beltramose retreated to tidy up the sleeping chamber.

"Markus Musa Giovanni, we four discuss matters of greatest import this night. You know me already, if only by reputation. This is Qalhara, my guardian and protector. And this is Ankhesenaten, representative of the Walid Set."

She must mean the recovery of the Sargon Codex. He had hoped his family could get it first, delivering it to Mount Erciyes or keeping it for study as the Giovanni elders best saw fit. Still, better to help Constancia recover the codex now than to allow Lazarus the time to make his play for divinity. "I intend no disrespect, but if you are here for the reasons I infer, is it not a matter for Cappadocians alone? What right does the serpent have to be here?"

"Please; I am sitting in the same room," Ankhesenaten offered them an exasperated smile. "Do me the courtesy of including me in the conversation."

"He acted as guide so that we would not be trespassers in his land, thereby sparing us from unwelcome encounters with others of his blood." Constancia cast a sidelong glance at the Setite. "Though that service has ended, he has come tonight on a new matter."

Ankhesenaten leaned forward, physically inserting himself into the conversation. "Yes, let us come back to that. As I said before we were interrupted by yon colorful Cappadocian, I was subject to base emotion when we parted these many nights past. I return armed with reason and courtesy, to announce my intention of cleansing this plain of the Lazarenes who infest it.

"Forces gather even now," he continued. "My brethren shall arrive within the week, and they will care not about any distinction between heretical Lazarene and loyal Cappadocian."

"So you urge us to flee before they get here." Markus shook his head in puzzlement. "What is your scheme, serpent? Would you not gain more praise to deliver them both Lazarus and Constancia in a single bold stroke?"

"You display your ignorance of the children of the Dark God. I bear your kind no ill will, but for those who seek to usurp what is ours by divine right. Despite our differences, Mistress Constancia has offered me respect in our dealings. I would prefer that such an arrangement continued to mutual benefit, rather than see her fall before the might of the Walid Set." The Egyptian vampire quirked one hairless brow. "Indeed, though we have not begun on the best of terms, I would not be averse to forming an arrangement with you as well."

Charming bastard, I shall grant him that. More than grudging respect, Markus felt chagrin at acting like an uncouth Latin— like so many of the louts he'd seen amid the crusading forces. He prided himself on his intellect. Was it nothing more than a thin veneer, that a few months in this strange land could strip it away with such ease?

"Your courtesy is appreciated," Constancia was saying, "and you do much to improve my opinion of you and your kind by offering it. But there is little chance that we will be caught in your assault. Now that Markus has emerged from torpor, we shall make our own move on the Lazarene temple tomorrow night."

Ankhesenaten looked from Constancia to Markus in surprise. "Toward what end? Now that you have this fellow, what do you hope to accomplish by going back?"

"Suffice it to say that the Lazarenes have stolen an object of great scholarly value to us. I must recover it, that it may be returned to Mount Erciyes."

"And just what is this object?"

Constancia waved a hand. "A treatise from a Chaldean scholar, laying some of the groundwork that established our clan's course of study. The Sargon Codex is quite old and surely of little interest to a Follower of Set. The value is simply as a museum piece for Cappadocians."

Ankhesenaten's shrug dismissed the codex as just another Cainite curiosity. "Their kind has also stolen from us. I would hope that you do not plan to take items of similar value to the Walid Set."

"I leave such things for you to recover in this impending assault of yours. Still, if you harbor suspicions, why not join us?"

A warm smile revealed brilliant white teeth against Ankhesenaten's caramel flesh. "You do me quite an honor, mistress. How could I pass on such a generous offer?"

"It is clear that you have many questions, Markus Giovanni."

"Not just of the past few nights, but even into these many months gone by." He glanced to the door through which Ankhesenaten had passed to address preparations for the next night's venture. Sitting with the high priestess, Qalhara a mute presence in the corner, a stillness fell across the room that centered him as surely as any ritual chant. He marveled at Constancia's effortless power, so different from the vibrancy of Lazarus. *And different also from we Giovanni. So then how...?* "I understand that you were essential in recovering me from Purgatory, mistress."

"My grasp of the spirit realm is restricted to the divining arts. If you had not striven, even on the verge of torpor, to return—and if the veil had been any tougher than parchment—you would have been lost to that place forever." Her pale eyes looked him over critically. "That was a most foolish endeavor, Giovanni. What possessed you to brave the land of the dead?"

"A keen sense of survival. My only other choices were to have my ashes mix with the desert sand, or join them." Like Infantino's betrayal, the incident was still too fresh in memory to contemplate now. Still, he would not soon forget the doubts that were raised during his time with the Lazarenes. "But enough of me for the moment. You must have divined that Lazarus has the Sargon Codex, that even now he makes plans for apotheosis. I am puzzled that you came here alone, though. Was this a diplomatic effort? Did you seek to dissuade him from making the attempt?"

Constancia's placid features shifted in what Markus could have sworn was consternation. Her aura rippled too swiftly for him to discern the telltale hues that would give him insight into her mood. She shook her head slowly, her features adopting the stern calm as before. "You are as perceptive as I was led to believe. I witnessed an oracle that predicted Lazarus would, in fact, attempt godhood. But success will not be what he expects. He shall not supplant God, though he will achieve power undreamt of. You spent many years in Constantinople; you are familiar with the so-called Dream? Well, it will take on a new form when Lazarus becomes like unto a god on earth. Lazarus's progeny shall supplant the children of Caine in a conflict that will rend the earth and destroy countless souls. In the end, the Dream will become a perverted nightmare, and the cycle will be forever broken."

"The cycle; Lazarus spoke of it as he tried to enlist my aid. He claims that Cainites break the cycle already with our very existence."

"It is a pity that such a tremendous mind as his might be driven to madness. It has happened more than once to our kind, though we seldom realize it until too late." She paused, sparing Qalhara a glance. "As you said, I came to beseech Lazarus. It is folly now, to think that there was ever a chance."

Something struck Markus as slightly off about the priestess's words, but he could not hope to understand the mind of a Methuselah. *After all, three nights with Lazarus and I understand him less than when he was a creature of rumor and legend. Should Constancia be any easier to evaluate?*

"What do you plan now?" he asked.

"We have no choice. Lazarus must not succeed."

Markus raised his hands in a slowing gesture. "Do you hope to destroy him? Surely he is too powerful for the few of us, especially with his followers at hand."

"You are quite correct. It is far more important that we recover the codex. Stripped of his chance, the events that I have foreseen will pass from possibility. In their place, a very different future will unfold."

"But that promises to be just as difficult to achieve. His entire reality revolves around Sargon's tablet." Realization struck. "By Christ and Caine. It has been so many nights… He might perform the ceremony at any moment!"

"Your unique escape put that off for the moment," Qalhara interjected, "if your pet ghost is to be believed."

Markus felt a wave of vertigo. "But Infantino—"

Constancia waved off his exclamation. "Your man calls it Falsinar. In fact, only he has proven able to exert any kind of influence over it. I cannot say that I am at ease with the arts your family studies, but the ghost has been helpful in this circumstance."

Though he had only scattered recollections of his sojourn

into the land of the dead, he remembered the ghost of Falsinar coming to his aid.

But I had not bound him; how is it that he lingers? Is his connection to Beltramose that strong?

He was eager to investigate this fascinating circumstance when more immediate matters did not demand his attention. "So Lazarus has been more concerned with how I got free than with achieving omnipotence?"

Constancia favored him with a cold smile. "The entire hive of heretics has been in an uproar. Only in the past few nights has it calmed."

"The perfect chance to strike, then, in those moments when they first relax."

"Qalhara said those very words. And with you returned to consciousness at last, we will have no better opportunity."

"I am still too weak to be of much help, mistress. Give me even another handful of nights and I might tell a different tale, but that still leaves us with a pitiful force compared to the Lazarenes."

"You need not worry on that score, childe. I have not been idle while waiting for you to recover."

Given his own talents, Markus had a few ideas of what one of Constancia's skill could achieve. "Even so, would it not be prudent to wait until I am whole?"

"Too long a wait and we shall miss our chance. I divined that tonight would offer the best opportunity for success, but you have only just awakened. No, it must be no later than tomorrow." She indicated the angry red marks that crisscrossed his hairy white forearms. "Your role shall not be that of combatant anyway. Only you are familiar enough with that place to show us where the codex may be found."

Markus was conflicted by fear and desire. Perhaps due to the deep slumber of torpor, he no longer felt the same desperate need to hold the codex. Its seduction was reduced to little more than a plaintive whisper. He might well have to endure that call for the rest of his existence—but what might happen if he sought the thing? Would he lose himself in madness as the Lamia had? "Surely Falsinar's ghost—"

"Your man says the spirit fears the codex. It will go nowhere near the thing. No, the ghost has found us a most attractive way inside the temple, but it shall be of little aid once we are inside."

"And the Setite? I admit that I may have been hasty in assuming he was of the same temperament as the serpents that attacked me. Still, was it wise to invite him to join us?"

"Ankhesenaten is more worldly than many of his kind, but he is still fundamentally a Follower of Set. He claims it will be a week of nights before his brethren arrive in force, but he could easily be… mistaken, shall we say, as to the actual time. With him at our side, we shall enjoy some degree of protection from his fellows. And he is canny enough to know that forming a relationship with us far outweighs the immediate gratification of our destruction."

"You told him nothing of the other prophecy."

"It seemed far more expedient to let him think his supposition was correct. Do you mean that you disapprove of my misdirection?"

A ghost of a smile flitted across Qalhara's face. "Not at all, mistress. There is no telling how he might react to the truth, had we even the time to relate it. He is far more pliant having convinced himself than he would be with persuasion."

"Let us hope he is swayed as easily to fulfill the second part of the prophecy after we have recovered the codex."

"Wake, Beltramose. I have need of some companionship amid all this strangeness."

Shaken from slumber, the ghoul could hardly keep from throwing his arms around Markus. "*Signore!* It is so good to see you up and about again."

"It does me well to see you also." He peered closely at the man. "Is that Falsinar?"

Beltramose nodded, far more comfortable having the spirit of his compatriot hovering by him than he ever was with the ghosts Markus had captured. "I do not always see him, but I can feel him nearby. It is a most strange sensation."

"Well, greetings to you also, Falsinar. My thanks for

intervening when I was at Infantino's mercy."

"He says—" Beltramose stopped himself. "Apologies, *Signore*. I expect you can understand him well enough."

"*He was mad,*" Falsinar had said, his words warped and muted by the barrier between them. "*We will never escape this land without you to lead us.*"

Markus heard the words with little trouble, but he was surprised that Beltramose had picked up the knack without any training. "Your loyalty is commendable. Let us hope we will be gone from here soon."

They stepped into the night and felt a gust of wind that promised dawn would soon follow. Markus walked in silence, taking in the simple construction of the few buildings that comprised the farm, the fields that lay fallow until spring, and the fresh graves that surely held the remains of those who had called this place their home. "Do you know where Constancia has gone with that pair of ghouls?"

"*Signore*?" Beltramose yawned. "Her servants have been sprinkling some concoction of blood and other odious substances across that portion of the desert plain. She went with them once before, though I know not what purpose it serves."

"Do you know what may be found over there? It seems like nothing but a featureless plain."

"The priestess and that demonic-looking woman were arguing the very night you escaped. Mistress Constancia said something about graves by the hundreds."

"Truly, you and Falsinar have been witness to a number of curious things." Markus clapped a hand on his retainer's shoulder. "Come; dawn is a good hour off. I would hear all that you have seen these past days and nights—especially any insights you may have about our newfound allies."

Chapter Twenty-Three

Temple of the Lazarenes
16 October, 1204

Markus could scarcely believe his eyes. One hundred twenty cadavers marched in the desert, promising violent death to any man or beast that crossed their path. Cappadocians were not militant by nature, but they were nonetheless capable of awesome displays of force. The legion of corpse knights had arisen just before the previous dawn and spent the day heading toward the Lazarene temple. From his seat astride a camel a quarter-mile distant, Markus could almost feel their ravenous hunger for destruction. "How could you create such an army alone?"

"The ritual is a challenge to learn, let alone master. Only those who have proven their skill after centuries may learn its secrets." Constancia looked no different from the night before, but she could not disguise a great strain in her tone. "It costs me greatly to keep them to their course. Do not pester me with any more questions."

A squad of ten peeled off from the main force and moved toward their group. Qalhara raised a bone wrapped in stained cloth—a charm the high priestess had created to allow her bodyguard to command a small group of corpses. "Come; we must hurry if we are to be in position when the corpse knights begin their assault."

Markus shot Ankhesenaten a wicked grin as he muscled his camel forward. "Your Setite friends had best hurry, or there may be nothing left for them to assault."

The passage followed the course of an underground stream, long since dried up. Hieroglyphs adorned the rough walls, suggesting that the temple may have been built by someone other than its current inhabitants.

Only Ankhesenaten and Goreb showed interest in the painted characters. Constancia and Qalhara were preoccupied with keeping the corpse knights under control, while Beltramose and the two Cappadocian initiates struggled with mortal concerns. Markus was lost in recollection; each step triggered a memory of his recent stay in the temple. Though he had seen no display of Lazarus's power, he had to wonder if all the forces that Constancia had marshaled would prove sufficient to defy him. The codex was a prize of too high a stake for either side to resist committing the fullest extent of their might.

"Falsinar says that we are very close," Beltramose whispered. "When shall the—"

A clamor of surprise echoed down the corridor—calls of an assault, panicked cries to rush to the temple's defense.

"I have sent the army of the dead at their main entrance and down another of the passages the ghost told us of," Constancia explained. "Once I release my control, they will attack anything with great fury, even us. The Lazarenes should be kept quite busy dealing with them."

Qalhara held the bone near the tunnel's low ceiling, where all could see it in the meager light thrown by the candle that Palladius carried. They held still, tense with nervous excitement, until the noises lost their immediacy.

"Go!" the Lamia ordered at last. The corpse knights under her command poured forth, fast drawing ahead of the more cautious Cainites and their servants. The raw stone of the tunnel soon gave way to the finished blocks of the temple itself. The somewhat larger passages and superior lighting from a series of lamps gave them confidence to move more quickly, though Qalhara let the animated dead remain their vanguard.

Constancia looked over. The extended ritual of summoning forth the corpse army had taken its toll. She and her servants had selected a number of mortals from the oasis community to provide the massive amounts of blood she needed to sustain a force of such size, but that had left little for her once the creatures were unleashed. She would find performing any other death magic difficult for the foreseeable future. It was a high price for what amounted to nothing more than distraction, but she knew of no other way to occupy Lazarus's attention while they made their try for the codex. "It is in your hands now, Markus Giovanni."

He heard the codex's murmurs no more loudly than at the farm, but the recent wounds in his flesh tingled as if held close to a flame. Following instinct and inspiration, Markus made his way deeper into the Lazarene temple.

The fates quite enjoy their little twists and turns, Constancia thought as they hustled along passages and up stairways. She had rushed to intercept the Giovanni's meeting with Lazarus, only to arrive too late. She had searched for some means to liberate Markus, only to find that he had freed himself. But his freedom mattered little, since Lazarus had the means for apotheosis in his grasp. And so they descended into the enemy's lair, committing to grave peril so that they might spare the world from ruin.

She had no time for divination in the past week, instead devoting her attention to raising the corpse army. She hadn't even an inkling of how this venture would turn out. *Do I rush to my own demise even now?*

Death hung heavy over their little group, that was certain—and in more than the literal form of the corpse knights that even now tore through a pair of Lazarenes and their handful of animated servants. Ignorance of the future gave Constancia a strange thrill, so rarely did she face it.

Even for those who can parse the threads of fate, the future remains a mystery.

By the time Markus finally discovered the room that held the codex, they had, incredibly, run into only two groups of Lazarenes—each no more than a handful of animated dead led by a pair of Cainites. Most of the Lazarenes were focused on repelling the massive diversionary force, which had allowed

Markus and the others to slip up from the lower levels largely unnoticed. So far the plan was a remarkable success, but much remained before they could claim victory.

"You are confident the tablet lies up these stairs?" Constancia asked.

"As confident as I can be. This group was placed here to guard something." He gestured at the remains of the Lazarenes and two of Constancia's corpse knights that littered the alcove. He did not explain that, while the song of the codex grew no stronger, Markus had nonetheless felt increasing certainty as they wound their way through the passages to this place.

"There is only one way to know," Ankhesenaten piped in. "Perhaps you should send a few of those warriors of yours to take a look."

"No!" Constancia's yell made even Qalhara jump as she made to order the animated corpses forth. "They may inadvertently destroy the codex in their rampage. We must go ourselves. Leave them to guard our retreat."

Markus expected disaster each time he took the next step up toward the darkened archway. But there was only pervasive silence.

The stairs ended in a wide landing, with a stout, iron-banded door on the other side. Markus moved forward and quickly determined that the door was barred and locked. Qalhara, whose Lamia blood granted her tremendous strength, took up the challenge of the door. The noise was tremendous, but soon enough the black mouth of a doorway yawned before her.

With not a little trepidation, the Cainites entered the chamber.

Given his traumatic first encounter with the Lilith shard, Markus expected some great agony or epiphany when he beheld the Sargon Codex. Alas, it looked surprisingly mundane, a well-preserved clay tablet on which were etched row upon row of tiny, cramped Chaldean characters. He couldn't even tell where the Lilith fragment fit until he noticed a chip out of one side. The missing edge stopped short of obliterating any of the text, but he could see how a clever individual had used it to extract the sliver with Lilith's name inscribed. Someone—Lazarus, he expected—had restored the fragment to its original place with some skill. Only a hair of an outline suggested it had ever been missing.

Only when he was spun around did he realize he'd been reading aloud the writings inscribed upon the tablet. Pale blue eyes seared into his own, and he staggered back from an elder vampire's unfettered fury.

"Do not look upon it ever again, if you value your immortal existence!" Constancia raged. "I care not what the oracles claim as your role in our fate, but I will not allow you to unleash some new disaster!"

Markus tried to explain the influence of the codex upon him, but he was too unnerved to form the right words.

Ankhesenaten had no problem speaking his mind. "Nothing but a museum piece, you say? I suspect there is more to this codex of yours, mistress."

"Not now, Setite," the high priestess replied. She unwound a long piece of cloth that had appeared to be just another layer of her robes and began wrapping the artifact with exceeding care.

"I believe now is a perfect time, lest you want the full might of the Walid Set dedicated to hunting you through eternity."

Constancia favored him with a delicate arched brow. "They will hunt me only if they have reason. If you suggest that you will flee to your brethren with claims of my outrages against the Setites, I will be forced to order your immediate destruction."

Goreb stepped before his master at the same instant Qalhara readied one of her short spears. Ankhesenaten trembled, but he managed a firm tone. "We are at an impasse, and time is running short."

"You seek to bargain with me here?" Constancia snarled, snatching the wrapped bundle to her breast.

"I think it offers me the best terms. Here is my offer: I will let you keep your tablet, and even offer safe passage from Egypt, in return for a single boon."

"And what is that?"

The Setite tossed up his hands in a shrug. "That we shall leave to the future. But you must grant my request no matter when it comes."

"You dare—?!" Constancia stalked forward until the tip of Goreb's weapon brushed against the cloth that now shielded the codex. Weakened by the summoning of such a force of corpse knights, it might take her precious moments to dispatch this foolish serpent. And then to get out of the desert with Lazarus and the promised Setite force on her heels? An impasse indeed. Her words were the growl of some predatory beast. "Very well, Ankhesenaten. But beware, lest your reach exceed your grasp."

Any reply was lost in the explosion of sound that erupted from the base of the stairs. Markus recognized the voice that bellowed above the screams and clash of arms. He scrambled to his feet, all weakness and confusion gone in the surge of fear. "Lazarus comes!"

Chapter Twenty-Four

Temple of the Lazarenes
16 October, 1204

Markus lunged for the doorway. "Back down the stairs—now!"

"You just said that Lazarus was down there," Ankhesenaten protested. "And if that shouting comes from him, he does not sound pleased."

"Stay here if you like, serpent, but it will be your tomb. Our only chance of escape lies this way!" Some cast about for another exit, but they saw what Markus had. The vaulted chamber was designed for security—there was no other possible way out.

He was a pace behind Akil and Palladius; the ghouls had originally been left to guard the doorway. Vampire and mortal fled down the wide staircase toward the sounds of battle and emerged into madness. Seven corpse knights remained, and they all fought with unfettered savagery against three Cainites. Markus had no trouble recognizing the Lazarene lieutenant, Osia. The well-built man with the pointed features next to her had a blazing aura that revealed him as Lazarus. The Methuselah's robes were nothing more than shreds of fabric, but his flesh remained whole. He appeared to have avoided all but a few minor blows from Constancia's creations. The third vampire was a twisted thing of wild hair and tatters. It lashed out with a fury equal to that of the animated warriors. Markus caught a glimpse of the creature's face and realized with some shock that it—she—was none other than the Lady Alexia Theusa.

By Christ and Caine, what has become of her? Where is the poise and reservation? She is little more than an animal!

He was happy to let pass the mystery of Alexia's degeneration in favor of finding a way out of this chaos. The corpse knights were holding back the vampires for now, but the space remained too cramped to attempt a dash to any of the three corridors that emptied into the room.

"We must push them back farther, into that tunnel," he commanded the Cappadocian initiates. They looked at the snarling mass of undead just two yards distant, then turned shocked eyes to him.

"He is right," Qalhara said from behind them. Her tone had a dangerous edge that motivated the ghouls immediately. Though terrified for their lives, Akil and Palladius remembered their duty and rushed to press the attack. The Lamia moved up as well, making room for her mistress as she readied an attack with her short spears.

Lazarus, acquitting himself well against four of the corpse knights, finally registered the intruders' presence just as Constancia stepped through the archway. He took in Markus's scarred form and the high priestess's wan countenance, betrayal and outrage twisting his face to something inhuman. A terrible roar burst from his lips: "Giovanni!"

"Now!" Qalhara ordered, thrusting high the bone charm for emphasis. The corpse knights gibbered and snarled in response while the Cappadocian initiates yelled incoherent battle cries. Osia was sucked into the animated warriors' deadly undertow. She was torn to wet gobbets of bloody gristle that imploded into ash as final death claimed her.

Akil and Palladius struck at Alexia, but the cramped confines restricted them more than it did her. She caught Palladius by the wrist, her touch sufficient to freeze him like a marvelously detailed statuary. The ghoul was thrown off-balance but could do nothing to correct his fall. The corpse knights knew no distinction between friend and foe; any who came within reach were fair game. They fell upon the immobilized Palladius with the same eagerness they showed Osia. Akil cried out for his fallen comrade, and Alexia seized on the distraction to slam a pair of needle-thin knives into the side of his head. He gobbled the air like a landed fish, then the maddened Alexia snatched him by the waist and darted around the corner of the opposite hallway.

The remaining corpse knights tore into Lazarus—or, at least, they launched themselves to do so. The ancient vampire was incensed beyond the bounds of reason at seeing the betrayer Markus alongside Constancia, with the Sargon Codex in hand. All restraint was gone; Lazarus sprouted the claws of a beast and slashed wide his palms. He slapped one hand on the forehead of the first lunging corpse. The thing's head exploded in a shower of gore while the body carried on its momentum. It dashed into the wall behind Lazarus, then collapsed as its animating force dissipated.

He swept his other arm wide at the same time, unleashing a glittering spray of crimson droplets. Each spot that the potent blood struck on the other three dead warriors sizzled like an ember for an instant—then the surrounding flesh detonated in spontaneous decay. Huge chunks of the corpse knights' bodies crumbled to powder, and what remained could no longer support itself.

Lazarus stepped over the twitching forms, blood dripping from his palms and the Beast dancing in his eyes.

Ankhesenaten and his bodyguard watched the carnage from the relative safety of the archway at the base of the stairs. Beltramose crouched even further back, murmuring to the empty staircase.

"We are surrounded by insanity," Ankhesenaten told Goreb. "These Cappadocians would destroy one another over some tablet while their servants carry on conversations with spirits."

The taciturn bodyguard grunted. "Pray that their madness is not catching."

"Quite the contrary, my friend. It would save us much time and energy if they could eradicate one another with no subtle urging from us. We might then devote our full energies to wipe out at last the minions of our Great Enemy."

Goreb replied with another grunt, but this time did not elaborate.

"Hmm; perhaps you are right," Ankhesenaten allowed. "These Cainites have a knack for sending even the simplest plans awry. We can rely only on ourselves to see the job done right. But for now, let us remain out of sight while this matter settles itself."

Constancia felt the pressure wave of Lazarus's aura as he moved to the center of the room. He was her elder by only a single generation, but it was a yawning gap when dealing in power on the scale of those just a few steps removed from Caine himself. She could also sense that Lazarus held himself in check by the barest strands of self-control. If not for the Sargon Codex—which she held forth like a shield—he would certainly have flung more of his virulent blood at her, and at Markus and Qalhara clustered with her.

"Giovanni," Lazarus growled, hands flexing in poorly restrained rage. "We could have unlocked the secrets of eternity together. Instead, you show yourself the pawn of the misguided."

"Lazarus, I beseech you," Markus said, stepping from Constancia's protective shadow—or, more accurately, from the one the codex cast. "There is more here than you know. Constancia is an avowed master of oracles. She has foreseen disaster should you strive for divinity."

"Of course." He spat vehemence at Constancia next. "Childe of Japheth. I am not surprised that you are at the heart of this. I know your misguided love for our progenitor. You cannot save him from himself. You will not leave with the codex."

Constancia stood firm despite a quaver in her soul. "You are mistaken, Lazarus. Godhood is not meant for one such as you."

"There will be no parley here, woman. Unhand the tablet willingly and you may see another night. Otherwise, I shall destroy you where you stand."

"And chance destroying Sargon's masterpiece also? I think not." She nodded toward the near passage. "Qalhara, we leave now."

"*No!*"

The cry surprised them all, as did the form that flashed like an arrow toward Constancia. Qalhara responded as quickly. It was the same pale figure that had attacked a sailor on the ship *Golden Virtue*—but this time the Lamia had her short spear at hand. Her throw was a blur that struck the attacker just as she reached the High Priestess of Bones. Alexia Theusa staggered, the spear embedded deep in the meat of her thigh, but it did not keep her from her goal. She snatched at the Sargon Codex with eager hands. "Return it now!"

Constancia heard the artifact creak in the tug-of-war as Alexia tried to tear it from her grasp. "Restrain yourself, my sister—or do you wish the tablet destroyed?"

"The codex is eternal!" A glimmer of lucidity flashed within the cracked madness of Alexia's eyes.

Lazarus twitched a hand, sending vitae to splatter a large red stain of warning on the ground. "Release it, Constancia!"

"You surround yourself with the weak-minded, Lazarus," Constancia shouted, struggling to keep hold of the codex without snapping it apart in the process. "And you, my sister. Do you think that this object will return your great love to life? Andreas shall return—but you will long be dust when he does!"

"You lie!" the madwoman shrieked, wrenching away the tablet with a mighty effort. Bloody froth spattered the cloth that wrapped the Sargon Codex as she cried, "With this, I may usurp God's will and be reunited with Andreas at last!"

Lazarus shook in a palsied fury as the women struggled. The Methuselah could control his rage no longer when Alexia Theusa stole the codex away. The Beast shattered the worn shackles of restraint in one terrible instant—and Lazarus flung a handful of blood in outrage. Reason returned immediately after, but it was already too late. Even one of Lazarus's might could not call back his deadly power.

Markus saw the Methuselah unleash his attack. Issuing an inarticulate cry of warning, he dove away from the arc of red. Qalhara moved as quickly, driving her mistress to the ground in a protective tackle.

Aware of nothing but her new prize, Alexia registered the attack only when the heavy crimson droplets splashed on her shoulder and face—and onto the upper portion of the Sargon Codex.

She had not even the time to scream as her upper body detonated in a cloud of decay. The vitae of Lazarus ate through the tablet's wrappings that same instant. Potent blood magic and divine artifact collided in a blast that shattered the world.

Clay fragments showered the antechamber amid a deafening peal like the thunder of heaven itself. All were tossed like a child's toys in the shockwave, and the very stone bucked and cracked around them.

Markus was staggered by pain both physical and spiritual. His body, still weak from its recent injuries, was battered as the temple started to implode in a shower of dust and stone. And the song of the codex was torn from him, leaving a gaping tear within his soul. The emptiness swelled, threatening to send him into a madness to rival Alexia's.

But his agony was as nothing compared to that Lazarus suffered. The Methuselah unleashed a cry of terrible loss. Blood surged from his wounds in a rising cloud that threatened to engulf the chamber and far beyond. The bizarre blood magic never took effect, however, because the ceiling caved in and a hundred tons of desert came crashing down through the collapsing temple.

Chapter Twenty-Five

Alexandria
1I November, 1204

E ven a month later, their escape from the fall of the Lazarene temple was a haze of splintered sensation in Markus's memory.

He'd been aware only of being pulled free of crushing debris and a frantic dash away from a massive sinkhole. Then everything was darkness and loss. It took him eight nights before he could cope with the gap in his spirit sufficiently to rise. They were well on their way to Alexandria by that point, Ankhesenaten staying true to his word and granting all who'd survived the event safe passage from Egypt. Markus shared an enclosed wagon with Qalhara for the journey, who had suffered grievous physical injury protecting her mistress from the worst of the collapse.

Beltramose and the spirit of Falsinar attended him along the way, explaining as best they knew what had happened. The staircase in which they and the Setites hid had protected them from the initial stages of the temple's collapse. Ironically, the chamber in which the codex was stored proved to be their best means of escape. A gap tore in its vaulted ceiling as the rest of the complex fell in, leaving a chasm up which they scrambled to reach the desert.

Ankhesenaten had, in fact, been less than truthful regarding the Setite forces. Some of the serpent bands already lay in wait. They rushed forward at his call to carry them all to safety.

A great rumbling hole appeared where the Temple of the

Lazarenes had been, a massive cloud of dust rising above. By the time the hastily assembled caravan struck out for Alexandria, the desert sand was already shifting to fill in the crater.

Of Lazarus and his followers, there had been no sign.

Markus felt conflicting relief and sorrow, not only at the loss of the codex, but at the possible demise of Lazarus. He hadn't agreed with all that the Methuselah had told him, but he nonetheless felt a kinship with a figure of such keen intellect. *Under other circumstances, what discoveries might we have made together?*

"I seldom see such depth of concentration in one so young," Constancia opined from the doorway to his chamber. She looked as composed as ever, garbed in a cream robe of Arabic cut. Thanks to her formidable constitution and her guardian's efforts, she'd survived with but minor injuries that were long since healed.

"Mistress! I did not realize you were there. How may I assist you?"

"I have come to bid my farewell, childe. Ankhesenaten has said that the *Golden Virtue* shall be ready to sail with the dawn tide. At my request, he shall take you to Europe."

Markus furrowed his wide brow. "I had thought it agreed that he would return you personally to Mount Erciyes?"

"Qalhara is still too weak to attempt travel by sea. We have made other arrangements. And the Setite hopes he might gain the ear of a member of an influential Venetian merchant family."

"Does he? Well; he has proven a pleasant surprise compared to others of his kind I have encountered." A smile quirked the dark thatch of his beard. "It might make for an interesting trip, to indulge in a dialogue with one such as he."

His tone grew more serious. "I had been told of your misgivings regarding my family, and I must admit some distrust of you in turn. But events at the temple, though they ended in failure for us, give me hope for the future of the Giovanni within Clan Cappadocian."

"Yes; the future of the Cappadocians…" Constancia withdrew in contemplation for a moment. "Your words remind me of something; a promise I made to a scion of another clan. I wonder if you would perform a task for me, in this spirit of realizing such a future."

"If it is within my power, mistress."

"Oh, it is a simple enough matter, but important in maintaining relations with the Nosferatu. Are you familiar with the scion of that clan, late of Constantinople, called Malachite?"

Markus nodded. "We are not close, but our past dealings were pleasant."

"In the wake of Constantinople's fall, Malachite has been set on a course that shall make him a figure of some importance in the Cainite world. Mount Erciyes would benefit from having a representative at his side in future nights." The high priestess turned her pale eyes to Markus. "It would do well for our clan—and reflect favorably on your family—if you would be that representative, Markus Musa Giovanni."

The ache of the lost codex ebbed a fraction in the swell of pride that Markus felt. "I would be honored, Mistress Constancia."

"Signore!" Beltramose hopped from the longboat and joined his master on the pier. "Such a fine ship is this *Golden Virtue.* It rivals anything our shipwrights might create."

"I forgive you your blasphemy, Beltramose. And remember, though we return in victory, it would not do to relax our guard a moment on the journey."

"Victory, *Signore*?" came the whispered words of Falsinar's ghost. "How can that be? The codex is destroyed."

"One must look upon the larger scope," Markus replied. He cast a glance at the wraith, who flickered next to Beltramose. He was proving as compliant as any ghost that Markus had bound in the past—yet Falsinar was not subjugated to Markus's will. Instead, the connection with his living compatriot seemed sufficient to sustain him. *It is inevitable that I bring him under my sway. Still, there is time to study this curiosity in more detail first.*

"The larger scope?" Beltramose prompted.

"Indeed. I have searched for means by which the Giovanni may garner the respect due them within Clan Cappadocian. The Sargon Codex would have been a tremendous prize, it is true, but I return far from empty-handed." He glanced around, but the sailors engaged in the predawn bustle along the docks had no time for eavesdropping. "I have earned the favor of High Priestess Constancia herself, after all. And I am the only Cainite to know what lies within the lair of Alexia Theusa.

"And while the Sargon Codex was ruined, who can say if its secrets may not be recovered some night?"

Constancia watched from the balcony as *Golden Virtue* made ready to sail. Streaks of light blossomed to the east, but she had a few more minutes before she must seek shelter from the dawn.

"You are certain that the Giovanni will keep the course to meet with the Nosferatu?" Qalhara asked. Though still weak from her injuries, she stood as alert and resolute by her mistress's side as ever before.

"He is enough in my thrall that a gentle request shall be felt as a most urgent order," Constancia affirmed. "It lies with Malachite now, to see that the Dream meets its necessary end."

"And what does the future bring us, mistress?"

"Lazarus failed in his bid for godhead, Qalhara. He may even have been destroyed for his temerity. But I have seen no change in the fate of our clan. Whether he is the cause, surviving by some miracle to exact his revenge, or some other Cappadocian who I have somehow overlooked, it seems our time upon this world shall run its course." Qalhara appraised her mistress. "Must this be the way of things?"

"Only God may say. But while there is time, there is hope. I have found new hope in the events of these past nights." Constancia looked back into the room, where pieces of clay tablet inscribed with tiny Chaldean characters poked from the open flap of a leather satchel. "There may yet be a way to set the future on a new course."

About the Author

Andrew Bates is a professional writer, illustrator and procrastinator. He is the author of the *Year of the Scarab Trilogy*, a popular modern horror adventure series. He has also been a designer on a number of White Wolf role-playing games, including *Trinity*, *Adventure!*, and *Mummy: The Resurrection*. Visit www.white-wolf.com and www.devilbear.net for more on his interests and accomplishments.

Dark Ages: Cappadocian is his first attempt at period horror fiction. With its completion, he plans on taking a long break before starting his next project.

Curious about other Crossroad Press books?
Stop by our site:
http://store.crossroadpress.com
We offer quality writing
in digital, audio, and print formats.